The

TORN
WING

❧

KIKI HAMILTON

Book Two of
THE FAERIE RING Series

This book is dedicated to you, Dear Reader, for sticking with me and caring enough to want to know what happens next with Tiki and her family.

Thank you.

Also by Kiki Hamilton

THE FAERIE RING

Key to Pronunciation and Meaning of Irish Words
(With thanks to irishgaelictranslator.com)

An fáinne sí (un FAWN-yeh shee)
The faerie ring

Na síochána, aontaímid
(nuh SHEE-uh-khaw-nuh, EEN-tee-mij)
For the sake of peace, we agree

Grá do dhuine básmhar
(Graw duh GGWIN-yeh BAWSS-wur)
Love for a mortal person

Óinseach (OWN-shukh)
Fool/idiot (for a female)

Nimh Álainn (niv AW-lin)
Beautiful Poison

Tánaiste (Tawn-ISH-tah)
Second in command

Cloch na Teamhrach (klukh nuh TYARR-uh)
Stone of Tara

LONDON
1872

Regent's Park

Camden
Town

Ki

Grosvenor
Square

Leicester Square

Piccadilly

St. James Square

Trafalgar Square

Green
Park

Birdkeeper's
Corner

St. James
Park

Hyde Park

Kensington

Buckingham Palace

Westminster
Abbey

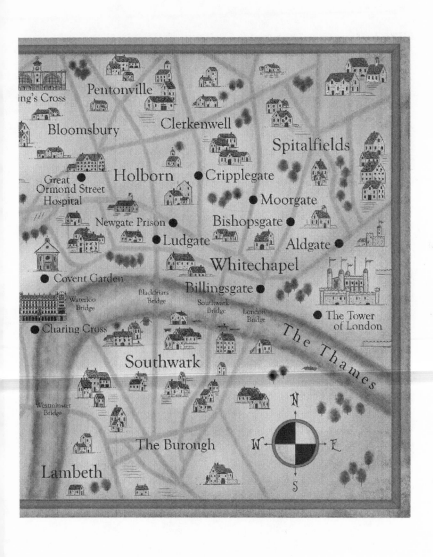

The TORN WING

Dear Reader,

The story told within **THE FAERIE RING series** is a combination of fact and fiction. Known as 'historical fantasy', I like to think of the books as a *'what if....'* kind of story.

Much of book one, THE FAERIE RING, is grounded in reality: **Queen Victoria and Princes Leopold and Arthur** were real historical figures. In fact, the story was set in the year 1871 because that was the year Prince Leopold was eighteen years old.

Many of the places referenced in the story: **Charing Cross Station, King's Cross Station, The World's End Pub, St. James Park, the Birdkeeper's Cottage, Buckingham Palace, Hyde Park, and the Great Ormond Street Hospital**, are real and can be visited today - should you be lucky enough to find yourself in London.

As you read book two, THE TORN WING, you might find it interesting to know **The Wychwood Forest** is also real and located in Oxfordshire, England. The Wychwood was a royal forest for centuries, providing a place for the sovereigns to hunt. It wasn't until 1988 that a public footpath was created through the Wychwood, though there was evidence of the trails being used by locals for centuries. "Milton Stone", used to build St. George's Chapel of Windsor Castle, was quarried from Milton-Under-Wychwood, a town located within the forest. Among the legends associated with the Forest today are tales of hobgoblins and faerie folk as well as witches and more.

Additionally, **Wydryn Tor**, also known as **Glastonbury Tor**, is a hill in England that has been associated with *Gwn Ap Nud*, the King of Faeries. The Tor is also said to be linked to Avalon of Arthurian legend, and is believed by some to represent an entrance to the land of Faerie.

The Hill of Tara is a significant historical site in Ireland and contains a number of ancient monuments. According to tradition, the Hill of Tara is the seat of the High King of Ireland. There are also stories naming the Hill of Tara as the capital of the *Tuatha Dé Danann* (the Irish race of gods in Irish-Celtic mythology who retreated underground and became known as the *Sidhe* or *Aos Sí*—more commonly known today as Faeries.)

The London Stone is a real artifact which dates back to the Middle Ages and was stored for many years in the wall of the St. Swithin Church. Today, the London Stone is still displayed and available for viewing on Cannon Street. The myths associated with the stone in this story are the same myths associated with the stone in real life.

Additional information you might find interesting regarding some of the **people, places and things** mentioned in THE TORN WING are listed in the Author's Note at the end, though to avoid any spoilers, perhaps best read **after** you finish the book.

Now—on with Tiki's story...

Chapter One

The Otherworld

The killer walked boldly down the corridor of the Summer Court, his steps measured and confident. His fortitude over the years as he'd lain staked and dying a slow, painful death in the depths of the Wychwood Forest would be rewarded tonight.

Floors, the color and texture of brook-fed moss, softened the approach of his booted feet. Vast columns, similar to those that graced the center front of Buckingham Palace, lined the passageway. Entwined with fragrant vines of honeysuckle, passion flower and wisteria, the great stone pillars supported a ceiling as blue and endless as the summer sky.

The killer's lip curled in disgust. The Seelie fey loved the sunlight and their mortal affectations. The UnSeelie's love of darkness and blood suited his tastes much better. A true UnSeelie would rather torture a mortal than befriend the thing. He, on the other hand, would prefer to eat its heart.

At the end of the hallway two guards stood at attention in front of a pair of immense arch-topped doors. They gripped a spear in each hand, arms crossed over their red-coated chests, their black eyes alert and wary. Curved backswords hung from their belts, the silver blades glittering in the torch light like deadly adornments. It was common knowledge the razor-sharp blades of their weapons were crafted of cold iron—poison to any fey. What the guards didn't know was that iron would have no affect on him.

The killer bowed to the guards, the golden tray he carried proffered for their inspection. Upon the tray rested a single golden chalice, the base and rim sparkling with rubies, emeralds and amethysts. "I deliver the King's nightly libation."

The taller of the two guards raised an eyebrow, one corner of his mouth lifting in amusement. "Sionnach, you've returned. I didn't know you were now also a serving wench."

Sionnach's lips curved but his eyes remained cold. The magical glamour Donegal had placed upon him provided the illusion of looking similar to the guards, allowing him to fit in.

"There is much you don't know about me, Olcán."

The second guard sniffed the concoction within the chalice then placed the tip of his smallest finger in the drink before touching his tongue. His face remained impassive as he tasted the golden liquid. He gave a sharp nod, his expression relaxing.

"As awful as ever, but the drink doesn't seem to be poisoned."

Sionnach pulled the tray away from the guard and spoke as though reciting a familiar litany. "King O'Riagáin believes consumption of mortal ale brings a clearer understanding of the human world and the threat they pose."

The taller guard's black eyes glittered and he spoke in a derisive tone. "Perhaps he should drink from the UnSeelie cup. It might be they who pose the bigger threat."

Sionnach inclined his head at the guard's assessment. "Well said, Olcán. You've heard the rumblings, too?"

"That the UnSeelies are threatening war?" His pointed features twisted in a contemptuous smirk. "They're always threatening something. I'll be glad when the Beltane celebration is over in a few weeks and our court returns to the Palace of Mirrors. The UnSeel-ies can slink back to the darkness and shadows where they belong."

Sionnach inclined his head again. "May we all be so lucky to find ourselves in the place where we belong." He motioned with the tray toward the door. "Gentlemen, may I pass?"

After searching the killer for hidden weapons, Olcán tugged open one of the great doors and allowed entry into the royal chamber.

Once the door closed behind him Sionnach's movements were swift and sure. He didn't speak as he approached, but pretended to trip just as he reached the royal bed where the king lay reclining. The cold liquid in the chalice drenched the king's face and chest, causing him to jerk upright sputtering and gasping in surprise.

Faster than the eye could track, Sionnach yanked out a razor thin length of wire that had been coiled in the heel of his boot and wrapped it around the king's neck. In a matter of seconds, the Seelie king was dead.

Sionnach's lips twisted in a cold smile. Donegal, king of the Winter Court, would be pleased with his success tonight, for the UnSeelie king planned to claim both the Summer and Winter thrones in an attempt to rule all of Faerie.

But Donegal's plans didn't stop there. The UnSeelie king had promised Sionnach his freedom in exchange for two deaths. The first was that of the Seelie king—now accomplished. The second was Queen Victoria, for Winter planned to claim a third throne: England.

The killer straightened and left the dead king prone on his opulent bed. London was the perfect hunting ground for someone with his desires and abilities.

He licked his lips in anticipation.

Chapter Two

London, April 1872

The scream of the wind drew Tiki onto the porch of Number Six Grosvenor Square. She shivered and pulled her cloak tighter as the gale shrieked around the corner of the building like the eerie cry of a dying beast. A storm was blowing in with alarming speed—it was as if the air crackled with dark magic.

Overhead, the afternoon sky was growing as black as the coal dust that often coated the City; Shadows loitered beneath trees and crept into corners like living beasts—hunched and watching. A strong gust yanked the hem of Tiki's forest green dress and threads of her long dark hair danced on the wind as if unseen fingers played with the strands. Unnerved, she pushed her hair out of her face and stepped back where she wouldn't be so exposed. Her imagination painted threatening, otherworldly faces in the clouds above London's myriad rows of smokestacks.

"Teek, why are you out here in this weather?" Fiona's voice was laced with worry as she joined Tiki on the porch. The fifteen year-old shivered and tugged the worn blue shawl tighter around her bony shoulders. Though food was plentiful now, their years of struggling to survive on the streets of London, not only for themselves, but also for the younger ones, Toots and Clara, were still evident in their wafer-thin silhouettes.

Tiki's brow furrowed as she glanced down the empty street. "Toots went out to play stickball with some friends. I hope he has enough sense to come in out of this weather."

Fiona gave a dry laugh. "He's ten. He's got no sense at all." Her brown hair, which in the past had been sawed off in uneven chunks and kept short as a boy's, was growing out in soft waves, framing her angular face. "This storm's a nasty bit, isn't it?"

"Can you feel it too, Fi?" Tiki shifted to stand closer to the other girl. Though only a year separated their ages, at sixteen, Tiki often felt older than Fiona—a result, she assumed, of her broader education from a middle-class upbringing. But she and Fiona had been through much together over the last two years, trying to survive by picking pockets and nicking food when they could. As a result, they shared a bond closer than most.

Fiona nodded. "It's like before, when you took the ring." She folded her arms tight across her chest and looked warily up and down the street. Though her education had not been derived from books, her street smarts were every bit as valuable. "Like we're being watched."

"Exactly," Tiki said. Nothing had been the same since she'd stolen the Queen's ring last December, which she'd later learned held an ancient truce between the world of Faerie and the British royals. That simple theft had unleashed a waterfall of events that had put London on the brink of war with the Otherworld. The ring was safely guarded once again, but an ever-present fear squeezed Tiki's heart as she waited each day for whatever was to come next. For *something* was very surely coming.

She watched the black thunderclouds boil across the sky, like the bubbling contents of an evil witch's cauldron. The skin at the back of her neck tightened in alarm. "I *hate* faeries," she said in a low voice.

Fiona crossed her arms and chewed on her thumb, a habit she'd developed whiling away the time in railway stations looking for pockets to pick. "Do you think it's Lark—"

"Don't even say her name, Fi." Tiki cut her off. "She's been captured. We don't have to worry about her anymore."

"Shamus says she's too clever to stay a prisoner for long."

"I know what Shamus thinks," Tiki replied, trying not to snap. As tall and gaunt as a sapling birch tree, seventeen year-old Shamus was Fiona's cousin. His white-blond hair was a startling contrast to the brown of Fiona's short locks, as much as his quiet nature was to Fiona's chattiness. It had been Shamus and Fiona who'd helped Tiki survive when she'd run from her uncle's house two years ago. "But there's no reason for—" Tiki dropped her voice— "*Larkin* to pursue us any longer. The ring has been returned and is guarded. We don't have anything she wants."

"I hope you're right, Teek." Fiona stepped toward the door and gripped the brass knob. "Unless she just wants revenge."

Thunder rattled in the distance with a series of guttural *booms*, like throaty laughter.

"She's in a prison somewhere, Fi," Tiki ground out in a low voice.

Against her will, an image of the faerie filled Tiki's head. Larkin had often worn a glamour—a magical illusion to make her look human—with blond hair hanging in perfect ringlets framing an attractive face. But in her natural state, Larkin had an exquisite beauty that was compelling; A splendor as breathtaking and fierce as a summer storm. Skin like fresh cream gave the mistaken impression the faerie was more fragile than a porcelain doll, but her eyes—a vivid, turbulent blue-green—reminded Tiki of the bottles of poison in Mr. Lloyd's apothecary shop in Leicester Square. "She can't harm us anymore," Tiki said. Beneath her breath she added, "I won't let her."

"If you say so." Fiona cast a worried eye at the trees thrashing back and forth in the wind. "Don't stay out here too long by yourself. It doesn't feel safe." The door banged shut behind her as she disappeared back into the warmth of the townhome.

Tiki scanned the street one more time for Toots. In the distance, a carriage clattered down the lane at an unusual clip. Shod hooves echoed against the cobblestones as the driver urged a faster pace. Their sides heaving, the black horses snorted white clouds into the cold air as they slowed in front of Number Six. The rigging of the elegant black coach creaked as the door swung open even before the iron-clad wheels had stopped rolling.

Rieker jumped to the street, his long coat swirling around his legs. Dressed in black, he blended with the shadows sifting into the City with the onset of the storm, making him look wild and dangerous. Tiki hurried down the steps toward him.

"You've returned early—are you all right?" she said. "What's happened?"

Rieker grasped her hand, his fingers warm against her cold skin. His dark hair was brushed back from cheekbones that looked more pronounced than the last time she'd seen him, as if he'd not been getting enough to eat. He reached a long finger up and smoothed a windblown piece of hair from her face.

"You're all right?" he asked.

"Yes." She nodded.

He shot a worried glance toward the townhome. "The others?"

"Fine—" her fingers tightened on his— "we're all fine. What's happened?"

The tension around his mouth relaxed and he slid a muscled arm around Tiki's shoulders. For a fleeting moment he pulled her tight against his chest and she inhaled deeply. Horses, expensive leather, the freshness of a summer breeze—his scent created a longing deep in her gut.

"I've news, but I'm afraid it's not good."

Tiki's heart hammered inside her chest. It was as she had suspected—something *had* happened. She stepped back so she could see his face. A scar stretched along the line of his jaw, faded white by time. "Tell me."

"Larkin has escaped."

Tiki had an odd sensation of falling. "But how?" she whispered. "They clamped her wings with iron..."

Rieker shook his head, his jaw clenched in distaste. "She tore her own wing off." He kept his arm around Tiki's shoulders and steered her toward the townhome. "Gather what you need—Leo has requested our presence at Buckingham."

Chapter Three

In less than an hour Tiki and Rieker were being ushered into Buckingham Palace. The opulence of the Palace was as overwhelming this time as the other few times Tiki had visited. Crystal chandeliers glittered from soaring ceilings. Gilt-framed pictures of dour-faced ancestors graced the walls, watching their passage with haughty regard. Rugs an inch thick rested on marble floors and hushed their footsteps as the doorman led them to the library where Prince Leopold waited.

"Ah, Wills, you've arrived." Leo pushed himself out of a chair in front of the fire and came to greet them. At eighteen, he and Rieker were the same age and had been chums since childhood. "Miss Tara." He gave her a beguiling smile, dimples appearing in each cheek. "Always a delight to see you."

Tiki dipped into a curtsy and bowed her head to the prince. "And you sir," she said with a shy smile.

"You look lovely," he said, bending over her hand, "but then, you always do." He did not release her hand, but instead led her toward the fire. "You remember my mother? Queen Victoria?"

At his words, Leo led her around the back of the chair opposite to where he'd had been sitting to face the occupant. Tiki gasped out loud. It was the Queen, in the flesh, sitting three feet in front of her. A small tiara of diamonds graced the sovereign's dark hair and she wore a gown of black, still in mourning for the passing of her husband, Albert, over ten years earlier. Next to her chair a small black and white cocker spaniel rested her head on her paws, watching Tiki with thoughtful brown eyes.

Leo swept his arm toward Tiki. "Mother, may I present Mistress Tara Kathleen Dunbar."

"Your Majesty." Tiki bowed her head low as she dropped into a curtsy, her heart racing a million miles a minute. Had Rieker known the Queen was going to be here?

"You may rise, Miss Dunbar," the Queen said in a rich voice.

"Your Majesty." Rieker was next to Tiki now, also bowing to the Queen. As William Richmond, he had grown up with Leo and Arthur and had often played in the gardens of Buckingham Palace. It wasn't until after his family had been murdered that he'd run away to the streets where he lived as Rieker, a pickpocket who helped the street children find food without getting arrested.

"Hello William." The warmth in the Queen's voice was unmistakable. "So nice to see you again." She tilted her head. "You look well. No troubles to report, I take it?"

"All is well at the moment, Madam." Rieker's lips curved in a confident smile and Tiki was filled with pride. Rieker was like a chameleon, changing colors to adapt to his environment. One minute he could be rubbing elbows with the worst of the lot who lived among London's underbelly in places like Seven Dials—the next, shifting seamlessly into the role of a young lord, chatting with the Queen like old friends. Tiki wondered what else she didn't know about the young man.

"Can I offer you something to drink?" Leo asked.

After chairs were pulled closer and a sweet tea served, he cleared his throat. "We've asked you here today to share a serious bit of news we've learned."

Before he could continue, the Queen interrupted. "No disrespect intended, Miss Dunbar, but perhaps we should speak to William alone on this matter." She waved a jeweled hand. "For the security of all, of course."

Tiki jumped to her feet and dipped her head. "Of course, your Majesty." Tiki was torn between emotions: wanting to stay and hear whatever the news might be and relief the problem didn't require her involvement.

The door to the library swung open and Prince Arthur, Leo's older brother by three years, hurried into the room. "Hughes said you'd arrived," he called across the room. "Wills, always good to see you, old chap, you're well, yes?"

"All's well here, Arthur."

Arthur stopped before Tiki. "And the lovely Miss Dunbar," he gave a short bow, "always a pleasure."

"I've asked Wills and Tara to join us today to give them the news." Leo glanced over his shoulder at Tiki as he poured Arthur a glass of tea. "Tara, you've a nickname, haven't you? Wills has mentioned it before."

Heat rose in Tiki's cheeks. To stand before three royals, one of whom was the Queen of England, and all who were staring at her, was a bit overwhelming. She focused on keeping her voice steady. "Yes, it's Tiki. Short for Tara Kathleen. My father gave me the name as a child."

"Yes, I remember now," Leo said. "Tiki of the faerie ring." He handed Arthur the glass then stepped over to the empty chair next to his mother. "I invited Tara here for a reason today. It was Mamie who identified the birthmark on Tara's wrist for me as *an fáinne sí*—which, in the Celtic world, translates to *'the faerie ring'*. Though I know few details, I believe Tara has as much of a connection to this mysterious realm as Wills. I was hoping she could shed some light on the whole mess." He sank into the blue upholstered chair and smiled at Tiki. "It might be best if she stays."

Queen Victoria's eyes narrowed and she studied Tiki. "I find the idea of your birthmark fascinating." A wave of nervousness made Tiki's skin prickle. "May I see it?"

With a shaking hand, Tiki slid the sleeve of her forest green gown up toward her elbow. Her arm looked thin and pale, the delicate black lines that twisted and wrapped around her wrist more pronounced than ever. The entire group leaned forward to peer at her mark, three strands woven like a Celtic knot. The Queen motioned for Tiki to turn her arm over so she could see the other side. Satisfied, the Queen sat back and fixed a steely gaze on Tiki.

"What do you know of the Otherworld?"

"N..nothing, really," Tiki stuttered. "I..I've always had the birthmark. I didn't know that it meant anything until..."

"I've been doing some research myself on the meaning of Tiki's mark." Rieker said, pushing himself out of his chair to stand next to her. His strong, straight nose was a perfect fit for the attractive contours of his face. Dark hair swept across his brow and a bit of a dimple winked from one cheek. Tiki took a deep breath, comforted by his support. "As you know, I was unaware of my own connection to the Otherworld until recently. Tiki and I are working together to have a better understanding of how our lives our intertwined—" he smiled at her, the skin crinkling around his eyes— "with the fey."

"Probably best to say it all in front of Tara, then, wouldn't you agree, Mother?" Leo spoke, pulling Tiki back to reality. He motioned toward her and Rieker. "It's obvious they've no secrets." Tiki smiled, but she wondered if Leo's statement was true.

The Queen frowned. "Fine."

Arthur stood behind Leo, one arm resting on the wooden back of the chair. His dark hair showed signs of receding early but he stood straight and tall wearing a jacket of deep red, a hint of color in each cheek making him the picture of robust health.

"We do rely on advice from Mamie quite often," he said. "If she has confirmed there is a connection between the fey and our friend here, then I think it must be to our advantage to have Tara on our side."

"Grand." Leo raised his glass of tea. "The decision is made." He nodded at Tiki. "Please be seated again." He paused while Tiki smoothed her skirts and sat down, then pushed himself straight in the chair. "I hate to inform you, but there's been some nasty business about lately—nighttime attacks, deaths—" he pressed his lips into a straight line— "something out of the ordinary about them."

"How's that?" Rieker asked, his brows knitted in a frown.

"We haven't found a connection between the victims yet other than the wounds are torn and jagged, as if they've been made with something rather than a knife."

A chill blew through Tiki, causing the hair on her arms to stand up.

"Like before?" Rieker asked. He didn't need to say anything more. Everyone in the room knew he was referring to the deaths that had occurred last December when the ring of the truce had been unguarded.

"Yes, similar." Leo lowered his voice. "But this time, the killer is taking a grisly souvenir."

"What's that?"

"He's tearing out their hearts."

Tiki bit back a gasp as Rieker grimaced. "Any leads?"

"Nothing substantial. The Palace Guards are looking for witnesses near the last crime scene over in Whitechapel. They think someone might have seen something but is afraid to come forward for fear of sounding deranged."

Tiki wondered if Leo was remembering the chaotic scene he had stumbled upon in Rieker's bed chamber when Larkin had been captured. There'd been a terrible row and a dead faerie named Marcus, had lain bleeding iridescent green blood on the floor.

"Which, given the circumstances, is understandable," Leo finished, looking rather green himself.

"Well, thank you for the warning—" Rieker started.

Leo held up his hand. "But that's not all. We've learned a terrible war has erupted in the—" he dropped his voice— "*Other*world. The world of Faerie."

"That would explain the weather," Rieker said. "The storms, the cold—the incessant wind. Quite unseasonable for the beginning of April."

Leo nodded. "Mamie has said as much. But, apparently, there is a new, more imminent threat."

Rieker frowned. "There's always conflict of one kind or another between the Seelie and UnSeelie courts in the Otherworld. What's different this time?"

Queen Victoria cleared her throat. When she spoke her voice was heavy with unease. "It seems our alliance with the Seelie court is in jeopardy."

"How's that?"

The queen's face was grim. "Apparently, the Seelie King's head is on a stake outside his palace. Donegal and the UnSeelie's want to rule all of Faerie."

Tiki clenched her fingers into a fist until her nails bit into the palms of her hands. She knew little of the fey world, but she did know Donegal was the Winter king, ruler of the UnSeelie Court. Rieker had told her he was especially deadly.

Arthur spoke, his face tight with worry. "The UnSeelies are the ones who want to destroy the truce, held by magical fire within the ring you now guard, Wills. The same truce made with the English royal family and the high kings of the Seelie Court, which ensures peace between our worlds in exchange for the right of their kind to walk among us undetected."

He crossed his arms and paced behind Leo's chair. "Mamie says this war in the Otherworld has waged for centuries. The Seelies believe joining with us will give them more power. The UnSeelies, on the other hand, feel our mechanical inventions have been replacing their magic; As our cities grow we're taking over their world. They want to take back what they feel mortals have stolen from them." His voice rang with a somber tone. "Apparently, they want to take back England."

Leo's usually smiling face was equally serious. "In the past, as long as the ring has been guarded by the bloodline of those who made the oath, the fey can't attack. But if the flame of the truce is extinguished, or unguarded—" his eyes lit on Tiki— "then it's war.

Tiki tried not to squirm under Leo's gaze. She had stolen the ring last winter, unaware of the magical bond held within the stone. When she'd taken the ring from Buckingham Palace, the truce had been considered unguarded and the fey had crossed over to London, preying on unsuspecting mortals. A shiver ran up her spine. She didn't want to go to war with the fey. From what she'd seen of them, she wanted to stay as far away as possible.

The young prince hesitated. "We've been informed the UnSeelie king has found a way around the truce." Leo's eyes shifted to Queen Victoria. "Word has it he intends to murder mother."

Chapter Four

"Why didn't you tell Leo that Larkin had escaped?" Tiki asked as soon as they were settled in the carriage. Rieker sat on the bench across from her, his long legs stretched into the small space between them, brushing raindrops from his sleeves. The black clouds overhead had finally given way and rain pelted the City as if thrown from above.

He shrugged, lines of concern etched between his brows. "I didn't see the point. Leo's already worried enough as it is. I don't believe he knows of our history with Larkin." The carriage lurched forward as they began the return trip to Grosvenor Square.

"But still, she's as much a threat as anyone. He should be aware she's out there—somewhere." Tiki sat back against the crimson velvet of the seat and stared blindly out the window at the verdant trees they were passing in Green Park, trying to calm the bubble of emotions that threatened to choke her. "Do you think she was involved in the murder of the Seelie King?"

Rieker drummed his long fingers on the arm of the seat. "The timing is certainly suspicious but we have to remember Larkin is wounded."

"From tearing off her own wing." Tiki shuddered. "That's ghastly."

A frown flickered across Rieker's face. "She's desperate, Tiki. To be locked in one of Donegal's prisons isn't just a gaol sentence—it's a living death. Especially for her. I'm sure she would have done anything to get free."

Tiki looked away. For a second, it almost sounded like he was defending the evil faerie. "Because of what she did?"

"Really, it was what she *didn't* do." His lips pressed together in a bitter line. "Donegal ordered her to murder my family, but she didn't kill us all. Instead, she saved me." Rieker's eyes looked black. "That's why the high king of the UnSeelie court had her arrested."

Tiki's heart twisted at the reminder of the loss Rieker had suffered. Larkin had killed his parents and two younger brothers as they crossed the Channel to Paris for the Christmas holidays four years prior. Their boat had capsized during a vicious storm and the others had drowned, but Larkin had held Rieker's head above the water. Rieker had told Tiki last winter that Larkin had saved him because she had *grá do dhuine básmhar*—love for a mortal person. A jealous twinge twisted in Tiki's chest. Even with the horrific things Larkin had done, was it possible for Rieker to be immune to her unearthly beauty?

In a sudden burst the rain turned to hail and a million tiny fists pounded the roof of the carriage. Outside, the white ice came down with such force the sleet bounced when it hit the ground.

A question burned on the tip of Tiki's tongue. "How did you come to know of her escape?"

Rieker's face was guarded—almost as if he were hiding something. "There are those who keep me informed on important matters in the Otherworld."

Tiki's eyes narrowed. This was news. "And how do they do that exactly?"

Rieker adjusted his position on the seat and picked invisible dust from his trousers. "He comes to London and——" he paused.

"Yes?"

Familiar shadows lurked in the depths of his eyes as his gaze met hers. It was as though a wall had gone up between them.

"And talks to me." Rieker shrugged. "That's all. His name is Sean. He's much younger than Kieran was, but he's been badly wounded at some point. He's got terrible scars on his face."

"You trust him?" Tiki's voice echoed with disbelief. Rieker had told her of Kieran—an old man he'd met while living on the streets of London. Kieran had been dying and Rieker had helped him find food, to stay warm. In return, Kieran had told him of the world of Faerie—the plots, the intrigues, the relationships. Much of what he'd shared hadn't made sense and Rieker believed the old man to be delirious. It wasn't until later Rieker suspected Kieran had deliberately placed himself in his path and that his incoherent ramblings were actually a warning.

"What this Sean person tells you could be a ploy to gain access to the Queen's ring you guard," Tiki said.

Rieker looked away, a shadow of irritation darkening his face. "We need to have some way of knowing what's happening there, Teek. Especially if Donegal has found a way around the truce." His jaw clenched and he gazed out the window. "Because if that's true, then we are all in danger."

Tiki's heart sank at his words, at the way he spoke so casually about a world so alien.

"Sean told you of Donegal?"

Rieker nodded. "He also knew of Kieran—told me things Kieran had mentioned before he died."

"So this Sean also told you of Larkin's escape?" Tiki wasn't sure why Rieker's honesty was so unsettling. Was it that he'd been in contact with the fey? That he actually *trusted* one of them? Or maybe it was that he reminded her of the old Rieker—the one with secrets.

Rieker nodded. "I came to find you as soon as I learned the news."

"And you believe him?" Tiki pressed again. "Trust what he's told you?"

A sigh of exasperation escaped Rieker's lips. "I don't know that I'd trust any faerie completely, but the Seelie fey are the ones who brokered the truce with us. They want to see the ring protected and to maintain peace between our worlds as much as we do."

Tiki was silent as she considered Rieker's answer. It made sense the Seelie fey would want to protect Rieker—someone who carried the bloodline of Eridanus, king of the Summer Court for a millennium before being murdered. It was that same bloodline which allowed Rieker to now protect the ring of the truce. Perhaps it was that she was just learning of this fey liaison now, as disaster was striking, that made the information seem so dangerous.

She brushed a strand of her long hair over her shoulder and peeked at him from the corner of her eyes. He sat in profile to her, gazing out the window, the fine muscles in his jaw flexing with his thoughts. His shoulders were back and he looked prepared for battle. So fierce, so wild, so handsome—he was everything she wasn't: rich, titled, powerful. In that moment, he seemed a stranger again.

"Does Sean think Larkin will return to London?" Tiki asked.

Rieker turned from the window and leaned his elbows on his knees. He braced his fingers together and stared at the steeple they formed. His response was terse. "As you know, Larkin is unpredictable, but I think we have to assume she'll return to London straightaway."

"But she was caught here before," Tiki protested. The faerie's pleading screams as she'd been captured by her own kind still echoed in Tiki's ears with a disturbing resonance. "Wouldn't London be the first place Donegal and his men will look for her?"

Rieker stared at his fingers with such concentration Tiki wondered what memories moved before his eyes. "I have no idea what the UnSeelie King will do first, Teek, but I know what we have to do." In a sign of frustration Tiki had come to recognize, Rieker ran a hand through his hair, mussing the dark strands.

She spoke before he could say something she didn't want to hear. "Well, all I know is that I don't want anything to do with them. I wish you could return the ring to the royals and let them deal with the bloody fey."

Rieker lifted his head, a look of disbelief on his face. "This situation is deadly serious, Tiki. Larkin has alluded to the fact your birthmark is important to the Otherworld. You can't pretend you're not part of this."

Tiki crossed her arms and pressed her lips together in anger. "I'm not—"

Rieker spoke over her, his eyes dark and serious. "Listen to me, Tiki—we know Larkin and the UnSeelie fey will murder to get what they want. We know they'll steal children. Old Kieran told me many things about the world of the fey, but in a veiled way that didn't always make sense." His voice became more urgent. "But there is one thing I do know." He pointed at her wrist. "Whether you like it or not, your mark links you to the Otherworld and we need to know what it means."

A chill crept through Tiki as the carriage jolted onto Grosvenor Lane, the uneven clopping of the horse's hooves against the cobblestones keeping time with her heart. She didn't want to know what her birthmark meant.

THE DRIVER STEERED the carriage through the back alley into the coach house that adjoined the upscale townhome.

Tension crackled in the air between them as Rieker assisted Tiki down the steps and led the way inside.

"Hello Charles." He nodded at the tall, robust butler who was silently approaching. "Once again you somehow magically know of my arrival."

"Welcome home, Master William." The man dipped his head in a bow. His black cravat and jacket were a sharp contrast to the crisp white shirt and gray vest he wore. A moustache had been greased to fine points below his rather bulbous nose. "I heard Geoffrey's arrival with the carriage."

"Please see to my bags." Rieker shrugged out of his long black overcoat and handed it to the older man who already held Tiki's cloak over one arm. Rieker reached back and took Tiki's hand, leading her down the hallway. "We'll be in the study." Lowering his voice he leaned closer to her. "I want to talk to you about what we tell the others."

Stiffly, Tiki followed him down the grand hall and through one side of an ornately carved pair of doors. Of all the rooms in the elegant home, the study reminded her most of Rieker: a mixture of strength, elegance and a touch of mystery.

Being in this room was like sneaking a peek into William Richmond's world of secrets. For a moment she imagined that she really lived here with him, rather than as a guest who needed temporary lodging. A longing pulled in her chest at the thought.

"Wills!" Bare feet pattered down the wood floor of the hallway as Clara raced toward the study. The four year-old ran into the room and threw herself into Rieker's arms. "Where 'ave you been? We've been waiting for you to come home for*ever!*"

"Have you now?" Rieker hugged the little girl close and raised his eyebrows at Tiki over her shoulder.

Clara leaned back to look him in the face. Pale blond ringlets wreathed her face. "Especially Tiki." Tiki's cheeks began to warm and she busied herself using the poker to reposition the wood in the grate.

Rieker chuckled, the corner of his mouth twitching. "I've only been gone a few weeks."

"Hallo, Master William." Mrs. Bosworth huffed, as she hurried into the room, smoothing the folds of the white apron she wore over her black dress. The middle-aged housekeeper smiled with unconcealed pleasure at the young man sitting with Clara in his arms. "I couldn't stop her when she'd found you'd arrived. Now, come along, Clara." Mrs. Bosworth clapped her hands together and made a shooing motion toward the door. "We've got cookin' to do."

Clara looked from Rieker to Mrs. Bosworth as if deciding. Finally, she slid off Rieker's knee and paused to lean close. "I'll make you somethin' good to eat," she whispered.

His eyes lit up with delight. "Brown frogs and worms?"

Clara jerked her head back with a horrified expression then burst into giggles. "No, you silly. Brown frogs and *slugs*." Then she turned and pattered from the room, her laughter drifting behind like notes from a musical instrument.

Mrs. Bosworth rolled her eyes at Rieker. "Thank you, young sir, for the lovely suggestion. Next thing I know, she'll be diggin' up me garden." She left the room shaking her head.

Tiki smiled at their antics. Mrs. Bosworth had cared for Rieker most of his life. Their familiar teasing set her nerves at ease. "Toots will be especially glad you've returned. I think he wants you to teach him how to ride a horse."

"To ride?" Rieker looked at her in surprise. "Has he ever been on a horse before?"

"No." Tiki smiled. "But he loves them. I think he fancies himself to be a gentleman like you."

Rieker barked out a laugh. "I'll have to be careful to set a good example. I could easily teach him the wrong things."

"No doubt about that," Tiki murmured. She pressed her lips together to hide the smile tugging at the corners of her mouth.

Rieker narrowed his eyes in a playful scowl. "I believe we've a case of the pot calling the kettle black." He pushed out of the chair to close the door to the study and his grin faded as he returned to his seat.

"We've got to make a plan, Tiki—to understand what your mark means, to be prepared for the worst."

Tiki smoothed the forest green folds of her dress, running her fingers across the fabric. She agreed they needed a plan, but she wasn't sure it needed to include knowing what her mark meant. She'd lived just fine for sixteen years without knowing. Would it really make that much difference now? What they needed to do was obvious: stay away from faeries. She let out a slow breath, trying to be patient. "What do you have in mind?"

"There are two people I can think of who might have some answers for us." Rieker tilted his head so he could see her eyes. "The first is Sean." He paused, waiting for a reaction, but Tiki didn't speak. "The other is Mamie, the woman who has tended Queen Victoria all these years. You heard Leo and Arthur today—they often get information regarding the Otherworld from her. She lives in the Birdkeeper's Cottage at the end of St. James Park. We could pay her a visit and see what she might know of your birthmark."

Tiki lifted her chin. Better to be clear now, rather than let Rieker think she was in agreement with him on their course of action. "What if I don't want to know what my birthmark means?"

Rieker's mouth opened in a startled expression. "*What?*" His dark eyebrows drew down until they were two slashes across his forehead. "You're joking, right?"

Tiki crossed her arms. "Not really." A conversation she'd had with Larkin when the faerie bargained for the ring of the truce echoed in her ears. *'An fáinne sí is a birthmark of Finn MacLochlan—a high king of Tara— the ancient Irish faerie court. That mark on your arm practically makes you royalty.'* Larkin's face had twisted with jealousy. *'That's why Adasara hid you in London.'*

Even now, the words made Tiki squirm in her chair. She tapped her finger on her arm and worked hard at keeping her voice level. "I don't really see how it will help, anyway. It's not like we're going to go do battle with them. We just need to stay as far away from the bloody fey as we can get."

For a moment, Rieker seemed at a loss for words. "But, it's not that simple—"

"Why not?" Tiki snapped. She didn't want to argue about this. After being attacked by Marcus last December and Larkin stealing little Clara when the child was deathly ill—of all people, Rieker should understand why she didn't want anything to do with faeries.

The rap of knuckles sounded on the door.

A growl of frustration erupted from Rieker's throat and through gritted teeth he called, "Come."

The door swung open and Charles, the butler, stood there. "Sorry to interrupt, sir. A Miss Isabelle Cavendish has arrived to see you."

Rieker frowned. "Isabelle?" He blew out a long sigh and ran his hands through his hair. "Thank you. Please show her in, Charles."

Tiki pushed herself out of the chair intending to leave the room.

Rieker stood as though to stop her, then seemed to think better of it and slid his hands into his pockets instead. "Will you stay, Tiki? I can't imagine Izzy will be here long and you and I have more to talk about."

Tiki's heart squeezed at the familiar way he addressed his visitor. Isabelle had grown up in the same wealthy circles as Rieker—a world almost as alien to Tiki as the Otherworld. She'd met the other girl at the Masked Ball held at Buckingham Palace last December and could still envision Isabelle's beautiful features. Her magnetic eyes and regal posture were hard to forget, as was her obvious attraction to William Richmond.

"Certainly—if you'd like." Tiki's words came out sounding stiff and formal. It wasn't often that she had difficulty making a decision, but how she fit into William Richmond's life was a puzzle she couldn't seem to piece together. Her middle-class upbringing, before becoming a pickpocket to survive, was a far cry from the privileged world of London's upper class in which Rieker had been raised. Tiki feared the day was coming that Rieker would reach the same conclusion. Lately, she'd been thinking it was time to find another home for her family of orphans.

"Hello William." A silky voice purred from the doorway.

Tiki turned with a gasp. She would recognize Larkin's voice anywhere.

Chapter Five

Isabelle Cavendish stood in the doorway, a coy smile twisting her lips. She was clad in an elegant midnight blue dress with matching jacket, her brown hair pulled away from her face to cascade down her back. Her features were the same chiseled perfection Tiki remembered, but the enigmatic blue-green eyes that stared back were unmistakably Larkin's. It only took Tiki a second to realize Larkin was wearing a glamour to look like Isabelle Cavendish.

"Larkin," Tiki said in a shocked tone, fear beating a rapid tattoo inside her chest. "Why are you here?"

A frown flickered across the girl's face as she glanced at Tiki. "Just who I was hoping to find—the thief." Her glamoured features tightened in distaste.

Rieker stared from one to the other in obvious confusion. "Larkin?" he echoed, swiveling to look at Tiki. "Are you sure?"

"Yes, William, she's right." Larkin sniffed as though a bad smell wafted beneath her nostrils. "Don't tell me she lives with you now—and no doubt, the rest of her little band of pickpockets." The faerie's words rang with a bitterness that was palpable. "Such a disgustingly sweet little family."

Rieker shifted his position to stand between Tiki and Larkin. "That's no concern of yours."

Larkin's eyes narrowed with a calculating look. "Though I do miss the little girl at times. What was her name? Clara? Tell me, does she ask after me?"

Red-hot anger surged through Tiki, replacing her fear. "No, she doesn't," she snapped. She glared at the faerie. "Thankfully, the nightmares of when you stole her have stopped." It was a lie, Clara had never had nightmares that Tiki knew of, but she couldn't stand the idea Larkin might have some twisted idea she mattered to the child. "Why would you come back to London? I heard you were wounded when you escaped—that you had to tear your own wing off to get away."

Larkin's poisonous laugh filled the room. "Do you *pity* me now?" She spat the words out as though she couldn't bear the taste of them on her tongue. "Guttersnipe, you can't pity what you don't understand."

"I don't pity you." Tiki's voice was raw with emotion. "You deserve every ounce of what you've got."

"*Isabelle*," Rieker spoke up, interrupting their conversation. "Why are you here?"

"William, where are your manners? Aren't you going to invite me in to sit down?" A small bag swung from Isabelle's wrist and she carried a fan in one hand that she snapped open with an irritated flick of her wrist. She moved slowly though, as if she were in pain.

"No, because you're not staying," Rieker replied, the muscles in his jaw flexing.

Larkin frowned. "Considering what we've been through together, it seems you could be a bit more charitable." Her eyes raked over Tiki. "Perhaps it's the unsavory influences in your life."

"You would have a clear understanding of unsavory, wouldn't you?" Tiki shot back, her anger bubbling to the surface again. Something flickered in Larkin's eyes and for a second, Tiki got the impression the faerie was laughing at her, as if she enjoyed Tiki's irritation.

"Larkin." Rieker held his hand up. "Not another insult." He was a head taller than the faerie and took a threatening step toward the other girl. Larkin, rather than retreating, leaned closer and ran a finger down his lapel, a teasing smile on her lips.

"Oh William, don't get your knickers in a knot. Let a girl have her fun."

Rieker ground his teeth and took a step back so she could no longer touch him. "Why did you come back to London? What are you after this time?"

Larkin contemplated them through narrowed eyes. "You both think you're so clever, don't you? Saved the ring and now you'll live happily ever after." Her lip curled like a feral dog. "Well, happily ever after doesn't exist in my world and soon it's not going to exist in yours either. I've come to warn you."

Rieker raised his eyebrows. "Warn us about what?"

"Donegal is on the move and if he's not stopped he will take everything that is precious from you." Larkin snapped the fan closed and tapped it against her fingers. "Believe me when I say there are worse things than dying."

"Now that you've warned us," Rieker said in a dry voice, "What is it that you want from us?"

The faerie blinked and then her lips twisted in a beguiling smile. It was as if the warmth of the sun suddenly flowed into the room. "Why, I want you to help me."

A chill ran up Tiki's arms. Her voice came out in a ragged whisper of disbelief. "*Help* you?"

"You don't seem to understand." Larkin snapped her teeth at Tiki as if she wished she could bite her. "I won't be able to stop him this time." Lightning fast, her mood shifted again, her tone becoming cajoling. "But if you help me, I'll help you."

"What do you mean *this time*?" Rieker said slowly.

Larkin's throaty chuckle echoed in the room, reminding Tiki of the thunder she'd heard during the storm. The faerie was dangerous, unpredictable and untrustworthy, yet Tiki held her breath, waiting to hear what Larkin would say next.

"It's time to face the facts. I *saved* your life, William. You *owe* me. The faerie blood that runs in your veins may allow you to guard the ring of the truce, but it also binds you to the laws of our world. You are beholden to me."

Tiki gasped. "*Saved* him? You *murdered* his family."

The faerie stood oddly still, her arms held close to her body. In the past she'd danced and twirled—a butterfly flitting from flower to flower—but now, she barely moved. Her icy gaze was frozen on Tiki. "How do you know that?"

Tiki motioned with her hand. "Rieker told me."

Rieker was silent, watching Larkin with a wary expression.

A ghost of a smile crossed her lips. "Oh, and does he tell you all of his secrets now?"

At Rieker's continued silence a tiny thread of doubt wove its way around Tiki's heart.

Larkin's lips twisted in perverse pleasure at the betraying play of emotions across Tiki's face. "I didn't think so." She leaned forward and spoke in a conspiratorial whisper. "Never forget, guttersnipe, I've known William far longer than you have. I know more than a few of his secrets."

Tiki's felt as though she were being pulled into a dark abyss.

Larkin's eyes dared Tiki to believe what she said. "*Donegal* drowned those people. Not me. I arrived too late to save any of them but William."

"You expect us to believe that?" Tiki snapped. She shot a glance at Rieker out of the corner of her eyes. Why wasn't he speaking up?

Larkin snorted with disgust. "Does it *ever* occur to you that the obvious is not always the answer?"

An odd sense of imbalance wobbled Tiki, as though she stood on a slippery slope. For a second, she wondered if the faerie spoke the truth.

"You're putting blame in the wrong place—" Larkin's voice almost sounded weary—"because that's the easy thing to do. Both of you underestimate the threat of the Winter king. I might have stopped him if I'd recovered the ring of the truce but now it's too late—he's gone too far. I need your help."

"That's enough, Larkin." Rieker suddenly came to life and moved toward the faerie as if to usher her out. "We don't want to help you. We just want you to leave us alone."

Larkin's lips twisted into a sneer. "You'd best be careful what you wish for, William, or you might wish away the very thing you want the most."

Rieker stiffened. "Are you threatening me?"

She fluttered the fan before her face, her eyes glittering like blue opals behind hooded lids, reminding Tiki of an exotic snake waiting to strike. "I'm quite sure you would find some of my secrets fascinating."

"Were you involved in the murder of the Seelie king?"

The faerie blinked in surprise. "So you already know." A fleeting smile flitted across her face. "That's what I like about you, William—always one step ahead of the rest of the lot. I've always said you would do well in my world."

Rieker didn't return her smile. "You haven't answered my question."

Larkin's smile faded. "No, I wasn't involved in the Summer king's murder. In the span of four years—less than a blink of time in the faerie world—*two* Seelie kings have been murdered—O'Riagáin and Eridanus. Both at the hand of one man: Donegal."

A low snarl emitted from her throat. "Now he sits on the Dragon Throne as we speak, claiming to rule all of Faerie. He is a madman, thirsting for power, surrounded by his minions—" she threw out an arm and flinched as though in pain— "mindless warriors who follow his commands." Her voice lowered. "But he won't stop with the death of O'Riagáin. Oh, no. He has bigger plans than that. He's coming after the Queen, the royal family and—" her words fell, diamond sharp— "he's learned there is someone marked with *an fáinne sí* hiding in London." Larkin raised her eyebrows. With an arrogant twist of her head she nodded at Tiki. "He's coming after *her*."

Chapter Six

Tiki gripped the back of a nearby chair. Surely she couldn't have heard Larkin correctly.

Rieker took a step forward, his hands clenched in fists. His voice rang with accusation. "How did he find out about Tiki's mark?"

"Donegal is after anyone who will further his power," Larkin replied. "Especially now, when he's found a way around the truce and believes he's invincible." She slapped the fan against her hand, a calculating look creasing her beautiful features. "He doesn't know who is marked or where they might be yet, but trust me, he is relentless." Her lips twisted in a smug smile. "Lucky for you, I know how to stop him. That's why you'll help me."

Tiki stood stunned. "But I thought you were part of the UnSeelie court. I thought—"

"You thought what?" The faerie cut her off with a snarl. "That I would forever live my life in the shadows and gloom? That I was bred from the monstrosities who make up the dark court?" Her upper lip curled with derision. "I was a *spy!*" She spat the word out like a gauntlet thrown to the ground. "I sacrificed myself to that miserable life for Eridanus, for Finn—" she stopped, a rare play of emotions blowing across her face. "But they didn't live to see my success and I will do what *I* think is right now."

"And that is what, exactly?" Rieker's voice was low, ragged with emotion.

"There's only one way to stop Donegal at this point. He has grown too strong. We need to put her—" she stabbed her long finger in Tiki's direction— "and the *Cloch na Teamhrach* together."

Tiki stepped back. She didn't understand what Larkin had said, but she knew better than to trust the faerie. Nothing Larkin had planned could be good for Tiki or her family.

Rieker spoke the foreign words with a surprising ease. "What is *Cloch na Teamhrach*?"

"The Stone of Tara."

At the sound of her name, dread trickled down Tiki's back like the icy brown water of the Thames, chilling her. She clenched her hands. "Tara?"

"Yes," Larkin said. "The stone is carved from the rock found beneath the Hill of Tara in Ireland, where the Seelie court originated. It is sacred to our world." The faerie's eyes narrowed, her expression becoming hard. "Legend says the rock will cry out when touched by a true high king or queen. All in Faerie, Seelie and UnSeelie alike, must bow to a sovereign named by *Cloch na Teamhrach.* "

"So where is this sacred stone?" Rieker asked, his curiosity clearly aroused, "and what does it have to do with Tiki?"

Larkin lowered her voice. "The location of the Tara Stone is one of the Otherworld's greatest secrets, but it is whispered that the stone is in the Palace of Mirrors."

"The Palace of Mirrors?" Tiki asked, despite herself. "What's that?"

A smile quirked Larkin's mouth at Tiki's interest. "The Palace of Mirrors is a fortress located on Wydryn Tor high above the Wychwood Forest. It stands on neutral ground between the Plain of Sunlight that the Seelie's inhabit and the Plain of Starlight where the UnSeelies live."

"The Wychwood Forest?" Rieker interrupted. "But that's over in Oxfordshire."

Larkin tapped her fan along the back of a chair as she moved toward the window. She stopped in a spill of sunlight, which turned her glamoured brown hair to the blond color Tiki remembered from past encounters. She swiveled toward Rieker.

"You're exactly right, William. The Royal Forest of Wychwood is an ancient parcel of land that was set aside as a place for the British sovereigns to hunt deer and stags. A place of magic your royals have long known about. The stone quarried for one of your world's most important royal buildings, St. George's Chapel at Windsor Castle, comes from a town within the forest. Protected by enchantments, even now." She snapped her fan open and fluttered the delicate blue silk before her face. "The Wychwood Forest is a grand place of immeasurable beauty—" her tone sharpened— "and terrible danger for those who don't know their way. The Wychwood is one of the true intersections between the mortal world and the Otherworld."

An intersection with the Otherworld? Tiki fought back a shudder. Was it possible such places existed? Where one could start walking in one world and end up in another?

"A..Are there," Tiki faltered, "other...intersections?"

"Of course," Larkin said. "For instance, Wydryn Tor is a crossroads with what you mortals call Glastonbury Tor, though time and space are measured differently in our world. But I was telling you about the Palace." Larkin snapped her fan closed against the palm of her hand. "The Palace of Mirrors provides the same function as your Queen's Buckingham Palace. It is where the ruler of Faerie resides."

She moved to the desk, drawing a long finger along the edge of the walnut wood. "In our world, control shifts during the year. The Seelies, also known as the Summer Court, rule from Beltane, which is the first of May, to Samhain, at the end of October. The UnSeelie's, the Winter Court, rule during the dark months from Samhain to Beltane."

Rieker stood with his hands on his hips. "I thought Donegal sat on the Seelie throne now?"

Larkin gave a sharp jerk of her head. "Which is the reason I'm here. Donegal has killed the Summer king just weeks before Beltane—the day when control of the courts should shift back to the Seelie's again. But he doesn't intend to relinquish control on the first of May." She held her long, delicate finger up. "We have one chance to take the throne back."

"And what's that?" Rieker asked.

The glamoured faerie stepped away from the desk to walk back toward Tiki and Rieker. As she moved a cloud covered the sun and the shaft of light suddenly disappeared like the snuffed flame of a candle.

"Donegal controls the courts through brute force rather than destiny. The stone did not speak for him, because he is not the true heir," Larkin said. "The last time the stone cried out was during the reign of Finvarra, the first high king of the *Daoine Sidhe*." She gave Tiki a pointed look. "He was Finn MacLochlan's father."

Tiki blinked at the familiar name. Larkin had mentioned Finn MacLochlan before—that the mark on her arm was also the birthmark of Finn MacLochlan—whoever he was. Tiki's heart pounded like a train racing down the tracks at full steam. "What does any of this have to do with me?"

"Should the stone roar, then all in Faerie, even Donegal, would be forced to acknowledge the Seelie Court has a new, true high king —" through slitted eyes Larkin's gaze locked on Tiki— "or queen." The faerie took a step closer. "I need your help because you, Tara Kathleen Dunbar MacLochlan, despicable little orphan girl, are Finn MacLochlan's daughter and therefore, Finvarra's, last true heir."

Chapter Seven

Tiki stood frozen, her mouth ajar. Nothing Larkin could have said would have been more shocking. Even Rieker seemed stunned by the faerie's announcement. When he finally spoke, it was in a tone of disbelief. "Larkin, what nonsense are you spewing now?"

The faerie moved, as if balanced on air, the silky folds of her dark blue dress billowing around her. "Really, it can't be that much of a shock." She sounded as if she were bored by their confusion. "You must have realized by now."

At their blank stares, her expression shifted. "Fine. Pretend you don't know. I'll explain it to you." She frowned at Tiki. "But repeating the facts won't change what is necessary at the end of the day."

"I'm afraid we have no idea what the 'facts' might be," Rieker said in an even tone. His eyes were bright with curiosity. "Are you saying Tiki is descended from a faerie king?"

"William." Larkin snapped. "Why do you sound surprised? You're descended from Eridanus, one of the greatest faeries who ever lived. Why should the news that Tiki has faerie blood be any different?"

"I have *a thread* of faerie blood in me," Rieker protested, "passed down over centuries. You're suggesting Tiki has significantly more."

"For the love of *Ériu* she is marked with *an fáinne sí*, after all," Larkin said. "It's obvious she's Finn MacLochlan's daughter."

Tiki capped her hand over her arm where the thin black lines of her birthmark twisted around her wrist. *An fáinne sí:* The faerie ring. A rare and undeniable connection to the fey, she'd been told. Yet she *had* denied it. She had not allowed herself to believe she had any connection to that unseen world, even though her mother had hinted many times that another world intersected with their own.

"But I'd never even heard of Finn MacLochlan before you mentioned his name—" Tiki protested.

"That doesn't alter the facts," Larkin said in a stony voice, "that you are his daughter."

Tiki clenched her teeth. "That's not even possible. I've lived in London all my life and—"

"Yes, well—" Larkin swept Tiki with a smug glance. "Where to start and how much to tell—"

Tiki's breath caught in her throat. Was she ready to know the truth? "Last winter you mentioned that someone named Adasara *hid* me in London. Why don't you start there?"

"Yes, my dear beautiful sister, Adasara." Larkin's voice sounded wistful. "I think you're exactly right. That is the perfect place to start."

Tiki sucked in her breath with a hiss. *"Sister?"*

A smile flitted across Larkin's face and she looked pleased with herself. "Oh, yes. Did I forget to mention that?" She smoothed the folds of her dress, her movements effortless and graceful. "Adasara was my older sister. She was very beautiful and very kind." Larkin flicked a strand of hair over her shoulder and tilted her head. Her eyes were bright as if she were enjoying herself immensely. "Not like me at all."

"Why did your sister have Tiki?" Rieker asked. "Did she steal her?"

An expression of innocence was painted on Larkin's features. "Adasara had Tara because she was her mother." Her enigmatic eyes shifted to Tiki. "Which, if my calculations are correct, makes me your aunt, doesn't it?"

Time stood frozen, as Tiki stared at Larkin in disbelief.

"*Tiki, Tiki, Tiki*." Clara's shrill cry echoed down the hallway. The spell broken, Tiki jerked toward the door, instantly alert to the panic in the four year-old's voice. She turned back to warn Larkin not to reveal her true identity to the child, but Isabelle Cavendish was gone.

"Rieker—where—"

"Come quick," Clara gasped as she exploded through the door. Her chest heaved as she grabbed Tiki's hand and tugged her down the hallway.

"Clara—" Tiki fought a rising panic of her own— "what on earth is the matter?" She pulled back against the insistent tugging of the child. "Stop and tell me what's wrong."

"I can't." Clara said. "We've got to hurry."

A sixth sense prickled along Tiki's spine. "Clara Marie, stop this instant and tell me what's going on."

Fiona appeared in the doorway, her face knitted in a worried expression. "Hello Wills." She nodded at the young man who stood next to Tiki. "Welcome home."

Tiki bent at the knees and scooped Clara into her arms, balancing the frail girl on one hip. "Fi, do you know—"

"It's Toots." Fiona said. "He hasn't returned from wherever he's got himself off to. Clara got it in her head that he's disappeared."

The little girl turned frightened eyes toward Tiki. "It's true," she whispered. "Mrs. B. sent me outside to tell Toots to come in an' I saw those blokes take 'im."

"Take him where?" Tiki asked in a sharp voice. Tears welled up in Clara's eyes.

"That's just it—I don' know. I can't see 'em anymore."

"Clara, love, there's no need to get so upset." Tiki smoothed a tangle of blond hair from the little girl's face. "He's probably just around the corner. I'm sure he's fine."

"But Tiki." Clara hiccupped. "He's *not*. I was watchin' from the horse house. They were standing there in the alley talkin', then one of 'em took Toots's arm and all three of 'em disappeared."

"Disappeared?" Tiki echoed.

Rieker stepped closer. "Are you sure?"

Clara gave a solemn nod, her blue eyes bright with tears.

Tiki didn't wait to hear more. She let Clara slide to the floor and clutched her little hand.

"Show me where." They hurried back toward the rear door, running out through the harness room, past where Geoffrey was brushing one of the black mares, to the large oversized carriage door that led to the alley. Clara pulled her out onto the narrow lane and pointed.

"Down there."

A tall, dense hedgerow protected one side of the narrow lane that was used to access the coach houses along the back of the building. There was never much foot traffic and at this moment the alley was empty in both directions. Tiki's heart skipped in her chest as she searched for the red-headed boy. Toots was full of energy and often wandered off. Years of surviving on the streets had made him unafraid to explore. But Clara was suggesting he hadn't simply wandered off but that he'd been abducted—perhaps by something otherworldly. Or—knowing Toots—had he gone willingly?

"Was he yelling for help?" Tiki smoothed Clara's tangled curls back from her little face.

"Oh, no, he was laughin' and 'avin' a good time, and then—" Clara motioned with her hands— "gone."

Tiki clutched Rieker's arm. "Do you think—"

"I don't know," Rieker said. "You check inside again. I'll look out here." He leaned down and opened his arms to take Clara. "I'm going to walk down the way a bit and see if I can find Toots. Want to come with me?"

"Yes." Clara nodded with a serious expression. "I'll be your 'elper."

Rieker lifted her small body over his head, sliding her legs onto his shoulders. "You don't have to hold onto my ears, either. I've got you." A guilty giggle escaped Clara's lips as she released her grip on Rieker's ears. Tiki's chest constricted with emotion.

"Teek, you stay at the house, in case he returns. And don't panic." Rieker gave Tiki a gentle smile. "You know Toots. He's tough and adventuresome. He's all right—wherever he might be." He lifted a tress of Tiki's hair and tucked it behind her shoulder, letting the silky strands run through his fingers. "We'll find him." She tried to force a smile but fear crept through her veins and she shivered.

Rieker walked down the street, Clara bouncing on his broad shoulders. "Toots! Tooottssss!" They called one way and then the other, their voices carrying above the wind. Tiki took a deep breath and forced herself to consider the unthinkable. Last winter Larkin had stolen Clara, intending to trade her for the ring of the truce. If Toots had been taken by Larkin, this time Tiki had nothing to trade for his return. Except, perhaps, herself.

Chapter Eight

"I'm concerned, Arthur. Even though mother is practically on house arrest and has guards with her at all times, I fear it's not enough." Leo led Diablo into the royal stables, one hand gripping the reins under the great black horse's jaw. The shod hooves were muted against the straw strewn over the cobblestone floor.

"I know." Arthur walked abreast, leading his own mount. They'd just returned from a ride through the Queen's parks. The weather had abated enough they were able to ride between downpours. "I've had the same worries. When we don't know how to recognize the face of the enemy we are at a distinct disadvantage. If the weather is any indication, then things are getting worse rather than better in the Otherworld."

"It's not just the weather." Leo handed the reins over to the stable master. "There's something else."

"Such as?" Arthur turned his horse over and pulled his leather gloves off as they walked the length of the stables to exit. Horses snorted and poked their heads over their stalls, hoping for attention from the brothers.

Leo leaned close and lowered his voice. "I have this feeling I'm being watched." He gave Arthur a sidelong glance. "Have you noticed it as well?"

Arthur's brows pulled down in a frown. "Are you serious? Have you noticed something out of the ordinary?"

"Nothing I can put my finger on. It's difficult to describe." Leo paused, searching for the right words. "It's a bit like having someone breathe down your neck, but when you turn, there's no one." He forced a laugh. "Probably my imagination. All this talk of faeries and war has got me spooked."

Arthur slapped his gloves against his leg. "As we all should be. Best to take extra precautions for now."

Chapter Nine

Tiki's thoughts were a whirlwind the next morning as she gave last minute instructions to Mrs. Bosworth about Clara. Could Larkin's claim be true? Was Tiki Finvarra's last heir? Was it possible that even now, the UnSeelie king could be coming after her?

"Tiki—are you coming?" Fiona called from the front door. "It's going to be noon by the time we get down to see Mr. Potts."

"Run along wit' ye, miss," Mrs. Bosworth said, shooing her reddened hands at Tiki. The middle-aged woman wore an identical black dress to the one she'd worn yesterday, covered by a white apron that was already stained with evidence of her hard work in the kitchen. Her stout legs ended in sensible black flat shoes. "Go see if you can track down young Thomas. I can't imagine where that lad's got himself off to. But while you're gone, I know how to care for the little one." She smiled down at Clara who stood clutching Doggie. Clara's long white-blond curls floated around her head making her look like an angelic cherub.

"Teek, I'm goin'ta help Mrs. B. cook somethun really good," Clara said with a wobbly smile as she reached for the housekeeper's hand. "It'll be a surprise for Toots when he comes home."

"All right, you two, that sounds lovely." Tiki bent down to kiss Clara's soft cheek. "I'll tell Mr. Potts you said hello." Tiki hurried toward the front door. Shamus had left at the break of dawn to make his deliveries for Binder's Bakery. He'd promised to look for Toots during his drive around the City. Rieker had also left the townhome before Tiki was up.

"Tell ol' Potts we need a new story to read, too." Clara called over her shoulder as Mrs. Bosworth led the little girl toward the kitchen. "I know Fi wants one with a 'andsome prince but I want one with a faerie in it!"

IT TOOK THIRTY minutes for Tiki and Fiona to walk from Grosvenor Square to Charing Cross railway station. They cut down Saville Row and over to Regent Street, the roads busy with carriages and omnibuses ferrying the masses through the heart of London. More than once Tiki looked over her shoulder to see if they were being followed, but there was nothing suspicious.

A funeral hearse rolled by, the black plumes on the cart shimmying as the matching horses stopped and started in the congested streets. Two-wheeled carts groaned along, their axles creaking under the weight of their loads, while barefoot children dodged the piles of steaming manure from the horses. Their shrieks filled the air to blend with the shouts of the drivers, the snorts and whinnies of the horses, the jangle of the rigging and the cacophony of iron-shod wheels clacking against the cobblestones.

"Where do you s'pose Rieker's been these last few weeks?" Fiona asked as they walked past a music hall, the tinkling notes of a piano and a woman's laughter spilling out the open door. "I thought he was to be gone for another week."

"I don't know," Tiki replied. She'd been annoyed last winter when Rieker had first started following her, but she'd gotten used to his constant presence and had come to care for the young man more than she liked to admit. His absence over the last weeks had been a more difficult adjustment than she'd expected—and that scared her. She'd learned to survive on her own. She didn't want to have to depend on someone else. There were times now, though, when he almost felt like a stranger again.

Fiona paused to stare through a glass window where a shop clerk straightened a display of ladies hats. "Does he still live on the street some of the time? He looks awfully thin."

Tiki sighed. "I don't really know, Fi. He told me once that he sometimes buys food and pretends he's stolen it just to feed some of the street children who are starving. It wouldn't surprise me if he still does that." Tiki pulled her hair over her shoulder and gripped the windblown strands with one hand as she stood next to Fiona and stared blindly at the window display. She'd noticed he'd lost weight, too. "You know, I was thinking we could start helping to feed some of these street children. I've got the money the Queen gave me for returning the ring. We can afford to share some bread and cheddar."

"That's a nice thought, Teek," Fiona said. "We could go over to Covent Garden and hand it out there. We know a few of the blokes workin' the market, though they wouldn't recognize us now that we're ladies." She dipped into a curtsy, grinning and Tiki couldn't help but laugh. Six months ago it would have been impossible to imagine others might consider them to be ladies.

Fiona looped her arm through Tiki's and pulled her down the street. "Do you think Rieker still picks pockets?" An attractive young man dressed in a black suit and a top hat set at a jaunty angle, approached. His blond hair was a bit longer than usual and one corner of his mouth turned up in a grin, as if he knew a secret.

Tiki's gaze lingered on him—there was something so familiar about his face—then her cheeks warmed as she realized he was staring back at her with an appreciative grin. She still wasn't used to the attention she received now that she dressed as a young woman again. During the two years she'd lived in the abandoned clock-maker's shop next to Charing Cross, she'd dressed as a boy and had been invisible. Moments like now, when she *wanted* to be invisible, was when she missed those days.

He lifted his hat and nodded as he passed. "Ladies." His voice was low, almost musical.

"Who's that?" Fiona whispered, nudging Tiki as she looked over her shoulder at the young man. "He looked like he knew you."

Tiki tugged Fiona along. "Stop staring," she hissed. "I have no idea who he is."

Fiona paused to primp in the reflection of another store window, pulling her curly waves behind her hair in a pretend up-do, and tilted her chin. "See—he thought we were ladies too. It's a wonder what a splash of water and a bit of fabric will do for a girl." She let her hair fall back around her face. "You never answered my question. Do you think Rieker still picks pockets?"

"Rieker's got his secrets, Fi. There's more about him that I don't know, than what I do." She hesitated. "But I do know why he returned to Grosvenor Square early."

Fiona turned, her curiosity clearly piqued. "Why's that?"

In hushed whispers Tiki told her of Larkin's return and the faerie's outrageous claim.

Fiona's mouth dropped open. "Do you believe her?"

"Of course not. Nothing but a pound's worth of poppycock."

"But why would she make something like that up?" Fiona sounded unconvinced. They walked another block, passing a shoe-maker's shop, the staccato pounding of hammers echoing out into the street.

"I have no idea."

Fiona sucked her breath in. "Do you think she has something to do with Toots gone missing?"

Tiki's expression darkened. "I can't help but wonder."

"But why—" Fiona growled. "That horrible creature. If she took Toots just to get to you—"

"I know." A gust of wind teased Tiki's hair, reminding her of when Rieker had so gently smoothed the strands from her face. She brushed her hair back with an impatient gesture. "There's something else we need to talk about."

"What's that?" Fiona asked. The rich smell of glue filled their noses as they passed the offices of a bookbinder.

A twinge of sadness filled Tiki's chest as she spoke. With Larkin's return and the secrets Rieker seemed to be keeping again, the decision seemed inevitable. "I think it's time to find our own flat."

WHEN THEY ARRIVED at Charing Cross, Fiona went to use the lavatory while Tiki paused to admire a basket of hothouse roses. As she bent to smell their fragrance a shadow shifted behind her, too close for comfort. The slightest pressure brushed her back, like invisible fingers touching her. Tiki whirled, ready to pull the knife she had hidden up her sleeve. A shadowy figure dissolved into nothingness as she blinked, leaving the space before her empty. Tiki glanced around to see if anyone was watching her but there was no one. Unsettled, she turned back to the flowers as Fiona approached.

"Teek, did you see that bloke leanin' against the wall over there?" Fiona's cheeks were as rosy as the dress she wore. She dipped her head and looked from beneath her lashes. "He's a handsome one, don't you think? He keeps watchin' us."

Tiki glanced in the direction Fiona indicated. The young man was about their age, dressed in trousers and a jacket that had seen better days. A cap covered his brown hair but Fiona was right—his face was attractive and he looked friendly enough.

"Nobody I know," Tiki said. "Let's get on to Mr. Potts and find out if he's seen Toots."

It was only a short walk to the bookstore. Mr. Potts had been selling books in Charing Cross for over twenty years. The old man had held the key to a world of hope at a time when Tiki had none. With no money or food, half the time, she'd spent may hours in the bookstore, imagining she lived in a different world.

Tiki glanced through the store's paned window as they passed to the front door. A bell tinkled as they pushed their way in. "Hallo, Mr. Potts," Tiki called.

The old man's stooped form shuffled out from between an aisle of books. At the sight of them his bent shoulders slumped even further. "Oh, g'day, ladies. Yer sounded a bit like a friend of mine." He turned back, a wrinkled hand scratching his bald head.

"Mr. Potts, it's me, Tiki."

"Eh?" The old man grunted as he turned to gaze at her again with narrowed eyes. He took a cautious step closer, taking in her pale blue dress and long dark hair. His eyes shifted to Fiona with a blank look then he glanced back at Tiki. "Is that yer, Tiki?" he asked.

Tiki laughed. "Of course it's me, Mr. Potts. Don't tell me that you don't recognize me just because I'm clean?" She twirled once, holding her skirt out.

The old man's face brightened and he straightened up. His eyes glinted suspiciously. "An' you've got a new friend."

"Actually, she's an old friend who just looks new." She dodged to the side as Fiona elbowed her in the ribs. "Fiona took a bath too."

Mr. Potts chuckled. "An' she's got hair now."

"Thanks, Mr. Potts," Fiona said, glaring at Tiki.

Tiki changed the subject. "Have you seen Toots about lately?"

The elderly man turned away to straighten the edges of the stacks of newspapers laid out on a shelf. "That red-headed boy you look after? The one wot looks like somebody flicked an orange paintbrush at 'im?"

"Yes, the one with all the freckles," Fiona said. "Have you seen him?"

Mr. Potts shrugged. "Not for a few weeks." He cleared his throat with a loud *harumph*. "He used to come in and run around with a coupl'a other boys. Probably up to no good."

"Well, he's supposed to be in school," Tiki frowned. "I'll have to ask him about that."

The old man stepped toward them, a smile of appreciation on his face. "Tiki, yer look so different when you're dressed like a girl." He caught both of her hands in his old wrinkled ones. "Yer remind me of Bridgit."

The name sounded familiar to Tiki. "Who's Bridgit?"

"She's my daughter. You look a bit like her."

Tiki smiled. "You've mentioned that before. Toots always said that's why you let me read your books for free."

Mr. Potts released Tiki's hands and shuffled back toward his little desk. "I've got a drawing of her over here." He pulled a drawer open and reached in to search the back of the space with his hand. His wrinkled fingers emerged holding a sepia-toned portrait of a young girl, the edges frayed and torn.

Tiki held her hand out. "May I?" He'd never shown her a picture of his daughter before.

"She's sixteen there." He pointed his crooked finger at the page. "Had it drawn just before the Christmas holidays as a present for 'er mum. Yer cain't tell, but she's wearing a blue dress too."

Tiki took the page and studied the face staring back at her. Fiona leaned over her shoulder to peer at the portrait.

"You're right, Mr. Potts," Fiona said. "She does bear a resemblance to Tiki—with her long dark hair and that pretty face. Where is she now?"

The old man's shoulders sagged as if the air had been let out of him. "She's gone. Disappeared in Hyde Park in '42."

Tiki frowned. "Disappeared? What happened?"

"Got caught by a nasty storm one evening, just 'bout this time of year. We were in the area known as the Ring. Lightning right on top of us, thunder loud enough to rattle yer bones. Blew in out of nowhere." He shook his head. "Bridgit stopped to talk to some young bloke. When we turned back, she was gone—" he motioned with his hands— "like smoke on the wind."

Tiki froze. "The Ring in Hyde Park?" That area was a favorite gathering spot of faeries. Tiki had met Larkin there once. By the expression on Fiona's face, Tiki could tell the other girl had made the same connection.

The old man's hands shook as he took the picture from Tiki. "Sometimes when the weather's really nasty I walk through the park, hoping the storm that took 'er will bring 'er back to me." He smoothed his bent fingers over the drawing, pausing to look one more time before he tucked it safely into the back of the drawer. "My wife went to an early grave because of 'er broken heart, she did." He heaved a heavy sigh. "Me? I'm still waitin' for Bridgit to come home."

Tiki patted the man's gnarled hands. "I'm so sorry, Mr. Potts."

He shrugged his bony shoulders. "I should be used to it by now—she's been gone a long time, but I still miss her." He gave Tiki a wobbly smile. "An' I miss havin' yer come pester me for books."

"That's one of the reasons we're here. We're going to make a point of coming by and bothering you more often." Tiki smiled at him.

"A friend of yours was asking after you yest'day," the old man said as he sank onto the wooden stool before his desk.

"A friend of mine?" Tiki didn't have many friends and certainly none who knew she'd lived in Charing Cross. "Did they leave a name?"

"Didn't catch 'er name. Pretty girl, blond ringlets. She asked if I'd seen yer about lately." Potts ran his gnarled hands along the edge of the wooden desk, worn shiny over time. "I tol' her I hadn't seen yer for a bit but she said not to worry, she'd track you down."

Chapter Ten

"It sounds like Larkin's been on the hunt for you," Fiona said as soon as they left the bookstore. "I don't know who else that could've been, do you?"

"No," Tiki said. The station was busier now and jammed with travelers. She swerved around a mother tugging two crying children followed by a father pushing a loaded trolley. "Larkin wants something from me," she said in a low voice as Fiona quick-stepped to catch up with her. "I'm sure she'll come 'round again and again until she gets what she wants." Something bumped hard into her side and Tiki jerked around in surprise.

"S'cuse me, miss." The boy who Fiona had noticed watching them earlier doffed his cap at Tiki. "Crowds are thick as a pea-souper, today." His face split in a charming grin revealing surprisingly good teeth before he winked at Fiona and hurried on.

"Well—" Fiona smiled at his departing back as he slid into a crowd of people— "he was a cheeky bit, wasn't he?

It took Tiki a second to react. "He's got my bag," she cried and took off running in pursuit of the pickpocket. She ignored the startled looks as she raced after the boy—skirts flying around her knees, arms pumping. She cut through the travelers moving through the station. There—she spotted the boy up ahead.

As if sensing her approach, the boy glanced over his shoulder. His eyes got as wide as two full moons before he bolted through the crowd to escape. But Tiki wasn't having any of it. She'd worked too hard for every coin in that purse to let some thief off the street steal it from her. It didn't matter that picking pockets used to be how she survived. She wasn't going to be a victim.

The boy was fast. He darted and squirted through tiny gaps in the crowd. Once, he just missed being run over by a trolley full of luggage. But Tiki had the advantage of knowing every hidey-hole there was in Charing Cross. She'd run from the bobbies too many times herself not to know the best escape routes.

She turned down a familiar hallway and to her surprise, the boy darted behind a tall potted plant. He was headed into the abandoned clockmaker's shop. Tiki's old home. The piece of wood suspended by a nail that acted as their door was still swinging when she pushed it aside and slipped in.

A watery wash of light from the station poured through the three windows above their door, barely illuminating the long rectangular room. There was just enough daylight to make out the boy's silhouette near the box stove at the back of the room. His sides were still heaving from his mad dash. He jerked his head up in surprise when Tiki entered and scrambled for the back door that led through the maintenance tunnels out into the alley.

"I want my bag back!" Tiki shouted. She jumped over a pile of worn blankets and shoved a rickety old chair out of the way to grab a handful of his coat.

"Take it!" he cried as he threw the handbag at Tiki's face and tried to jerk away. She let go of his jacket to catch the bag. Free of her grip, he raced to the far wall and slid out the back door.

Tiki yanked open the drawstrings to check the contents, her breath coming out in small gasps.

A low voice spoke from a dark corner behind her. "Of course the guttersnipe returns to the gutter."

Tiki whirled and reached for the blade hidden within her sleeve, squinting to see through the darkness. She'd learned her lesson last winter with Marcus—she would never be unprepared to protect herself again.

"Larkin?" It didn't surprise her that the faerie had found her again already—it was obvious she was desperate.

A snarl came from the corner and Tiki clenched the knife tighter, bracing herself for an attack. A wavering impression of Larkin emerged in the dark shadows. Her faint image came into focus and then dissolved again into a thousand pieces before she shifted into view again, closer to Tiki. This time she looked as Tiki remembered. Her blond hair was long and tangled. She looked windblown as though she'd just stepped out of the storm that had buffeted London the last few days. Or perhaps, Tiki thought, she was the storm. She pointed the knife at the faerie.

"Where's Toots? Did you take him now?"

Larkin laughed under her breath. "So brave," she said in a mocking tone. "I have no idea what a *Toots* might be." Thin straps stretched over the creamy skin of her shoulders and held a green dress that draped in simple lines down to her ankles, revealing bare feet. Even in the dim light she shone with a delicate beauty that was mesmerizing.

"His name is Thomas. He's a young boy who lives with me." Tiki readjusted her grip on the knife and raised her voice. "He's part of my family and he went missing yesterday—just about the time Isabelle Cavendish visited. Do you know where he is?"

"I will never know what William sees in you." The faerie said, raking Tiki from head to toe with a scathing gaze. "So disgustingly sentimental about *mortals.*"

"How ironic," Tiki said, "coming from you. But you didn't answer my question."

Larkin contemplated Tiki with narrowed eyes. "You think you're so clever, don't you, little orphan girl? Let me tell you this—you're going to be in the battle of your life. I'll make the offer again: If you help me—I'll help you."

The muffled noises of the railway station rumbled in the distance as though in another world. In the abandoned clockmaker's shop, Larkin's words pulled at Tiki like a web tightening around her.

The faerie's lips pressed into a thin line. "But you've got to make your mind up soon, or there won't be anything left to save. We've got to reclaim the Seelie throne before the Beltane feast on May first or we'll never get Donegal out of the Palace of Mirrors." Then Larkin shimmered out of view.

Chapter Eleven

Tiki was exhausted by the time they returned home. Between her concern for Toots and Larkin's unexpected appearance, her head felt like it was ready to explode.

As they walked in the front door, a familiar voice drifted from the other room. Tiki and Fiona looked at each other in surprise.

"Is that—" They hurried to the kitchen to find Toots sitting on a stool near a large wooden table with Clara. Mrs. Bosworth stood at a nearby counter. He was waving his hands about the bright orange locks of his head, talking as fast as he could, telling a story that had his audience enraptured.

"Toots!" Tiki cried. "You're home!"

At the sound of her voice, Toots paused and glanced over his shoulder. Tiki and Fiona both rushed to hug the boy.

"I was so worried about you," Tiki whispered in his ear, trying not to cry. "Are you all right?"

"Yeah, Teek." He wiggled out of her grasp, his face lit up with excitement. "I'm fine. I thought I was only gone a coupl'a hours, but they're telling me I've been gone for two *days*." His voice held a note of wonder.

Tiki held Toots at arm's length, her hands braced on his shoulders as she searched his face. "Where were you?"

"I don' know exactly, but I had the time of my life!" He laughed with glee. "There was a whole field of horses—" his eyes were round with wonder— "their manes sparkled and glittered like the stars and they ran so fast their feet didn't touch the ground. An' Teek—I rode one! You should have seen me. She was beautiful— white as snow—and her mane and tail swept the ground they were so long! It was like we were flyin'."

He spoke so fast Tiki had a hard time following what he was saying. "Her mane was braided with bells that jingled as we rode an' I swear the bridle—that's the part that goes in their mouth—was made of pure gold and sparkled like it was covered with the Crown jewels."

Toots grinned and cast a quick glance over at Mrs. Bosworth as he spoke out of the corner of his mouth. "I thought about trying to nick it and bring it home but I wasn't sure how to get it out of the horse's mouth." His eyes got wide. "Have you ever seen the size of their teeth?"

"That's wonderful, Toots, but where were you?" Tiki asked again.

The little boy sobered then, a guilty expression twisting his features. "I don't know exactly. But it was sunny and there was lots of green grass for the horses an'— "

Now Tiki wasn't smiling. "Who took you there, Toots?"

"Dain brought him home." Clara spoke up. She stood on one side of Toots, clutching Doggie to her chest and listening with an enraptured expression. She wore a little blue dress with shoulder straps over a white blouse. "An' I got to see him too."

At Tiki's questioning look Mrs. Bosworth shook her head. "I didn't see nothin'—not the horse nor the chap who brought 'im home." She stood at the counter, her large hips wrapped in her familiar white apron, kneading bread dough. "But I knew he'd come back sooner or later. Off on a lark, just like I said."

"Tell her, Toots." Clara fisted her little fingers and planted a hand on each hip. "I'm not making it up. Dain was here and I got to see the pretty horse too. Just like Toots said. She was all white and grand with red ribbons in her mane—just like the horse that Tam Lin rides in the story you tell us, Teek." Her young voice had a stubborn ring to it.

"It's fine, I believe you, Clara," Tiki said. "The important thing is that Toots is home safe." Her brows pulled down in a frown. "But who is Dain?"

"Why, he's the boy who comes 'round sometimes," Clara replied innocently. "Haven't you seen him, Teek? He's tall with blond hair. He's a friendly sort. Doggie likes him."

Tiki returned her focus to Toots. "What about a blond girl? Did you see anyone like that? Her name's Larkin?"

Toots's freckled brow wrinkled with thought. "Nope, I didn't see any girls, Teek."

Clara lifted her head from petting Doggie, her little voice sweet and pure. "I can call Larkin if you want to talk to her."

Tiki and Fiona swung their heads to look at the child. Tiki had never openly discussed the time Larkin had stolen the little girl for fear of upsetting Clara.

"What do you mean, you can call her?" Fiona asked.

Clara shrugged as she tightened two swatches of fabric around Doggie's neck. "Larkin told me she would come if I ever needed her. Alls I 'ave to do is call her." The little four-year-old held her stuffed animal out as she ran around the table. "Look, Doggie can fly because I made her some wings."

Tiki was suddenly alert. "Why would you ever need Larkin?" Her voice sounded shriller than she intended.

"Oh, you know—" Clara slowed to a stop, letting Doggie land on the corner of the table near Tiki. "She said to call if I was ever lonely or scared or—" the little girl's lips quirked in a smile— "if I wanted to hear a faerie tale." She shot a quick glance at Tiki out of the corner of her eyes to check her reaction.

"That's very funny, Miss Clara Marie." Tiki reached out to tweak the little girl's nose.

Clara giggled. "I'm tellin' the truth."

"Clara," Fiona said with a doubting snort, "how exactly, would you call Larkin here?"

The little girl twisted the wings she'd put around Doggie, the shiny fabric sparkling in the lamplight. "She told me all I 'ad to do was whisper her name and ask 'er to come to me."

Fiona raised her eyebrows. "You think if you say 'Larkin, come to me', she'll magically appear?"

Tiki smiled at the little girl. "Maybe *that* was one of her faerie tales."

Clara giggled again and smoothed the worn fabric on the top of Doggie's head. "That's not 'er name, silly."

Tiki tensed. "What do you mean?"

"Well," Clara said slowly, "that's not 'er *real* name."

"Larkin told you her real name?" Fiona's voice was hushed with disbelief. To know a faerie's name was to possess the faerie. It wasn't possible Larkin would have revealed her true name to a child.

For a moment Clara looked uncertain. "Yes. But she told me to never tell *anyone*." Her blond curls swayed as a coy smile lit her face. "But I trust you." She stretched her small arms wide and whispered softly in a sing-song voice, "A'ine Fiachna Eri—"

"STOP." Tiki pressed her fingers against Clara's lips. She leaned toward the little girl and said, "We don't want Larkin here right now." Tiki didn't know whether to believe the little girl's claims or not, but she wasn't going to take any chances. "And I don't want you to ever call her unless you talk to me first, all right?"

"All right, Teek," Clara said, looking crestfallen as she sat down in a vacant chair. "I just thought since you were talking about 'er an' all…"

"Yes, thank you, that was very helpful of you. Now—" Tiki motioned toward the door, "let's go read a story about—" she paused and her eyes fell on Fiona— "a handsome prince. *Anything but a faerie tale*," she muttered under her breath.

IT WAS LATER, after supper, that Tiki questioned Toots further. They were ensconced in the parlor, the fire crackling cheerfully from the grate. Rieker still hadn't returned. Tiki had lit all the lamps to chase the shadows from the corners of the room. Shamus was asleep in an armchair, his open mouth emitting soft snores.

"Toots, who was it that you went away with?" Tiki asked. No one had actually said the word "faerie" yet.

Toots shrugged. He was on his stomach on the floor playing checkers with Fiona. "Just one 'a the blokes I play stickball with. He asked if I wanted to ride a horse."

"Then what happened?" Tiki sat in a chair before the fire, alternating between trying to make sense of all she'd learned and trying not to think about any of it.

Toots lifted his head. "Well…. that part was a bit strange. One minute we were standing on the street and the next we were in a big meadow with the horses."

He turned round green eyes toward Tiki. The freckles splattered across his nose stood out brightly against his pale skin. "I don't know how we got there. Didn't really look like any of the parks around here." He shrugged, his skinny shoulders lifting the thin material of his shirt. "But it was sunny and warm, and they let me pet the horses."

His brows knotted in confusion. "It's a bit hard to keep it all straight now. But after awhile this Dain chap came by and asked me if I wanted to ride. He let me ride behind him on the great white horse and we rode like the wind."

"Is that when he brought you back here?"

Toots grinned from ear to ear. "Eventually."

"I told you it was Dain." Clara chimed in from where she was threading a string through two pieces of shiny fabric. "He talked to me when he brought Toots home."

"Nobody talked to me," Fiona snapped. "Or took me to ride a horse—" she glared at Toots— "that could fly." She moved a red checker piece with a grumpy look on her face.

"There," Clara said with satisfaction. "My faerie wings are ready now." In one deft movement she swung the string over her head and positioned the shiny fabric over her back. "Tiki, watch me fly," she cried as she held her arms out from her sides and ran around the room.

"Clara, watch it! You're going to bust our game up." Toots waved the little girl out of the way as she neared their spot on the floor.

"No I won't," Clara said. "I'll fly right over the top of you."

"Clara—stop!" Fi said.

Tiki sensed disaster as the little girl headed straight for the older children.

"Clara, come back towards me, so I can see your beautiful wings shining as you fly," Tiki called. With a mischievous grin the little girl banked her arms at the last minute and made a sweeping turn and headed back toward Tiki.

"Toots and Fi saw me because I had my glamour on," Clara whispered as she came closer to Tiki. "I *let* them see me."

Tiki thought she was going to faint. "Your *what?*" she exclaimed.

"Shhh." Clara put a finger to her lips and frowned at Tiki. "You don't want to make people supicous."

Tiki drew a deep breath. "Do you mean suspicious?"

Clara brightened. "Yes, that's what I said."

"Did you hear that word somewhere?"

"Oh yes, Dain told me."

"I see." Tiki wasn't sure what to think about the little girl's shocking comment. "It seems Dain told you lots of things. Did he tell you about glamours?"

Clara nodded with a proud smile. "Yes, when he was explainin' how Toots can see those boys 'e plays stickball with." She placed a small hand on Tiki's knee and looked up at her with innocent blue eyes. "He said it's just like playin' dress-up." She giggled. "An' some-times, he said even grow'in ups play."

Tiki's stomach heaved. How could one of those horrible crea-tures have been talking to Clara and she hadn't known? She lifted the little girl up onto her lap. Clara turned sideways and snug-gled close as Tiki wrapped her arms around the child. Tiki's heart pounded as she forced the words out of her mouth.

"What else did you talk about?"

"Oh, he asked me about Rieker."

Tiki inhaled sharply. "He did?"

"Um-hmm. He called him William, though. Wanted to know if he was 'round often." Clara looked up at Tiki, her blond waves falling back, her little face glowing. "I tol' 'im you were best mates." She grinned, clearly pleased with herself.

Tiki kissed the little girl's forehead and ran her hand over her silky hair. "If you see Dain again, you need to come find me, all right?"

"All right, Teek."

"And don't tell him anything else about Rieker. Let's keep it our secret."

"I can keep a secret," Clara said in her sweet, innocent voice.

"Good girl," Tiki whispered. Another faerie too close to them. What did this one want? Was he after the ring? A spy for Donegal?

Working with Larkin? There was no way to know for sure. Toots had returned home safe this time, but what about the next? And the next after that?

Tiki closed her eyes and fought the urge to squeeze Clara as tight as she could. She would do anything to keep Rieker, Clara and her family safe. Anything.

LATER THAT NIGHT Tiki lay in bed and stared into the darkness while Larkin's words replayed over and over in her mind: *I suppose that makes me your aunt. Soon there won't be anything left to save. You're Finn MacLochlan's daughter.* She shivered with a chill no blanket could ever warm. To think she might be *related* to that creature— Tiki couldn't finish the thought. She punched her pillow and rolled on her side, trying to ignore the worry that had become her constant companion. Rieker still hadn't returned.

Chapter Twelve

Tiki slept in the next morning. She'd laid awake deep into the night thinking about all that she'd learned and what it meant for the future. She awoke to the sound of Clara's giggles in the hallway. Tinkly notes of laughter were punctuated by loud *shush's* from Toots, followed by more giggles.

She smiled as she listened to the merriment coming through the door. Her smile faded though, as she thought again of Larkin, of the secrets she'd revealed. What was the truth? Tiki didn't want to admit it, but the faerie had even made her doubt Rieker. They'd barely had time to discuss Larkin's visit before Rieker had disappeared himself.

Tiki's idea that she could just avoid the fey had faded. It seemed apparent now that she was part of whatever grander scheme Larkin had devised. Unable to stay still, Tiki shoved the blankets aside and sat up. If Rieker was right and understanding the meaning of her birthmark would give her some ability to protect her family, then that was what she needed to know.

As soon as she moved, the door to her bedroom swung open. Clara and Toots came scurrying in, making her suspect they'd been watching through the crack, waiting for her to get up.

"Tiki," Clara called. She clutched Doggie in one hand. "Yer finally up. We've been waiting *forever.*"

"Yeah Teek." Toots hair was brushed back and his face as clean as she'd ever seen it, making Tiki wonder if Mrs. Bosworth had taken a scrub brush to him. "We thought you might be dead."

"Alive and well, as you can see." Tiki sat back on the bed and patted the covers for them to join her. With giggles of glee Clara and Toots bounded onto the mattress next to her. "What is so important you need to wake me from my beauty sleep?" She squinted toward the door. "And where is Fiona?"

"Fiona's got a gent'man caller," Clara whispered in a hurried rush. "That's what we've been waitin' to tell you."

Tiki's mouth dropped open. "A what?"

"He's a very 'andsome young man," Clara said in a voice that was a spot-on imitation of Mrs. Bosworth. "He even brought her a rose."

Tiki looked at Toots. "What do you know about this?"

Toots shrugged, his overly-innocent expression making him look guilty. "His name's Johnny. He's a bloke I know from Charing Cross." He held out his hands to Tiki. "But I swear I don't know how he met Fi, or how he found out where we live."

TIKI WALKED DOWN the stairs with an uneasiness churning in her chest. Where could Fiona have met a young gentleman? She straightened her back as she entered the small parlor, not sure what to expect.

Fiona was seated in a chair by the fire. Her pale skin glowed with a faint blush and even from the doorway Tiki could see how her eyes sparkled. She was wearing a dress of pale blue that was a lovely contrast to her creamy skin. These last few months had transformed the young girl. A boy's back was to the door, a mop of tousled dark hair crowning his head. At the sound of Tiki's arrival he jumped to his feet and turned toward her.

Tiki blinked in surprise. It was the boy who had stolen her bag in Charing Cross.

"What are *you* doing here?" The words exploded out of her mouth.

"Tiki." Fiona jumped to her feet. "This is— "

"Johnny Michael Francis O'Keefe, Miss." He bobbed his head, his cap clutched in his hands. His face had a boy-like charm to it, but Tiki didn't miss the hollows under his cheeks and the way his second-hand clothes hung on this thin frame.

"Johnny O'Keefe?" Tiki eyes narrowed. "Also known as Johnny the Thief? I've heard of you before."

Johnny tugged the lapels of his rumpled, threadbare jacket straight. A nervous smile creased his lips revealing teeth that were surprisingly clean. "I swear I don' know where you heard such a thing as that." He waved a hand in her direction and cleared his throat. "Being the lady you are, an' all."

Fiona snickered, then guiltily raised a long-stemmed red rose to her nose to hide her smile. Tiki chose to ignore her. Johnny the Thief had quite a name among the pickpockets who worked the streets of London. Not only for his quick hands—but also for his close escapes. There'd been more than one tale of Johnny eluding the bobbies by the seat of his threadbare pants.

"It doesn't matter where I've heard it. We've met before—at Charing Cross." Tiki wasn't smiling now. "I believe you stole my bag."

Johnny's cheeks turned red. "About that..." He turned his crumpled cap in his hands and shuffled feet that looked too big for his lanky body. "I only did it because the blond lady promised me a quid. She was the one who told me to lead you to that little room."

He held his hands out from his sides and his face twisted in a look of disgust. "But in the end, it wasn't even worth it because I lost the bloody money. Put it my pocket and found a dead leaf there later."

Tiki frowned at his mention of the blond lady. "What did this woman say to you?"

Johnny shrugged. "I don' know. She just came up and offered me a quid. Showed me the little room with the back door then pointed out you two fine-looking ladies."

Fiona blushed, and Tiki didn't miss the pleased expression on her face. Tiki threaded her hands together, still standing stiffly erect. "How exactly did you find out where we lived?"

"Oh, that part was easy. I just followed you home." Johnny gave her an endearing grin. "Then I waited for a chance to talk to Miss Fiona."

Tiki's stomach twisted at the thought that they were being followed by Johnny and hadn't even noticed. Who else could have been following them? She would need to be more alert in the future. But right now Fiona's face was bright with excitement for the first time in a long time. Tiki tapped her thumbs together, trying to make a decision as she eyed the painfully thin boy. Finally she heaved a sigh. It hadn't been long enough since their fortunes had changed that Tiki had forgotten what it felt like to be hungry all the time. "Have you had breakfast?"

SHAMUS JOINED THEM at the table as it was Saturday and pulled a chair up next to their guest as they nipped into platters of sausage gravy over biscuits. In typical fashion, Mrs. Bosworth had cooked enough for everyone to have seconds, so there was plenty for an extra mouth.

Tiki cut a bite of gravy-soaked biscuit listening to Fiona and Toots chattering on while Johnny practically inhaled his food. "Where are your parents?" she finally asked.

Johnny paused with a bite halfway to his mouth. "Debtor's prison." His voice held little emotion. Tiki noticed he handled a fork with practiced ease and swallowed his food before he spoke. "Didn't see m'self living in that place so I set about my own business." He elbowed Toots. "Went to Charing Cross and met a few blokes in the trade." He took another big bite of food and swallowed. "I've done all right for m'self so far." He grinned. "Not dead or in prison yet."

"I see." Tiki moved the food on her plate around, her appetite suddenly diminished. There were so many children who were orphaned or living on their own. The conditions in the slums of London, as well as the workhouses, were hardly fit for an animal, let alone a young boy on his own. "How old are you?"

"Fifteen this summer." He shoved another bite into his mouth.

Tiki looked around the table. All of them were orphans. Fiona's mother, a seamstress, had been beaten to death by her employer. Her cousin, Shamus, had been on his own since his father, a mudlarker, had died in a drunken brawl in a pub. Tiki had found Toots in Trafalgar Square after his mother had kicked him out of the house at age nine because she had too many other children to feed. Clara had been curled up in a pile of garbage on a side road near Charing Cross where Tiki had almost tripped over her. She'd brought them both home and now they were a family.

"I met him over in Covent Garden," Toots said around a mouthful of food, nodding at Johnny. "He was pickin' pockets at the market, just like we used to do." Toots swallowed and took another big bite, oblivious to the stares suddenly directed his way.

Johnny's mouth froze mid-bite and his gaze went from Toots to Tiki then back to Toots again, a question in his eyes. "What'd you say?"

"Toots." Tiki nodded at his full mouth and raised her eyebrows.

"Yeah, Toots, don't talk with your mouth full," Clara chimed in. She sat across from him, balanced on a large book. Doggie rested on the table next to her plate. "It's not po'lite."

With a big gulp he swallowed his food and glared at Clara. "Hush up, Clara."

Clara stared back belligerently. "It's the rules—"

"Thank you, Clara." Tiki smiled her. "I think Toots remembers now." She turned back to the new boy as if nothing untoward had been revealed. "What are your plans now, Johnny?"

He put his fork down, his brows knotted in a serious expression. "Have you ever heard of Rieker? He's the best bloody pickpocket in all of London." His blue eyes sparkled with excitement. "I want to work for him."

Chapter Thirteen

Tiki and Shamus both choked on their food at the same time.

"You do?" Toots asked, his mouth forming an 'o' of surprise. "But I thought—" he swiveled around to look at Tiki, his orange locks shifting with his movement.

"I know Rieker," Clara chimed in, her mouth half-full. "His real name is—"

"Clara." Tiki cut her off and shook her head, putting a finger to her lips.

Shamus set his fork down and leaned back in his chair. "An' what would you be doin' for Rieker?"

"Pickin' pockets, o' course." Johnny smiled at Tiki. "An' I'm good at it, too. With Mr. Rieker's connections and working as a team—" his eyes lit up with enthusiasm— "he's the best of the lot, you know."

"The best of what lot?" Rieker's voice caused them all to turn. His tall form filled the doorway. He was still wearing his long black traveling coat.

"Rieker!" Clara wiggled out of her chair and ran over to throw her arms around his knees. "Yer just in time to meet Johnny."

Johnny's fork clattered to the plate, as his mouth dropped open. He eyed the well-dressed aristocrat who stood in the doorway. "R.. Rieker?"

"I have no idea what you're talking about," Rieker said with a straight face as he bent down and lifted Clara up in his arms. He stepped close and patted Toots on the back. "Welcome home, Toots. Glad to see you're back safe." His gaze circled the table, pausing on Tiki briefly before stopping on the visitor. "Johnny?"

Tiki sat quietly in her chair. Purple shadows colored the skin under his eyes and he looked like he hadn't slept since she'd seen him last. She noticed he didn't seem surprised to see Toots at all.

Johnny hopped to his feet, knocking the chair over in his haste. "Johnny Michael Francis O'Keefe." He said it so fast it was barely intelligible. "Sir."

Everyone started talking at once.

"Johnny brought me a rose," Fiona said, holding her flower up.

Toots pointed across the table at him. "He's a pickpocket too. I met him down at the station and——"

"Johnny is a friend of Toots *and* Fi's." Clara's high voice rang with childish innuendo.

Fiona flushed and looked down at her plate. Like normal, Shamus remained silent, leaving the chatter to the others.

Rieker raised his hand for silence. "You sound like a bunch of squabbling chickens—I can't make out a word you're saying."

Tiki stood and motioned to Rieker. "I need to talk to you." She nodded at the rest of them. "You lot carry on with breakfast." Rieker let Clara slide to the floor and followed Tiki to the library.

"Who is he?" he said, the minute she closed the door.

"He was here when I came down this morning." She couldn't keep the worry out of her voice. "He stole my handbag at Charing Cross the other day. When I chased him into our old home Larkin was there hiding. He told me today that a blond lady said she would pay him to lead me in there."

Rieker raised his eyebrows. "No surprise, really, given who we're dealing with." He paced to the hearth and leaned an arm against the mantle, staring down at the kindling laid in the grate. "How did he find where you live?"

Tiki moved across the room to stand near him, the skirts of her lavender skirt sweeping the floor as she walked. "He said he followed us home."

"Possible. Unless he was sent here."

Tiki caught her breath. "You think he might be—"

"I don't know what to think." Rieker pushed off the mantle and shoved his hands into the pockets of his trousers. "I'm suspicious of everyone now, *especially* Larkin."

Tiki told him what Toots had said about his disappearance and Clara's comments about Dain and glamours. She fingered the lace on the hem of her blouse. "Clara said this Dain fellow was asking about you." Her voice softened. "I was worried—where have you been?"

Rieker's jaw was set and his eyes were dark with concern. "I've been looking for Toots, trying to get the latest news on what's happening. Larkin won't quit until she gets what she wants from you."

"Do you believe her?" Tiki braced her shoulders. "Do you believe I'm Finn's daughter?"

The shadows shifted in Rieker's eyes and something that looked like truth flickered there. His voice was quiet, but firm when he answered. "Yes, I do, Tiki."

LATER THAT NIGHT Tiki lay awake in the darkness of her bedroom, tossing restlessly.

"Have you made up your mind yet?"

Larkin's voice came from within the deepest shadows in the room—the words disembodied and floating—almost as if they came from the very air itself.

Tiki jumped, but in truth she wasn't surprised to hear from the faerie. She'd known it was only a matter of time before Larkin came back for what she wanted. The faerie's anticipation was so palpable Tiki could almost feel it reaching for her, like fingers—or claws—ready to sink into her skin.

Tiki pushed herself into a sitting position, reaching for a night robe that hung on the bed post. She leaned over and lit the candle stub that was in the holder on the small nightstand next to her bed. Her dagger with the iron blade rested next to the candle and she slipped it into her pocket where she could grab the handle easily if necessary.

"Tell me why you took Toots to the Otherworld," she said. It wasn't a question.

Larkin gave her a sideways glance from the corner of her eyes, as if calculating her response. "The boy is horse-crazy and wanted to ride." She lifted her chin and waved her hand as if to dismiss the incident. "He needed to see a *real* horse. One who can run on the wind—"

"You can't just *take* a child!" Tiki snapped.

"I didn't take him." Larkin sounded insulted. "And from what I heard, he *wanted* to go."

"He's ten years old! He doesn't understand the dangers." Anger and frustration bubbled in Tiki's chest. Larkin couldn't possibly be that obtuse. Everything she did was for a reason. "He didn't even know where he was."

Larkin sniffed. "I don't know why you're so upset. He's home again, safe and sound."

"You took him because you wanted to get my attention." Tiki said. "If you want my help, don't ever take him again."

"Fine." Larkin snapped. "I didn't come here to be lectured." She pursed her lips as if trying not to lose her temper. "Have you thought about what I said? Have you made up your mind?"

"I have thought about it," Tiki said. She'd hardly thought of anything else. "From what you've described there's a terrible war going on in the Otherworld right now. I'm not going to show up just to be slaughtered. I've got responsibilities here." Tiki's voice wavered as she thought about leaving Clara and the others. "You've got to tell me what it is you expect me to do before I'll agree to go."

The truth was she had already decided. She couldn't risk the life of the Queen of England if there really was some way she could stop this madman. Nor could she take the chance that someone else—like Rieker, or her family—might be injured. She'd never be able to live with herself. But she wasn't going to let Larkin know that yet.

The faerie emerged from the shadows, her hair windblown and tangled, hanging like a golden mantle around her shoulders. As she moved, the flame of the candle shivered, throwing dancing shadows of light against the walls. Larkin appeared to float across the room to sit on the end of Tiki's bed.

She sat oddly still, her weight making no impact on the soft down-filled mattress, as if she were simply wrought of air. Tiki was used to the faerie twirling and dancing—taunting her—a mocking smile gracing her beautiful face. Now, it was as though she were a shadow of herself.

"I'll tell you what I can." Larkin's voice shifted to a whisper. "Donegal has been plotting this coup for centuries. The deception within the courts goes very deep. Back to when Finn was murdered."

Tiki tensed at the name.

"His assassination could not have been easy to carry out. Finn had the Macanna, his own group of warriors, who protected him." There was a thread of respect in Larkin's voice. "Those men and women would have died for him."

Tiki smoothed her fingers along the stitching of the quilt that covered her bed. She sensed there was much more that Larkin wasn't telling her. "What of Adasara?"

"Addie was trying to get away," Larkin said softly. "She managed to avoid them long enough to hide you in London, but eventually they found her too..." Her voice faded. "It wasn't long after Addie died that they came after Eridanus." Larkin's tone shifted. "It's obvious Donegal hasn't known of you before now or he would have hunted you down years ago. Addie was successful in that much, at least."

Tiki shivered. She wanted to ask about Rieker, about the secrets to which Larkin had alluded, but she wasn't sure she wanted to know the answers.

A smile twisted the lips of the faerie. "We're not so different, guttersnipe."

"Yes, we are," Tiki snapped. "I can be trusted."

Larkin leaned toward her, an annoyed look on her face. "Well, I'm here telling you the truth, aren't I? At no small risk to myself, I might add."

"Whenever you take a risk, Larkin, it's because you expect to gain something in return."

A smile flitted across the faerie's face. "True, perhaps, but if you come with me, we will both gain something."

"If what you say is true, that I'm the daughter of Finn MacLochlan, then why don't I look like a faerie? Why don't I remember anything? Why can't I *do* anything?"

Larkin's eyes slid over Tiki, her lips turned down in a disapproving frown. "It's not as if you haven't been able to *see* things. You've seen them all your life and chosen to ignore them." The faerie cocked her head at Tiki. "Your lack of knowledge is simply because you've never thought of yourself with those abilities."

Tiki felt rooted to the floor as she stared at Larkin's unearthly beauty. "But why don't I look like a faerie?"

Larkin gave a graceful shrug of her shoulders then grimaced, as if in pain. "Faeries are shape-shifters—chameleons. When outside of our world we instinctively blend with our surroundings. My sister was very powerful. I'm sure Adasara put an impenetrable glamour on you before she hid you in London. As you grew, you knew no other way to look. You unconsciously shifted the glamour to grow into the image you believed to be of yourself." The corner of Larkin's lip lifted in a mocking smile. "But I'm sure if you were to stay in Faerie long enough, you'd shed the glamour, and begin to look *normal* again."

Tiki ignored the girl's barbs. "Why don't I have wings?"

Larkin sobered and silence stretched between them. Tiki was just wondering if the faerie was going to ignore the question when she spoke. "The purpose of wings has evolved over the centuries. Long ago they were a symbol of power—the size, the shape, the color—all gave an indication of the faerie's status within court. But over time, the importance of wings diminished. Now they're only worn for vanity. A faerie has wings just like a mortal has long hair. It's so they may look a certain way." She shrugged. "I can live without them. Adasara must have torn yours off when she brought you to London."

Tiki listened, trying to keep her face blank, to not reveal the shock that roiled around inside her at the idea that she was...not human. "But," she finally choked out, "I don't know the first thing about your world, these people—" she flung her hands out— "this war you're fighting."

Larkin grabbed Tiki's hands and clasped them in her long fingers. Tiki couldn't remember the faerie ever voluntarily touching her before, other than to scratch her. Her skin was cool to the touch and soft, like a stone worn smooth by water. "That's where I can help you. I can teach you the things that you know deep inside— help you to remember."

A deep unease stirred in Tiki's gut. She wasn't sure she would trust Larkin to teach her anything. "But what is it you expect me to do in the Otherworld with this … this Tara Stone?"

"It's simple. All you have to do is touch it. When the stone roars then Donegal must relinquish the throne until Samhain."

Chapter Fourteen

Leo glanced up in alarm as lightning cracked the sky above his head. This latest storm had blown in quickly and settled directly over Buckingham, making the afternoon as dark as night. He pulled his coat tighter and glanced around. The uncomfortable sensation of being watched that he'd experienced over the last few days had grown even stronger.

Protection around his mother and the Palace had been increased. No strangers were allowed through the doors without being accompanied by the Queen's guard. Leo had found it was even getting difficult for him to leave the Palace. He'd slipped out a side door for this visit to the mews.

Dark shadows wavered across the path as he neared the stables as the lamps had not yet been lit for the night. His desire to check on his favorite horse, Diablo, who had recently shown signs of going lame, had driven him outside. But now, he was having second thoughts.

"Rubbish," Leo whispered to himself, "Wills would never jump at a few shadows." He put his head down against a gust of cool air and trudged on.

The first blow hit him square across the back. He let out a cry of surprise as he was knocked to his knees. Before he could turn to see who had accosted him, another blow caught him across the shoulder and flipped him onto his back.

For a fleeting second he saw a dark figure standing above him, swathed in shadows. Leo put his arm up to shield himself, squinting to make out his attacker, but the person lunged at Leo's face with blurring speed.

Leo let out a scream of pure terror as red hot pain burned from his neck. Then, everything went black.

Chapter Fifteen

T he streets were teeming as Tiki and Rieker's carriage wound its way back toward Grosvenor Square. They were returning from Covent Garden where they'd gone to give away some bread and cheddar to the homeless children who haunted the market, even in winter.

In the summer months, the beggars teemed like fish swimming upstream, sleeping in the baskets of the fruit, flower and vegetable vendors, dodging the constables and fighting for the rotten and damaged goods. Tiki, herself, had spent many a day at Covent Garden, trying to fill her cap and pockets with fresh fruit when the costermongers weren't looking.

As they made their way down busy Regent Street shouts from the drivers rose above the noise of the street as omnibuses loaded down with passengers jockeyed for position among the cabs, private carriages, and goods wagons.

When they turned onto Maddox Street, which became Grosvenor Lane, the roads quieted as if they'd entered a different world. Stately buildings stretched like soldiers at attention, providing an aura of gentility not found in other parts of the City.

As they approached the entry to the stables, Rieker sat forward in his seat.

"We've got company."

Tiki peered around his shoulders and saw the large, ornate carriage parked ahead in the driveway. Three footman and a driver stood next to the coach, their red coats and white breeches a bright spot of color in the dark, drizzly day.

"I believe it's either Leo or Arthur," Rieker said. He disembarked from the carriage and Tiki followed him into the drawing room where a young man in a grey suit stood staring down into the fire. "Arthur," he called. "How nice to see you. Is Leo with you?"

Prince Arthur turned at the sound of Rieker's voice. Tiki could tell from the Prince's expression that something was wrong.

"Wills," Arthur said, in a tone of pleasure and relief mixed. His eyes traveled past Rieker to where Tiki stood in the shadows.

Rieker motioned for her to join them. "What a pleasant surprise, Arthur. What brings you up to Grosvenor Square?"

Tiki dropped into a curtsy and could feel the heat crawling up her cheeks. She still found it a bit intimidating that Rieker had grown up with royalty.

Arthur leaned forward. "I wanted to catch you as soon as you returned."

"Why?" Rieker sank into a chair across from the prince. "What's happened?"

"It's Leo. He's been attacked."

Tiki gasped. "What?"

Rieker jerked forward, his expression becoming serious. "Tell us what happened."

"He was on his way to the mews this afternoon to check on his horse. Apparently, the assailant was hiding in the shadows along the building." Arthur's expression was terse, worry heavy in his eyes.

"The bloke knocked Leo to his knees from behind, then attacked him."

"Is he all right?" Rieker's voice was thick with disbelief.

Tiki's heart raced so fast she could barely breathe. Larkin had told the truth.

"He's not seriously hurt. His shouts brought the guards and scared the man away. He's bruised, banged up and totally out of sorts." Arthur pushed himself out of the chair and paced to the fireplace again. "Understandably. But the worst of it is a deep cut on his neck."

"The assailant had a knife?"

Arthur shook his head and turned to face them. "The wound doesn't have clean edges like a knife cut. The skin is jagged and torn— " he took a deep breath— "punctured, almost. More like what a claw might make, I imagine. The biggest problem however, is that the physicians can't get the wound to stop bleeding."

A horrible image of a clawed creature attacking Leo filled Tiki's mind. Donegal and the UnSeelies were attacking the royals. They were all in great danger. Was the Queen next?

The young prince shoved his hands into his pockets, rocking back and forth on his feet as he stared at Rieker. "I'm afraid Mamie's warning has come true."

LATER THAT NIGHT, after the others had gone to bed, Rieker and Tiki sat together in the library. Rieker paced in front of the fire, his long legs covering the distance in just a few steps before he turned and repeated the pattern. His brow was scrunched with worry.

"Arthur seems convinced Leo's attack was connected with the war in the Otherworld."

"It does make it seem like Larkin is telling the truth," Tiki said.

Rieker's lips pressed in a thin line as he came to a stop in front of where she sat near the fire. "I've thought of that. Which makes me wonder if Larkin didn't stage the attack for exactly that reason."

Chapter Sixteen

Tiki went from room to room and checked on Clara, Toots and Fiona before she retired to her own bedchamber for the night. Shamus had said goodnight earlier, as he rose before the sun to get to his job at the bakery. She had told Rieker of Larkin's nighttime visit and he'd insisted she leave her bedroom door open, in case she needed to call for his help during the night.

"Do you think Larkin is telling the truth?" she'd asked. "That all I need to do is touch a stone?"

Rieker had given her a doubtful look. "Nothing is ever simple where Larkin is concerned."

Juliette, the housemaid, had turned down the covers and Tiki ran a hand over the smooth sheets. It was a different world that Rieker lived in; an elite and privileged one to which she would never have access should she and Rieker part ways. The distance had grown between them since Rieker's return, making her realize how deep her feelings for him went. But with that realization also came insecurity. What if Rieker didn't always feel the same way about her? Was there a place for two people with such different backgrounds to make a life together? The need to be prepared for their eventual parting was stronger than ever.

Tiki sighed and slipped into her night dress, her toes curling away from the chill of the floor. Only time would tell what the future held for her and Rieker. The rain was still falling and there was talk the Thames might flood. She pulled on a pair of socks and walked to the window to pull the drapes tight. As she grabbed a handful of the thick velvet fabric to pull the curtain, a movement outside caught her eye.

She paused and stared through the diamond panes toward the tree-filled square. A gust of wind caused the light from the street lamps to flicker as the rain blew sideways. Who would possibly be out on a night like this?

The dark figure of a man stood unmoving beneath the giant arms of an elm tree. He appeared to be wearing a long coat with his hands shoved in the pockets. Tiki squinted through the darkness but the shadows were so deep it was impossible to see his face. A chill ran down her arms, turning her skin to goose flesh. The questions that seemed to swirl constantly in the back of her mind got louder. Who had attacked Leo? Would they come after her?

Suddenly afraid, she stepped back and tugged the curtains together, blocking out the stormy weather and unusual shadows.

"WHAT SHALL WE do today?" Tiki asked as they were finishing up breakfast the next morning. Rieker had left early to check on several business matters as well as to visit Leo. "The rain has finally stopped and I think I actually saw a bit of sunshine out there. Shall we go to the park?"

"Yes," Clara cried, jumping up and down in excitement. "By the water where the black swans swim. Do you remember Tiki? Not far from where we used to live."

"You mean St. James Park," Fiona said, smiling. Her eyes were bright and there was color in her cheeks. Tiki had never seen her look happier. "Yes, I think that's a brilliant idea. And after, we could go visit Mr. Potts—so Tiki can get a new book to read to us."

"That sounds good as long as I don't have to read it myself," Toots said, in between shoving the last bites of oatmeal into his mouth.

"Excellent point, Toots, it is time for you to work on your reading again." Tiki pushed clear of the table, the corners of her mouth turned up in a smile. "Fi, you don't want to go to Charing Cross because someone named Johnny might be there, do you?"

"That's right," Toots exclaimed, his spoon scraping against the bottom of his bowl. "Johnny lives in the old abandoned clockmaker's shop where we used to..." The young boy stopped and shot a guilty look over his shoulder at Mrs. Bosworth, who stood at the sink washing dishes, giving no indication she'd heard their conversation. He raised his voice. "Mrs. B., could I take him some bread and cheddar?"

"Of course you can, Thomas," the middle-aged woman replied. "If you can take it without spillin', I'll send a crock of stew along for him as well."

"I THINK WE'D better go to Charing Cross and deliver the food first," Tiki said as they walked down Brook Street and turned onto Regent. The sky overhead was gray, but the rain had stopped and a few spears of light shot through the clouds. It was only a thirty minute walk from Grosvenor Square to Charing Cross and the exercise was a welcome relief from the questions that churned relentlessly in her mind. What was Donegal plotting? What was Larkin plotting? Was it really possible she was Finvarra's heir? Would a stone roar if she touched it?

Clara skipped along beside Tiki, holding her hand, Doggie clutched in the other. She wore a pink dress that reached her knees and she reminded Tiki of a little spring flower. "Let's ask ol' Potts for a new story today."

Tiki grinned down at the little girl. "Yes, I thought I'd buy a new book as a gift for Rieker, since he's allowed us to stay in his home for now."

"Do you think Potts will give him another story about pick-pockets?" Toots asked, as he ran back and forth, trying to keep a wheel balanced with a stick. Mr. Potts had recommended the story, *Oliver Twist*, to Rieker last time he'd visited the shop.

Fiona walked next to Tiki, carrying the bag of food for Johnny. "Do you have money to pay for a book?" she asked. Her hair was a tangle of soft waves around her face and she wore a blue hat with a ruffle on the side that tied under her chin. She looked every inch a middle-class girl and not someone who had been picking pockets to survive just a few months ago.

"I have the money the Queen gave me, for," Tiki assumed a proper voice, "'assisting in the return of an article of importance to the monarchy.'" She laughed. "I suspect Rieker was the one who suggested they "reward" me but I was happy to take it. We shouldn't have to pick a pocket ever again."

"Amen to that," Fiona said, "but I have to admit, there's times when I miss wearing boys' trousers. They're just so much easier to get around in."

"I know." Tiki replied. "There are times when I miss being invisible. When we dressed in our rags, everyone looked through us, like we weren't even there. Now people smile and nod, especially men. It's exhausting sometimes."

"It's 'cause yer pretty, Teek," Clara piped up. "That's why they stare at you."

Tiki laughed and squeezed the little girl's hand. "Your ears are working pretty well today, Miss. Did Mrs. Bosworth clean out all the potatoes in them?"

Clara burst into giggles. "I haven't got potatoes in my ears." She pointed her little hand. "Toots does."

WHEN THEY REACHED Charing Cross Tiki sent Toots into the abandoned clockmaker's shop to see if Johnny was there. Before he returned a familiar voice spoke from behind them.

"You're looking as beautiful as a spring day, Miss Fiona." For a second Tiki was reminded of when Rieker used to sneak up on her while she sat in this same bench. The girls turned to face Johnny. He swept his cap off his head, pulled a rose out of it and presented it to Fiona with a flourish. "A rose for the lovely lady."

Fiona's cheeks turned pink but she accepted the flower with a pleased smile. "Thank you."

"Did you nick that from Mr. Colpitts?" Clara asked in her high voice. "It's got the tag wot he puts on his flowers."

"Hush, Clara," Fiona said. She held the bag out. "We brought you something, too."

Two dimples appeared in Johnny's cheeks as he smiled, giving him a charming air. "For me?" He took the bag and peeked in. "Slaved over the stove all day, did you?"

Fiona giggled, her cheeks even rosier.

Tiki smiled as she stood up. "Clara and I are going over to the bookstore. Fi, can you sit with Johnny while he eats and wait for Toots? He should be back any time."

Fiona cast a shy, sideways glance at Johnny, who was already moving around the bench to take Tiki's seat.

"Brilliant idea!" he said with gusto, reaching for the bag from Fiona.

Fi playfully slapped at Johnny's hands. "Hold on, let me get it out before you spill everything."

"Come along, then." Tiki said to Clara. "We're not needed here." Slipping her hand into Tiki's, Clara skipped along as they walked the short distance to the bookstore. The bell above the door jingled as they entered.

"Hallo Mr. Potts," Tiki called. After a moment, the old man shuffled out from between the stacks.

"Well, if it ain't Tiki and the littl'un." A smile wreathed his face. "I recognized you as a girl this time." He braced his hand on his desk as he sank down onto his stool, his hips cracking with the movement.

Tiki patted the man's gnarled hand. "How have you been?"

The old man shrugged his bony shoulders. "People comin', people goin'. I miss havin' yer come pester me for books." He gave her a wobbly smile.

"Well, I'm here to make a purchase today. A gift for a friend of mine."

The old man's eyes narrowed. "Are you still visitin' with Oliver Twist?"

Tiki blinked in surprise. "Well yes, actually, that's who the gift is for. What do you recommend this time?"

Mr. Potts pushed off from his stool and moved slowly into the interior of the store.

Tiki raised her eyebrows at Clara who gave an innocent shrug in return, her vivid blue eyes round with curiosity.

A moment later Mr. Potts returned with a thick volume. "'ere yer go." He placed the heavy book into Tiki's hands. "It's been around for awhile. Written by a French chap."

"That's a fat book," Clara said. "Has it got faeries in it?"

"*The Count of Monte Cristo*, by Alexandre Dumas." Tiki read out loud. "I've not heard of this one."

"'Bout a bloke with more than one identity." Mr. Potts quirked a gray eyebrow at Tiki. "Your friend should like it. I'll sell it to you half off today."

Tiki bit back a laugh and handed him a silver shilling. Rieker would also enjoy the man's sharp wit, she was sure.

"An for you," he tweaked Clara's nose, "I've got a book over here with a type of faerie in it." He shuffled to a different section of the store and brought back a thin book. "This is called *The Field of Boliauns*. 'Bout a little chap called a leprechaun. Tricky sort, that." He slid the book into Clara's hands and waved away Tiki's offer to pay. "You hold onto them coins so you stay outta trouble."

They visited for a bit longer and then promising to return soon, Tiki and Clara held hands as they headed back into the station to find Fiona and Toots. There were fewer trains in Charing Cross than King's Cross and the station wasn't as busy. Tiki couldn't help but glance at every traveler they passed and wonder if Larkin was disguised in a glamour somewhere nearby watching them.

But instead of Larkin, her eyes fell on a different familiar face. It was the young man who had tipped his hat at her when she and Fiona had walked to see Mr. Potts a few days ago—she was sure of it. His suit was neat and he wore a hat on his head like a gentleman. His blond hair was a bit longer than most, making him easy to recognize, but there was the same nagging sense of familiarity.

He leaned against a storefront corner, watching her, his arms crossed in a relaxed, slightly arrogant fashion, one side of his mouth turned in an appreciative grin. Suddenly Clara tugged on Tiki's hand and pointed at the young man. "Look, Tiki—it's Dain!"

Chapter Seventeen

Tiki's knees went weak. "Dain?" she echoed softly. "The Dain who brought Toots home?"

"Yep, same one," Clara said in a happy voice. She tugged Tiki toward the young man. "Let's go talk to 'im. Maybe he's got his pretty horse outside so you can see."

Tiki hesitated, then gripped Clara's hand tighter. "Yes, you're right. Let's have a word with Dain." Clara skipped along beside Tiki as they approached the young man, waving happily. Dain pushed off the wall and straightened, sweeping his hat off his head.

He knelt down and smiled at the little girl. "Hello Clara, what a surprise to see you here today. Are you traveling?"

"No, we came to see ol' Potts and to feed Johnny."

Dain's eyebrows flicked in a frown. "Who's Johnny?"

"He's a friend of ours, especially Fi." She gave him a sweet smile as she held out her book. "See? I got a book 'bout faeries, 'cept they're really called lep'reecons."

Dain made a show of looking at the book. "Leprechauns are tricky sorts — you best be careful around them or they'll steal all your gold."

Clara's laughter trilled like wind chimes. "That's wot ol' Potts said too." Dain smiled up at Tiki. "Is this pretty girl your sister?"

His direct question took Tiki by surprise.

"That's Tiki. She takes care of me." Clara smiled brightly at Tiki as Dain pushed himself to his feet. "She's like my mum, aren't you, Teek?"

"Miss Tiki, is it?" He inclined his head at her. "Brendain Browne, but my friends call me Dain. I hope you will too." His voice was low and musical, as if there was a thread of laughter underlying his words. Up close, he was taller than Tiki expected and she had to tilt her head to look into his face. "Clara is lucky to have someone as kind and attentive as you to care for her." His eyes were blue and guileless and Tiki felt the heat rise in her cheeks. He was extremely attractive, from the firm line of his jaw, to the chiseled features of his face and she was sure he knew it.

"Do I know you?" Tiki asked coldly. There was something familiar about this young man that made her want to know more—which told her one thing: he was dangerous. Only Rieker had ever had this effect on her.

Dain seemed non-plussed at her rude behavior. "I don't believe we've been formerly introduced, but I look forward to getting to know you better." He smiled, revealing a dimple on the left side of his cheek.

"But you know Toots?" Tiki persisted.

"Toots?" A puzzled frown brushed across his forehead. "I'm sorry—"

"Thomas." Tiki shook her head to clear her thoughts. "He's a ten year old, loves horses, has bright orange hair and freckles."

Dain's face went blank. "Why do you ask?"

It felt like a rock landed in Tiki's stomach. Dain's reaction to her description of Toots was too controlled. It was obvious he knew exactly who she was talking about.

"You are the one who brought him home, aren't you?" she said. Tiki took a step back and pulled Clara along with her. "What do you want?" Fear sharpened her wits and suddenly she could think again. Why was he here, *now*—when Tiki and her family were here?

"Dain, did you bring your white horse today?" Clara asked. "With the pretty red ribbons and the bells? I want to show her to Teek."

Dain's eyes were locked on Tiki and he seemed unsure how to answer.

"Are you following me?" Tiki snapped. Somehow, Dain was involved in Toots' trip to the Otherworld. That alone was enough for Tiki to consider him dangerous. He wanted something—but what?

Tiki squatted down and lifted Clara into her arms, wondering if she should pull her knife from where it was hidden up her sleeve as she backed away. "Just leave us alone," she said in a low voice.

"Why do you want him to leave us alone, Teek?" Clara asked, giving Tiki a confused look. "I like him and Doggie does too."

Dain fingered his hat as he debated his answer, his eyes never leaving Tiki's face. "I'm here to help."

Tiki put her hand up. "We don't want your help." She turned and hurried away.

Chapter Eighteen

Tiki's thoughts swam in confusing eddies as they returned to where Toots and Fiona sat with Johnny. Though his glamour had been flawless, Dain was fey, she was sure of it. He'd known who she was talking about when she'd asked about Toots and he'd avoided a direct answer. What did he want from them?

"We found Toots, Miss Tiki," Johnny said with a mischievous grin as Tiki approached.

She gave a weak smile in return. "Good." It was all she could think to say. Earlier, she'd considered inviting Johnny back to Rieker's townhome for another hot meal but Shamus had warned her not to reveal any more of Rieker's real life as William Richmond to the boy. Now, with this Dain fellow possibly following her, she needed to be extra careful.

"When Rieker starts his free school, maybe you could attend with us," Fiona suggested to Johnny as they were leaving.

"Why would he want to do that?" Toots asked "Who *wants* to go to school?"

Johnny smiled at Fiona. His brown hair was long and shaggy, a thick layer of bangs covering his forehead, but his eyes sparkled and he was quick with an engaging smile. "That sounds tempting, Miss Fiona." He handed her the bag with the empty stew crock in it, his fingers lingering on hers. "Thank you again for the meal."

Fiona nodded, her teeth tugging at her lower lip.

"Good-bye, Johnny," Tiki said, slipping her arm through Fiona's and pulling her away. "Take care."

He doffed his cap at them and gave them a mock bow. Though his clothes were threadbare and a string wrapped around his boot held the sole to the bottom of his shoe, he had a certain rakish air about him. "Until we meet again."

Tiki nudged Fiona as they pushed their way out the doors of Charing Cross into the afternoon. She glanced once over her shoulder to see if they were being followed but Dain was nowhere in sight. "He's a cheeky bit, that one. You better be careful around him, Fiona."

"Don't worry, Teek. Fi's waitin' for a 'andsome prince," Clara said, holding tight to Tiki's hand. "Johnny's not dressed right."

Fiona remained unusually silent.

RIEKER WAS HOME when Tiki and the others arrived. Like usual, Toots went out to the coach house to see if Geoffrey would let him pet the horses and help feed or brush them, while Clara and Fiona went in search of Mrs. Bosworth to tell her how much Johnny had loved the stew.

Tiki knocked on the door to Rieker's study.

"Come in," his low voice called.

Tiki pushed the door open and peered in. Rieker sat at his desk, his jacket thrown over the back of a nearby chair, his sleeves rolled to his elbows, the fabric of his white shirt strained by his broad shoulders. His dark hair brushed his collar as he bent his head to work, a gas lamp lighting the wood surface of the desk.

"Am I interrupting?"

Rieker glanced over his shoulder, and immediately stopped working. "No, I'm just finishing up some paperwork." He waved a hand in the direction of the chairs. "Come in and sit down."

Tiki closed the door and moved soundlessly across the plush Persian rug that covered the floor. She slid into the overstuffed chair, enjoying the manliness of the room. Dark bookcases lined the walls between huge windows that looked out to well-tended gardens. A nearby table with two chairs on each side had a chess game in progress.

Rieker waited as Tiki sat down. Dark circles shadowed the skin under his eyes and he looked as though he hadn't slept. Worry had created fine lines between his brows and his eyes were darker than normal, reminding Tiki of when she'd first met him.

"How was Mr. Potts?" Rieker smiled and his face transformed, as if he'd pulled a mask on to hide his concerns.

Tiki held out the book she'd just purchased. "He sent you a new book," she said, then affected Mr. Potts' accent, "'bout a bloke with more than one identity.'"

Rieker blinked in surprise, one corner of his mouth lifting in a half-smile. He reached for the book and examined the title with curiosity. "The Count of Monte Cristo?"

Tiki shook her head. "I haven't heard of it either."

Rieker put the book on the edge of the desk. "Well, if Mr. Potts recommended this one, it's sure to be good."

"How was Leo? Did you learn anything more?" Tiki slipped her shoes off and tucked her feet beneath her, snuggling deeper into the chair. For this moment she felt safe, alone in this room with Rieker, almost like they were hidden in a world of their own.

He shook his head, the muscles in his jaw clenching. "They still haven't been able to stop the bleeding."

Tiki frowned. "That's not good."

"The physicians are calling it hemophilia but the Queen has never shown any signs of the disease nor did Leo's father before he passed." Rieker tapped his fingers on the arm of his chair. "Arthur is convinced that *'other forces'* are involved."

"I don't think there's any question, do you?"

Rieker shook his head. "Not really. He's asked us to attend a party a week from next Saturday, to see if we can spot anyone who might be 'out of the ordinary' is how he put it."

Tiki hesitated. "Speaking of 'out of the ordinary', I keep seeing one young man in particular lately."

Rieker stiffened. "Who's that?"

"I first noticed him when Fi and I went to Charing Cross last week. Then I saw him again today. Clara waved at him and called him Dain." Tiki raised her eyebrows. "Apparently, he's the chap who brought Toots home from the Otherworld."

"Does he seem threatening?"

Tiki shook her head. "Not really...not yet—" she hesitated— "but he wants something."

"Curious faeries are usually a problem."

"He said he'd come to help."

Rieker grimaced. "Helpful faeries might even be worse." He quirked an eyebrow. "Dain, you said his name was?" Tiki nodded. "Keep your distance from him and tell me if you see him again."

"I told him to leave us alone."

"It's good you let him know you're not afraid of him, but maybe even better if you pretend you can't see him at all. By the way, Arthur thought we might be able to visit with Leo in a private drawing room for a short time while we're at the palace." Rieker gave her a teasing grin. "Arthur knows Leo enjoys seeing you. He probably thinks that will help him get well."

Tiki's cheeks warmed. "I think Leo fancies any girl, not just me."

Rieker chuckled. "That's true, but I think Leo fancies you more than most." A soft smile stretched Rieker's lips as he tilted his head to see Tiki's face. "You've enchanted him." His voice got softer. "Just as you've enchanted me."

Surprised, Tiki's eyes flicked to Rieker's. His gaze was steady on her and there was a vulnerability in his expression that she'd rarely seen. A warmth spread in her chest until she could feel it heating her cheeks, as well.

Rieker seemed to catch himself, and the mask that hid his emotions was back in place.

He looked away and ran his fingers through his dark hair, making the wavy ends stand up.

Tiki searched for something to fill the awkward silence. "What I don't understand is how Donegal has found a way around the truce."

"I know." Rieker sighed. "Unfortunately, I suspect Larkin is the only one who would be able to answer that question."

"Did I hear someone mention my name?"

Chapter Nineteen

"Larkin." Rieker's voice came out in a growl. "Is there never any peace from you?"

The blond faerie strode out of the dim shadows from the corner of the room. "Really, William—" Larkin's voice was disapproving— "you seem to forget that you want something from me." She ran a finger along the back of his chair, leaning forward to speak into his ear. "A little respect, a little gratitude, would go a long way in encouraging me to confide some of my secrets."

Dressed in a simple gown of moss green silk that seemed to float around her, the faerie was barefoot. Her hair hung long down her back in a wild tangle of golden waves. Her face glowed as if the sun shone down solely on her and once again, Tiki had a hard time dragging her eyes away from Larkin's beauty.

"Do you ever stop spying on us?" Rieker snapped. "Don't you need to sleep occasionally? Or are you part vampire as well?"

Larkin jerked her head back and hissed at him. "You push me, William, with your insults." She put a razor-sharp fingernail under his chin. Her lips pulled back in a snarl. "Pray that you don't push me too far one day."

"Don't threaten him, Larkin." Tiki sat straighter in her chair. Larkin wanted something from her—for once she had the upper hand. "Or you might push *me* too far."

Larkin looked at Tiki, her head tilted like a bird. "What's this? Has my little faerie queen finally gathered some courage?" She circled Tiki's chair and gazed at the other side of her face. "Do you bite and scratch now?" She poked a finger at Tiki's arm.

Lightning fast, Tiki's fingers stretched like a cat's claws and flew to clamp around Larkin's wrist. The faerie let out a cry. Tiki squeezed hard, intending to inflict pain. She spoke through gritted teeth. "If that's what I need to do to keep my family safe, then the answer is yes."

For a moment she stared unblinking into the faerie's mercurial eyes, then Larkin threw back her head and let out a wild cackle of laughter. Tiki loosened her grip and Larkin jerked her arm free. Tiki was surprised by the gleeful smile that stretched across Larkin's features.

"I feared perhaps you'd inherited too much of Adasara's gentle nature, but no—" Larkin twirled once, lifting her skirts so they swirled around her legs. As her long hair flew free Tiki caught a glimpse of what looked like two terrible wounds that slashed across Larkin's back before the faerie faced Tiki again and clapped her hands— "I see Finn is alive and well in you. Your father was a warrior. As fierce and wild as a midnight storm—"

"Larkin," Rieker interrupted, "why are you here?"

"Ah yes, that." Larkin stilled. "I came to tell you there is a party going on in the Palace of Mirrors, as we speak. Usually the celebration of Beltane, the onset of summer, is hosted by the Seelies as they regain power of the courts, but instead, Donegal is hosting a lavish feast." She pointed her long, delicate finger at Tiki. "It is the perfect opportunity for you to touch *Cloch na teamhrach*."

Tiki took a deep breath. "How do we get there?"

Both Larkin and Rieker looked at her in surprise.

"What?" Rieker gasped.

"A sensible choice," Larkin said, stepping closer to Tiki.

Tiki pushed herself out of the chair, needing to move, to put space between herself and the faerie, to try and dislodge the terrible fear churning in the pit of her stomach. "I can't stand by and watch the people I care about be hurt. But you'll have to help me. Tell me how to find the stone and what to do."

"You're not going without me." Rieker jumped up from his chair.

"There are some things I won't have to teach," Larkin said, standing perfectly still. "You're beginning to believe in yourself."

Tiki's brow furrowed. "What do you mean?"

Larkin held up her wrist and pulled back the flowing sleeve. Green blood oozed from the painful looking punctures in her skin. "Look what you did."

Tiki bit back a gasp as she stared at the faerie's arm. She glanced down at her own fingers. They looked perfectly normal now, but she'd felt the transformation in her hand when she'd reached for Larkin's wrist—the blinding speed with which she moved, the ferocity of her grip—almost as if claws had sprung from her fingertips.

"So, you see," Larkin said with an enigmatic smile, "it has already begun."

"You will not go without me," Rieker said again, looking from one to the other.

Larkin circled Tiki, looking thoughtful. "You'll need to be disguised. We can't take the chance of you being recognized."

"Then put a glamour on me. Or better yet, teach me how to apply a glamour."

Larkin measured her through slitted lids. "Perhaps you should just shed the one you wear?" There was a tone in the faerie's words that sounded like a dare.

"*What?*" Tiki and Rieker spoke at the same time.

Tiki bit down hard on her lip. Larkin didn't need any more of an advantage. "Don't be ridiculous," she snapped. "Can you disguise me or not?"

Larkin nodded, tossing a long strand of silky hair over her shoulder as she slowly paced. "I can disguise you, but the Palace of Mirrors is exactly what the names implies: a palace of enchanted mirrors. The mirrors reflect one's true form. It is a place where lies become truth." She let out a trill of laughter like wind chimes, as if she'd told a joke. "To stop anyone from entering court who might be in a glamour and mean to do the king harm, of course."

She moved behind Rieker's back as effortlessly as if she floated and for a second Tiki couldn't see her. Then the faerie peered from behind him, giving Tiki the odd sense they were playing a game of hide and seek.

"What do we do then?" Rieker asked, stepping closer to Tiki, pulling her away from Larkin.

"First, we will avoid the mirrors. They are primarily in the Great Hall, where court and all the festivities are held. It will be tricky, but we can still accomplish what needs to be done." She snapped her fingers. "But we need to go now, while the opportunity exists. The Palace of Mirrors will be the last place Donegal would ever expect to see one of us."

IT ONLY TOOK a few seconds for Larkin to apply a glamour to Tiki. With a feather-light touch she ran her hands over Tiki's hair and along her arms down to her feet, chanting indistinguishable words. As she worked, the faint smell of clover permeated the air. Tiki felt as if she'd been infused with a glowing light. But instead of being warmed by the light, a cool breeze blew across her skin—as if she stood in front of an open door.

"Hmmm." Larkin appraised Tiki. "You do look a bit like my sister now, though lacking in any natural grace or true beauty, of course."

"That is amazing," Rieker breathed in a tone of astonishment. "Teek, you don't even look like yourself anymore."

A nervous excitement bubbled inside Tiki. She desperately wanted to look in a mirror, but there were no mirrors in Rieker's study. She looked down at her hands, but they didn't look that different—her fingers were longer and more slender, the color of her skin more golden. Her hair reached all the way to her waist, but was still her familiar dark color. She now wore a dress the color of midnight blue, embroidered with threads of silver that sparkled and twinkled in the lamp light.

"How do I remove the glamour?" Tiki asked.

"When you arrive in the Otherworld, your glamour will naturally shift a bit more—to blend in with your surroundings," Larkin said. "I've applied it in a way so it will fade when you return to London."

She turned to Rieker, and rested a finger on her chin. "Now for you. Finn's best friend was a young man named Fraoch O'Donoghue. He was about your size—" she looked Rieker up and down— "and had the same sort of arrogance about him. He can be our inspiration." Rieker frowned, but Larkin only smiled and stepped close, cupping his face in her hands. "I do so enjoy touching you, William. Always so handsome."

Rieker moved to brush her arms away, but Larkin hissed at him as she jerked her hands toward his head and he froze. As Tiki watched Larkin ran her fingers along the perimeter of his body and he melted into someone else. Suddenly, a young man stood before her with a crop of long, wild brown hair that brushed his shoulders. A braid hung on one side and another part was pulled back with a strip of leather. His face, though marked by several vicious scars, was sculpted with wide cheekbones and a hearty grin, as if he'd just told a joke.

Rieker looked at Tiki. "How do I look?"

"Different," she said faintly.

"Yes, that will do nicely." Larkin swirled her hand in front of herself and suddenly a much older woman stood there, stout of hip with an aging face. Beautiful, but not anywhere near the breathtaking exquisiteness that usually illuminated Larkin's features.

"Oh," Tiki cried, putting a hand to her mouth. "Should I tell the others we're leaving?"

"Not to worry, guttersnipe," Larkin said. "You'll be back before they'll ever know you were gone."

Chapter Twenty

"Since you both have faerie blood," Larkin said, "you are able to travel through the gates on your own, but for now, since you don't have the most basic knowledge—" she sounded annoyed— "I'll take you." Larkin gripped their wrists. "Speak only if you have too. Avoid the mirrors and no matter what, stay close to me."

Rieker's study shimmered out of view and Tiki found herself standing in a shadow-laden thicket.

"Welcome to the Night Garden—" Larkin spoke in a low voice— "the depraved creation of the UnSeelie world." She held up a finger in warning. "Don't touch anything, unless you want to feed the plants with your own blood." A smirk lifted one corner of her mouth. "Or worse, become their next meal."

Tiki shivered and stepped closer to Rieker.

Even the light of the moon seemed hesitant to enter the garden and cast only a watery glow upon the immense tangle of barbed vines and thorned bushes. Here and there, a few magnificent flowers bloomed, their exotic blossoms emitting an alluring luminescence through the dim light. Upon closer inspection, Tiki saw that the edges of their petals were saw-toothed and blood-stained.

Dread weighted Tiki's footsteps. What were they doing in a place like this? The haunting sound of music floated through the night, like a piper leading the lost and weary home. "Where is that coming from?" she whispered.

"It's the plants," Larkin replied. "They're nocturnal—they sing at night to call their prey." She turned and started down a path lined with broken and uneven stones. "This way."

Rieker, taller than both Tiki and Larkin, ducked as they walked beneath twisted trees that hunched and loomed above the walkway, their claw-handed branches outstretched as though to grab an unsuspecting passerby.

Larkin paused at a bend in the path and Tiki glanced up at a stone statue that stretched above their heads, casting them in a web of gloom. The carving was of a woman, her face twisted in agony, reaching for the heavens. One great wing stretched from the left side of her back, as if she meant to take flight, while the other lay broken on the ground beside her.

"Danu," Larkin said, pointing to the statue. "The original goddess of Faerie—the mother of the *Tuatha De Danaan*. She was captured by a human who tore off her wing to keep her in the mortal world. The UnSeelies celebrate her as a reminder to hate all mortals."

Tiki covered her mouth with her hand.

Rieker reached over and took her other hand in his. "Why are we here, Larkin?" he whispered harshly.

The faerie pointed a long finger. In the distance stood an immense building, great stone pillars lining the front. Darkness dripped from every corner as if a black veil had been thrown over the structure. "Because we're going there—to the Palace of Mirrors."

The palace was perched on the pinnacle of a rocky mountain, a sweeping panorama stretching in both directions. To the right, Tiki could see a band of brilliant light radiating across the sky. To the left—only darkness.

"When the Seelies hold court here at the Palace, the sun rarely sets and the gardens are lush and overrun with flowers." Larkin pointed toward the glowing horizon. "When they're not occupying the Palace, the Summer Court lives there—in the plain of Sunlight." She swiveled and pointed the other direction. "That is the Plain of Starlight—" her lips twisted in distaste— "the never-ending darkness that the UnSeelie's call home."

She spread her hands. "We stand on Wydryn Tor. All around the Tor lies the Wychwood Forest—the unclaimed land between the Plains—and also the hunting ground for hags, goblins, kelpies, redcaps and every other sort of fey creature. Even witches and other unspeakables are found there upon occasion." Larkin lowered her voice. "It is rumored that from this forest is where Donegal found his assassin."

Rieker stiffened. "The one he's using to get around the truce?"

"Yes." Larkin's tone was matter-of-fact. "The same one who murdered O'Riagáin. The assassin is neither mortal nor fey. He is one of the oldest creatures known—a *liche*—a creature of the night who sustains himself by consuming the flesh and blood of others. It is rumored that Donegal found this one in the forest, a stake of ash through his chest, but still alive." Her lips curled with distaste. "The *liche* seems to like eating the hearts of his victims. Maybe he thinks that will replace having a stake driven through his own."

Tiki sucked in her breath at the grisly image. Was the *liche* what had attacked Prince Leopold? Could such a creature be loose in London—hunting the royals or anyone else who protected the ring?

"All the more reason to be successful tonight," Larkin finished. Though her glamour looked nothing like the real Larkin, her blue-green eyes glittered in the watery moonlight making her look half-mad. "Follow me and don't speak."

LARKIN CONTINUED DOWN the winding path of the garden. Vines writhed underfoot, like snakes, and Tiki stomped on several to stop them from wrapping around her ankles. More than once, the sound of footsteps scuttled through the underbrush and Tiki spotted glowing red eyes watching them from the depths of the tangled vines.

"Alms for the poor?" The words were scratchy, as though the voice had been worn out asking the same question.

Tiki jerked her head toward the sound. Just off the path, a wraith-thin body sat, wrapped in dirty rags.

"Scat!" Larkin hissed, shooing at the creature. "You risk your life begging this close to the palace." The creature hunched its shoulders as if to protect itself from a blow. "You'll have better luck at one of the villages in the wood." She took a threatening step closer. "Go now."

With a squeak of terror, the creature disappeared into the vines.

"What was that?" Tiki whispered.

"Beggar." Larkin marched forward. "Come along."

The deformed trees moaned and sighed as they passed, as though blown by the wind, but there was no breeze. Instead, the night air seemed to hold its breath as if in anticipation. Tiki practically ran up the steps behind Larkin to the grand entrance—anything to escape the garden.

Though dark-suited guards stood at attention at the enormous entry doors, spears in their hands and swords dangling from their belts, they allowed passage with little more than a shifting of their black eyes.

Rieker walked close to Tiki as they followed Larkin down a vast corridor, as majestic as any passageway Tiki had ever seen in Buckingham Palace. But despite the grandeur, this palace was swathed in shadows that clung to corners like spider webs. Torches, mounted in golden brackets, lined the walls, but the tongues of their flames emitted dense smoke, scenting the air with the acrid smell of fire and the stench of decay.

The few people in the hallway stood in small clusters, their glances like sharp pokes as Larkin's group passed. At the end of the corridor another set of grand doors were propped open. Music washed down the hall like a flowing river, rising and falling, swirling and dipping. The poignant sound of flutes met the eerie cry of bagpipes before being dashed away with fiddles and drums and a frenzy of other instruments. An unexpected craving filled Tiki, drawing her forward.

They passed through the doors into a great hall that stretched before her. Soaring black and gold fluted columns lined each side of the rectangular room, supporting an arched ceiling embellished with macabre paintings.

Tiki stared in horror at the painted facade above, dread coiling in her stomach. In one section, huge black dogs with pointed fangs, snarling snouts and red glowing eyes, chased what looked to be a terrified human male running through the forest. Winged creatures flew above the dogs—grotesque caricatures of birds, or fish, she wasn't quite sure which—with spiked beaks, outstretched claws and misshapen bodies.

In another section a pond was painted with a long-haired cadaver, covered in green slime, pulling herself out of the water to capture a young boy who stood nearby with his back to her, unaware of the danger. Tiki's gaze stopped on the image of a beautiful woman, her lips smeared with bright red lipstick. There was something unsettling about the pose, the way the woman was hunched over and slightly turned away. Tiki bit back a gasp as she realized the woman was holding a dead man in her arms, drinking the blood from his neck, as if bestowing a lover's kiss.

"Don't look." Rieker slid an arm around Tiki's shoulders.

Tiki hid her eyes against Rieker's shoulder, trying to erase the images from her mind. "What is this place?" The music filled her ears and pulled at her even as she looked away. Lilting notes of a flute, the trill of a panpipe, and the strums of a fiddle teased each other in a flirtatious melody that floated around the hall until she fought the urge to twirl in time to the music. She clung to Rieker's arm as if he were the anchor that could stop her from drowning in the madness.

"Welcome to the UnSeelie court," Larkin whispered. "There's a reason it's known as the dark court. Not only do the UnSeelies rule during the dark months of the year, but Donegal likes to bring the comforts of home when he lives here. During winter, court is a reflection of life in the Plain of Starlight—dark, evil and deadly. Luckily, Donegal only allows a select class to attend court. You won't find any Redcaps or Leanan-Sidhe from the Wychwood here."

Tiki lifted her head and looked around cautiously. Carved red ribbons, the color of blood, arced and danced along the walls above alcoves that were decorated with intricate designs of gold and silver. Huge mirrors were tucked into every alcove, reflecting the shivering firelight of the torches over and over again.

The room was crowded with finely-dressed men and women—conversing, drinking, shifting and moving as if in an exquisitely choreographed dance. There was something discordant about the atmosphere, however, like an orchestra with the instruments out of tune. Tension hung in the air as heavily as a London fog.

"Who are these people?" Tiki asked.

"Many are from the Seelie court, those who had come early to celebrate Beltane and the changing of the courts," Larkin said. "Now they are captives forced to publicly pledge their servitude to a new king. It pleases Donegal to humiliate people."

Tiki surveyed the room. Some were dressed as regally as royalty, their gowns of silk, satin and velvet embellished with threads of gold and silver. Others were clearly courtiers, draped in gowns that revealed more than they hid, reflecting the wearer's hope to improve their positions through flattery or whatever means necessary.

Larkin waved her slender hand to encompass the activity around them. "It's here that the game of war is plotted, by those who have taken power—for now." Her voice held a threat. "This is where the pawns are manipulated and the gambits begun."

"How can you tell UnSeelie from Seelie?" Rieker's eyes skated over the occupants of the room, evaluating what threat they could pose. He held tight to Tiki's hand but his shoulders were back and he moved with a careless grace that reminded Tiki of a panther— coiled and dangerous.

"You can't tell by just looking. Many are UnSeelie and all of the guards are Donegal's men." Larkin shot a warning glance at Rieker. "These men are hand-picked and look for an opportunity to protect their king. Don't start anything you can't finish."

Rieker's lips turned up in a half-smile. "Thanks for the warning."

Larkin nodded. "Usually faeries like to insult and humiliate each other—it's more entertaining to plot a revenge that might last several centuries than to outright murder someone. But Donegal's plan seems to be to kill anyone who resists him. He's surrounded himself with a blood-thirsty and relentless inner circle."

She pointed to a great beast of man with flaming red hair. "That's Bearach. His *tánaiste*. A vicious man. If he thinks a solider isn't doing enough, or might be questioning his tactics—he doesn't threaten the soldier—he threatens their family. People just disappear."

Tiki eyed the hulk of a man, laughing and drinking from a giant flask. He reminded her of MacGregor, a mean drunk, a woman-beater, whose pockets she'd picked last winter just to prove to Rieker she could do it. Fiona's mother had worked for Mac-

Gregor as a seamstress and though Fiona had never admitted it, Tiki suspected MacGregor had been the man who'd beaten Fi's mother to death.

Tiki's gaze went to the ceiling again to a painting she'd noticed earlier. A hulking red-headed giant held a spiked mallet in one hand, and wore a multitude of chains. Suspended from the chains around his waist, like some ghastly belt, were the severed heads of his victims.

She pointed a shaking finger skyward. "Is that him?"

Larkin glanced up and a smile flitted across her face. "No, that's a Jack-in-Irons, but you've got a point—Bearach must have a few hanging from his family tree."

"What does *tánaiste* mean?" Rieker asked.

"His second-in-command. Part of Donegal's inner circle that includes Sullivan, Cruinn, Scáthach —all monsters with ferocious capabilities. The Winter King never travels without them." Her blue-green eyes, the only part of her body that resembled the Larkin who Tiki knew, snapped with a fiery anger and she whispered a threat under her breath. "But they don't know what's coming for them."

Chapter Twenty-One

A guard, dressed in black and heavily armed with glittering knives and more than one sword, stared belligerently at Tiki. She dropped her eyes, fearful her bubbling stomach might come out her mouth. She focused instead on a court jester—dressed in a gaudy combination of colorful stripes and patterns—weaving his way through the crowd. His comical hat was festooned with a multitude of bells which created music as he bowed and danced in their direction. Wings arched from his back, spider-webbed with black lines, like a stained-glass window. They were adorned with sparkle and fluff as if a reflection of his brilliant wit.

"Remember to avoid the mirrors," Larkin murmured under her breath as she led them deeper into the crowd.

"How can we avoid them?" Tiki whispered. "They're everywhere."

"On the other hand—" Larkin gazed back over her shoulder at Tiki— "perhaps a quick glance would do you good."

"What's that supposed to mean?"

Larkin raised her eyebrows. "I think you might find it intriguing to see what the mirrors reveal."

Tiki jerked her head away, unsure of her response. Did she want to know what she would look like without the glamour Larkin swore she wore?

"Show us what Tiki needs to do and get us out of here," Rieker said in a harsh whisper.

Larkin jerked to a stop. "William, you might find it interesting to know what the mirrors don't reveal."

"Really?" Rieker's voice echoed with doubt. "And what might that be?"

Larkin waved her hand to encompass the room. "What the mirrors don't reveal is the squalor hidden beyond the court. That beggar you saw in the Night Garden is just one of thousands. The realm is not what it used to be. Things started changing centuries ago when Donegal took power in the UnSeelie Court, but when Eridanus died, things deteriorated more rapidly."

She walked through the crowd, head held high, as if she were born to Court. "Those who 'have', live in their world full of illusions, while those who do not, scrap and beg for the means to survive." She glanced at Tiki from the corners of her eyes. "Not so unlike London."

Tiki blinked in surprise. "You mean you have different classes here?"

"Just like any society." Larkin's lips pressed together in a thin line. "There is much of our world not reflected within these magical mirrors."

"Ah, my lovely lady." The court jester drew near and took Larkin's hand. With a flourish he bent at the waist to make a show of kissing her fingers. Now that he was closer, Tiki could see the man had wrinkles around his eyes and appeared older than many of the others in the room. He reminded her of someone she'd seen dressed in a similarly gaudy outfit at a street fair in Brompton outside the Victoria and Albert Museum one time. She wondered now if he'd crossed over for a day of entertainment in the mortal world.

Painted-on rays of bright yellow arced out across his eyelids and cheeks, making his eyes appear to be miniature suns. "Beautiful bird, your return to court is welcomed by many—" his voice lowered— "but the wings of a dove are no match for the talons of a hawk."

Tiki wondered if somehow the man could see through Larkin's glamour.

Larkin studied the jester for a long moment. "Unless, Fool—" she leaned close to the man's ear and Tiki strained to hear her words— "the dove has the heart of a fox." Though the title she'd bestowed upon the man seemed an insult, her voice held no rancor, nor did the jester seem to take offense.

The man held a finger aloft. "But do those with the heart of a fox see through the illusions of the cunningly ambitious?"

Larkin flicked her wrist as if to brush a piece of lint from her sleeve. "Be gone with your puns and shrouded advice. I don't wish to draw attention at this time."

The jester's eyes flicked to Tiki and then on to Rieker. Tiki could see curiosity burning there before he bowed to Larkin. "I await the moment to bask in the graciousness of your beauty, and that of your friend—" he nodded at Tiki— "another day." He swept away, pulling three colorful balls from a pocket in his vest and began juggling to the amusement of another group of people.

Larkin leaned close to Tiki. "Your reflection in an enchanted mirror is not what I brought you here to see." She pointed to the far end of the hallway. "There—at the end—do you see it?"

Tiki and Rieker squinted through the shadows to where Larkin pointed. Elevated above the throngs of people dancing, drinking and eating, was a platform against the far wall. Great steps led up to a massive slab of rock twelve inches thick. Centered on the rock was a huge golden throne in the shape of a dragon, its head turned to the side and roaring, spiked horns protruding from its snout and lining the back of its neck. Great golden wings were outstretched and the stout legs were crouched as if the beast meant to leap into the air at any second. The short front arms were thrust forward, like the outstretched talons of an eagle, above a seat that protruded from his belly.

Four guards, armed with bladed spears, surrounded the dragon and stood at attention on each side of the raised dais. Their faces were stern, given the party atmosphere that surrounded them.

"That seat?" Tiki asked.

Larkin's voice was soft. "That 'seat', as you so casually refer to it, is the Dragon Throne—where those who rule Faerie sit. It stands on *Cloch na Teamhrach*—The Stone of Tara. You might note that even Finn's name Mac*Loch*lan references the *cloch*, or stone." She wrapped her long fingers around Tiki's wrist as she drew her near to whisper in her ear. "An inescapable destiny." Tiki shivered as Larkin's cool breath brushed her skin. "In just a few moments, *niece*, you will touch the stone and it will roar once again."

"But the throne is so well-guarded," Rieker said, his voice heavy with concern. "How will she get close enough to touch it?"

"We will find an opportunity," Larkin said airily. Then softer, under her breath, "or we'll create one."

Someone bumped Tiki's arm and she turned. Standing, not a foot away, was a young man. Tall and thin, his straight hair was raven-feather black and pulled behind his head to reveal a large scar that sliced from his ear to his chin, causing one side of his mouth to pucker. Two more scars slashed through his eyebrow and across his forehead, in a gruesome testament to some horrific battle, but it was the familiar blue eyes that made Tiki stare. He opened his mouth to speak when a shrill voice interrupted.

"Sean!" A dark-haired faerie threw her arms around the young man's neck and locked her lips on his. It took him a minute before he got his hands on her shoulders and pushed away.

Tiki's jaw dropped open as Rieker jerked around. *Sean?* Was this the faerie who had been providing information about the Otherworld to Rieker?

"Sorry, miss." The young man said to the dark-haired girl as he held her shoulders, stopping her from throwing herself at him again. "You've mistaken me for someone else."

The girl was devastatingly beautiful: sloe-eyed, with cinnamon skin and lips the color of crushed cherries. She rested one hand on the young man's hip and teased his chin with a strand of her hair. "I don't think so. It's been a long time, but not *that* long." She wrapped her arms around his neck, and slithered close, oblivious to the others around them.

"It's me, Pashan." She rubbed her hips against his and Tiki felt her cheeks flame. "Surely, you haven't forgotten the times we've shared, have you, Sean?"

"Sean?" Tiki had not meant to speak out loud. She would swear those blue eyes were Dain's.

The dark-haired faerie spun around to face Tiki. "And who are you?" She looked Tiki up and down. The expression on her face made it clear she didn't consider Tiki any competition.

"Pashan." Larkin's voice was firm. "Leave us. Now."

The dark-haired faerie opened her mouth to argue then thought better of it. She pressed her lips together and flounced away.

Rieker took a step toward Sean. "What are you doing *here*?" His shoulders were back and he seemed coiled to react.

"I need to tell you—" Sean started.

Larkin flicked her hand at the newcomer and interrupted. "Not now." She slipped her hands through Tiki and Rieker's arms and pulled them in the other direction. "We can talk later. There are more important things to attend to first."

Chapter Twenty-Two

"Another body has been found." Arthur stood at the end of Leo's bed, his face grim.

There was no answer for several heartbeats.

"And?" Leo said in a weak voice.

"Same as the others. Slit from neck to navel, as if by a claw—the heart removed." Arthur rubbed his forehead with his hands. "That makes four now. The last one was the same night you were attacked." He loosened his cravat. "Four murders, four missing hearts, not one bloody suspect."

He paced to the door and back again. "He disappears like the mist in the night. No clues, no trail to follow. Not a single drop of blood outside the bodies." Arthur stopped and propped his hands on his hips, his long tweed coat pushed behind him. "I think you're the only one who has seen him and lived to tell about it."

"I barely saw him," Leo said in a whisper. "He was on me like a wild beast, all dark shadows and claws." He tugged his purple robe tighter across the bony ribs of his chest. "He was there to kill me, too. I know it."

Arthur propped himself on the end of Leo's bed. "I have to agree. Mother is so well-protected—he can't get to her, so I'm afraid he attacked you instead." He sighed. "Mamie warned us."

"The murderer is obviously not of this world," Leo said in a weak voice, "nor is he fey." Rain suddenly pelted the window, like fingers tapping to get in. "He must be some other kind of creature."

"But what?" Arthur said. "And how do we stop him?"

Chapter Twenty-Three

Dancers claimed the floor in the Great Hall of the Palace of Mirrors, twirling and weaving with wine-induced exuberance. The music of fiddles, flutes, horns and bagpipes filled the air, notes trembling like a million birds fluttering overhead.

Guards stood at attention beside each of the tall, black and gold fluted columns, surveying the crowd. Some clutched spears, others held spiked mauls, a few were outfitted with bows and arrows. All of them had daggers and sheathed knives hanging from their belts.

As Larkin led them through the room, Tiki dared a glance into one of the huge mirrors that filled the niches between the columns. But just as she passed, two dancers moved between her and the mirror, blocking her view. The musicians started playing a waltz and Larkin pulled them to a stop. The throne was still a distance away and the crowd was thicker at that end of the hall.

"We need to get closer to be ready when the opportunity presents itself," Larkin said.

The music shifted and a new group of dancers claimed the floor as Larkin led them forward again. The sheen of satin, taffeta and exquisitely embroidered brocade reflected the torches that surrounded the raised dais, giving the impression the material was made of flame. The men's trousers were straight legged, the color of bark, with colorful jackets and tails that flared behind them as they turned. Their boots flashed with gold buckles that matched the gold buttons and embroidery on their jackets. Bottles of blue faerie wine were handed about freely.

Tiki spotted a man sitting on the elaborately carved Dragon Throne. He held a goblet of gold in one hand that matched the circlet of gold which sat upon his shoulder-length black hair. He had to be Donegal. Dressed in rich black garments which shimmered as he moved as though made of iridescent black silk, his eyes were dark and slitted, reminding Tiki of a snake. An aura of evil emanated from him like a putrefied scent. Two men fanned him with giant wings.

Larkin edged them closer and nodded in the king's direction. "Those are O'Riagáin's wings."

Tiki stared in macabre fascination. The man looked utterly content being kept cool with the wings of the murdered Seelie king.

Donegal's gaze paused on their group. His thick black eyebrows pulled down in a frown, his eyelids half-closed, like a predator evaluating its prey. His gaze flicked to Rieker, and then to Tiki.

Tiki took a step backward into the thick of the crowd. "He's looking at us," she whispered.

"You there."

Tiki froze as the UnSeelie King's gritty voice echoed around the room. Donegal was staring right at her. She clutched at Rieker's sleeve. "He's seen me."

"Stay calm," Rieker said, putting his hand over her fingers. "He doesn't know who you are."

Donegal raised his hand to stop the music and rose from his chair.

"You." He pointed in Tiki's direction. Whispers buzzed through the hall. "In the blue dress. Approach."

"Now's our chance," Larkin whispered. "Just touch the stone that his throne stands upon."

The crowd around Tiki and Rieker backed away, magically creating space where moments before there'd been none.

"I'll be right behind you," Rieker whispered in Tiki's ear. He gripped her elbow and moved them toward Donegal. "Be careful. If it's not possible to touch the stone, don't try."

"My lord." Rieker bowed from the waist, pinching Tiki's arm for her to do the same. From the corner of her eyes Tiki saw two guards moving through the crowd in their direction, brandishing iron-bladed spears. "We are honored by your presence."

Tiki's heart skipped in her chest like a stone over water. The guards grabbed Rieker's arm and then hers. Rieker's brown thatch of hair fell over his forehead shadowing his eyes as they were yanked forward, but a smile played upon his lips. "Don't fight them," he whispered out of the side of this mouth.

"Halt." Donegal uttered when Tiki and Rieker were a few feet away. There was no way she could cover the distance and climb the steps to stand on the stone before the guards stopped her—most likely with a blade through her heart.

Donegal gazed at her with narrowed eyes. "Who are you?"

Tiki sucked in a quick breath. They'd never discussed the possibility that Donegal might question her. Was this a trap? Had Larkin deliberately put a glamour on her that would attract Donegal's attention?

An eerie silence hovered in the room. In that instant of pure quiet, all the reasons she stood there flashed before Tiki's eyes. She raised her head, suddenly more confident than she'd ever felt in her life.

"My name is Tara, sir." Rieker's hand tightened on her arm.

Donegal peered down at Tiki. "You dare say your name is Tara?" His black eyes stared at her. "That is a powerful name. Surely you must know you have to earn the right to claim such a name."

Tiki's mind raced. She hadn't been sure how she would gain access to the throne to touch the Stone of Tara, but maybe the opportunity was just going to present itself—like a pocket, begging to be picked.

"I do," she said in a firm voice. "In fact, I can prove my claim." She was surprised to hear some of Larkin's arrogance in her own voice. "May I approach?"

"Don't—" Rieker reached a hand out to stop her, his voice urgent. Tiki motioned for him to be still.

Donegal swept her up and down, looking for any hidden weapons. "Tell me."

Tiki shook her head. "I have to show you."

The room was silent, everyone mesmerized by the contest being played out before them. Even Larkin remained silent. Tiki glanced over her shoulder but she couldn't see the faerie among the crowd.

Finally, the dark king nodded. "Slowly."

The guard followed Tiki, the sharp point of his spear pricked against her back. One shove would send it through her heart. She lifted the hem of her dress and climbed the steps one by one. In that instant, all the stories she'd been told as a child raced through her mind like voices from the grave. All the magic, the whispered innuendo from her mother suggesting there was something more, that she had a special connection; the shadows that had shifted on the edges of her vision, the faces there one minute, then gone the next—she remembered and pulled from them. She *was* the daughter of Finn MacLochlan. She *was* marked with *an fáinne sí*. She *would* save the Queen and Rieker and her family.

Tiki was one step away from the stone upon which the throne of the Faerie world sat. One step away from *Cloch na*

Teamhrach—the Stone of Tara. She *would* claim her place in the Otherworld.

She slowly lifted her left arm. The sleeve of her dress hung gracefully over her slender wrist, covering her birthmark. Donegal stared at her in cautious fascination.

Now was the moment.

She took a deep breath and stepped up onto the Tara Stone.

Silence.

The Stone didn't roar.

"What is it?" Donegal snapped, his face twisted in an expression of annoyance. "Is there something up your sleeve?"

A terrible sinking sensation filled Tiki and she swayed, suddenly dizzy. She clutched at the arm of the throne to hold herself upright. Had it all been a lie? Had Larkin known all along?

"REMOVE YOUR HAND IMMEDIATELY!" Donegal roared, ready to explode. The guards jumped forward with their spears forcing Tiki to step back. "What is it you will show me?"

Tiki's heart pounded like a kettle drum. She had risked everything to touch the stone and *Cloch na Teamhrach* had remained silent. Now what should she do? She couldn't reveal her mark to Donegal—and she couldn't walk away. She had put herself in an impossible situation.

Chapter Twenty-Four

"Donegal!" The cry split the room. Every head turned toward the speaker. "You have something of mine that I want returned."

Larkin sat perched on a gold platform shouldered by four large men, which elevated her to the same height as the Dragon Throne. They carried her through the room as the party-goers fell away to allow them passage.

She was dressed in a body-hugging gown of gold that glowed as if lit from within. Her blond hair hung in wild abandon reaching to her hips. She looked like a goddess descended from the sun.

Donegal's head jerked up in surprise. The guard's grip on Tiki's arm weakened as he looked to see who dared confront the Winter King as an equal. Tiki chanced a quick look at Rieker. His head was bent as the colorfully-costumed court jester whispered in his ear.

A delighted smile creased Donegal's face. "Ah, Larkin, my little dove, there you are. I've been expecting you."

A buzz like a million bees filled the hall as servants and party-goers alike discussed this unusual turn of events. The story of Donegal's imprisonment of Larkin had fed the rumor mills for months, only intensified by Larkin's dramatic escape.

"It is always such a delight to parry with you, my dear," Donegal said. "Like a chess match come to life."

"Or perhaps a duel without swords," Larkin said.

Donegal's smile widened, though his black eyes remained cold. "A duel? To the death this time, I wonder?"

Larkin inclined her head. "Until there is a clear winner."

The smile faded from the Winter king's face. "There aren't many brave enough, or foolish enough, to challenge me in my own palace." He swept his hand out to encompass the room. "Tell me, which of my possessions would you want to take from me?"

"Just one," Larkin responded coldly. "I want my wing back."

A collective gasp rose and hovered in the room.

Donegal sat back against the throne, clearly surprised by her request. "Sad, I was hoping for a matched pair. Surely there are more valuable items for which you might wish to parley?"

"I am prepared to negotiate," Larkin said.

Tiki marveled at the fearlessness in the blond faerie's words. Just looking at Donegal made her shudder. To be imprisoned by him would be her worst nightmare. Why would Larkin take such a risk?

Donegal lips curved in a smile of pure enjoyment.

"Ah, Larkin, that's what I find so entertaining about you. Always the challenge." He tapped his ringed fingers on the gold arm of the chair. "So you want to negotiate for something you chose to leave behind. But with what, I wonder?"

"A trade." Larkin's words were firm. "I have information that you seek."

Donegal threw his head back and laughed.

Tiki's mind raced. How could she get to Rieker and escape? There were so many guards. Several had moved to stand in front of Rieker, their spears tilted to bar passage. Even if they somehow miraculously got clear of this room, how would they get back to London without Larkin?

The UnSeelie king's laughter died away. His expression darkened like one of the thunderclouds that had plagued London lately. "Such a tempting offer from one so beautiful—yet you have deceived me in the past, Larkin." His words became scathing. "Pretended to pledge your allegiance to my court when you really served Eridanus." His voice rose. "Pretended to love me when you really loved a *mortal*."His voice softened. "You will pay for that."

Larkin's feet hung over the edge of the platform, her legs crossed in a leisurely fashion, looking elegant and seductive. "What occurred in our past, Donegal, was nothing more than two adversaries battling for the ultimate prize: the crown of the Seelie Court." Larkin put her hands on her slim hips. "Surely you didn't just expect me to bow down to you? Where's the fun in that?"

Donegal slowly stroked the black hair that grew to a point on his chin, oblivious to the silent crowd who watched him.

Tiki edged down a step, but the pointed pressure of the guard's blade on her back stopped her.

Donegal lifted his hand toward Larkin. "Tell me then. What information do you have?" The dark king swept his arms wide to encompass the entire great room— "I'm already the ruler of both courts."

"Beltane has not passed yet, Donegal. You've yet to claim the Dragon Throne during Summer."

"Simply a matter of time." He crossed his arms with an air of supreme confidence. "There is nothing I need from you any more, my lovely Larkin."

Larkin's golden gown glittered in the light like a thousand miniature suns. "That's where you're wrong." Her voice rang out strong and clear. "Have you forgotten the ring of the truce?

A surge of anger filled Tiki. What was Larkin doing? She glanced at Rieker. His face was impassive. Another shocked buzz of conversation filled the hall as faeries craned their necks and shoved each other, trying to see both Larkin and Donegal.

"SILENCE." Donegal's roar quieted the crowd. His voice was deceptively mild when he spoke again. "You speak of the ring of the truce, Larkin. Is that what you offer me?"

"I know it's your greatest desire to destroy the truce binding our world to peace with the mortals."

"It *was* my greatest desire." Donegal slowly stroked his beard. "Fate has smiled upon me, however, and shown me another way to achieve my goals."

"Have you forgotten there are other secrets in the ring of *Ériu*?" Larkin's words sounded like a taunt. Her lips curved in a mocking smile. "Powerful secrets, which I know how to release."

"Do you threaten me, Larkin?"

"I offer you a trade. I know where the ring is kept now."

"You forget that I am the king here and you shall do as *I* command. I don't have to negotiate with you." He stabbed a finger in Larkin's direction. "*SEIZE HER.*"

Donegal's soldiers rushed to do the king's bidding. The crowd swayed and shoved, trying to get out of harm's way. Tiki could see Rieker struggling as he was pushed away from the throne by the guards, who seemed happy to use their spears as clubs. Screams and cries of help punctuated the air above the melee.

Sensing her chance, Tiki darted down the steps toward Rieker but before she could reach him, someone grabbed her arm and pulled her in the opposite direction. "This way," a low voice whispered.

Tiki jerked around to find Sean's scarred face inches from hers.

"I have to get to my friend," Tiki said. She tried to tug her arm free, but his grip was too tight. "Rieker!" She stood on tiptoes, waving to get his attention as he fought the surging crowd.

"He knows how to get back," Sean whispered harshly in her ear. "We need to get you out of here now."

"He doesn't," Tiki cried, hopping up and down to get a better view. "Larkin brought us—we need her to return to London."

Sean jerked painfully on Tiki's wrist as he pulled her to a stop in the shadow of one of the great columns.

"Ow—" Tiki glared at him. "That hurt. Let go of me—" She tried to wrestle her arm free, but Sean's grip only tightened.

"You've got to listen to me." He leaned close to her ear. "William has been here before. He knows how to get home on his own."

Tiki stared into Sean's sky-blue eyes. How had this faerie known Rieker's true name?

"He's been here before?" she whispered. All those times when Rieker had disappeared without explanation swirled through Tiki's memory. The times when he'd come home looking so gaunt and tired. The times he'd somehow known what was happening in the Otherworld—known how to contact Larkin. The secrets she'd wondered about—the secrets she could *feel* he was keeping—he'd been here.

"I've brought him several times during the last few months," Sean said. "He can come and go on his own now."

Tiki felt like she was sinking into a pit of quicksand. She stared across the floor at Rieker as he shoved and twisted, trying to work his way through the crowd toward them. A horrible realization hit her: Rieker had been the first to tell her the meaning of *an fáinne sí*—the first to pursue the ring of the truce. Now he protected the ring and whatever secrets it held. Had that been the plan all along? Had she been a pawn in a greater game for him to collect the ring? Was this quest for the throne simply the next move?

"FIND THE GIRL ALSO!" Donegal voice's roared above the noise. "I WANT THE GIRL WHO DARED TO APPROACH ME—*ALIVE*."

Sean yanked her behind the column. "We need to get out of here. He'll meet us in London."

It was hard to think straight. Donegal wanted her captured—did he realize what she'd almost revealed? She peered around the column at the crowd again, torn with indecision. Rieker was looking straight at her and waved for her to go.

Sean tugged on her wrist again, harder this time. "He's telling us to go—to get to safety."

"You're sure?" Tiki asked. Her body felt like it might split apart from the weight of her indecision.

Donegal roared again. He was standing in front of his throne now – staring into the middle of the Great Hall. "WHERE IS LARKIN?"

"I'm positive. Come." Sean pulled her through the shadows away from the chaos.

Soldiers were yelling answers back to their king. People were screaming, running for any way out they could find, while guards blocked the exits.

Tiki followed, trying not to think for fear her head might explode. A beautiful young woman suddenly appeared in front of her, blocking her way. By the stricken look on the girl's face, it was obvious she was trying to find a way to escape, too. Sean pulled Tiki in the other direction and the girl disappeared into the shadows.

Passing behind the great black and gold fluted columns, the faerie took Tiki through a small hallway that led behind the Great Hall where the Dragon Throne stood. Her heart pounded wildly as Tiki glanced over her shoulder to see if they were being followed, but the hallway was winding and shadowed.

"The next hallway has a door that leads outside," he whispered. "It's our only chance—they're looking for you now." As if to accent his point, a distant shout sounded from the Great Hall.

"Where's the girl?" The sound of running feet approached.

Tiki's pickpocketing instincts kicked in. She yanked her hand out of Sean's grip. "I can run faster if my hands are free." She kicked off her shoes and clutched them in her hands, her bare feet quiet against the stone floors. Sean nodded and hurried forward.

He stayed close to the wall as he crept down the winding passageway, Tiki on his heels. They turned a corner and another grand hallway stretched before them with soaring ceilings and great columns along one side.

Tiki's mouth dropped open. The hallway was lined with doors. "How in bloody hell are we going to find our way out?

Chapter Twenty-Five

Sean looked over his shoulder. "I know the way." The sound of running feet grew louder in the hallway they'd just left. Sean pulled her deeper into the shadows behind one of the soaring columns.

"Get down," he whispered.

Tiki crouched, pulling her dark hair over her face to hide her pale skin. Sean shielded her with his body, a knife clutched in his hand. Soft words of Gaelic fell from his lips. Was he creating an illusion to shield them?

A rough looking soldier sprinted into the hallway, a spiked maul on a chain in one hand, a curved sabre in the other. He glanced up and down the long corridor, his gaze brushing past their hiding spot. "Sullivan, the side hall is clear," he called out. "Head to the front, I'll check the back hall. Shoot to stop her—not to kill."

An answering call echoed in the distance.

Sean pressed his hand against Tiki's arm. Only when the echo of the retreating soldier's footsteps faded did he pull Tiki to her feet. He put his finger to his lips.

Tiki followed him silently down the hallway. The faerie hurried past twelve doors before he stopped. With slow precision he turned the gold handle. The cold wind blew in through the open door. Tiki let out a sigh of relief.

They slipped through the crack and Sean carefully turned the handle to close the door noiselessly. Tiki slid her feet back into her slippers. From the light of the waxing moon, she could tell they were on the side of the Palace and much closer to the edge of the precipice on which the building was perched. The trails were not well-defined on this side and she gazed doubtfully at the maze of impenetrable brambles that stretched before them.

Sean led with sure steps, though the path was dark and confusing. Thorns tore at the silky cloth of Tiki's dress as she fought her way through the prickly path, always listening for the sound of pursuit.

He was ahead of her as they neared the edge of the stone mountaintop when Tiki stopped to tug her skirt free from a grasping thorn. When she looked up again, Sean had disappeared. Panic flared through her like a match to paper. Where had he gone? She looked up and down the trail but there was only darkness and shadows.

Tiki held her breath as she inched forward and peered out over the edge of the cliff. Had he fallen? Far below, through the watery light of the partial moon, she could see the tops of the giant trees that made up the Wychwood Forest. She felt like a bird, perched in some otherworldly cloud fortress.

In the distance shrieks and cries echoed as party-goers spilled out onto the palace grounds. Tiki crept closer to the edge, clutching her skirts, and peered cautiously into the void. Suddenly, a hand appeared and Sean's voice drifted up to her.

"You have to jump. Take my hand and I'll help you."

Jump? Tiki's breath caught in a gasp. Jump over the edge? The angle of the moonlight didn't illuminate the darkness of the mountain below the gardens. She couldn't see where she was supposed to jump to, but she could see enough to know if she missed, she would suffer a very painful death.

Tiki reached out shaking fingers to grip Sean's hand and squinted hard to see the treacherous path that lay below her. Her slippers slid on several loose rocks and she clamped down on her lip to stop from crying out. Shouts grew louder in the distance accompanied by the bark of a dog. She took a deep breath and plunged over the edge.

Though Sean held tight to her fingers, those seconds suspended in air felt like a lifetime. To miss the trail and plummet off the edge was certain death. Sean caught her in his arms as she landed. Relief flooded her and she clutched his shoulders to steady herself. As she became aware of how close their bodies were pressed together she hurriedly pushed herself away.

"Th...Thank you," Tiki said as she brushed at her skirts. The awkward moment was quickly replaced with dismay as she realized the path before them was nothing but a goat trail cut out of the side of a vertical mountain. She pointed. "Are we going down *that*?"

She thought she heard him chuckle. "It's our best escape."

"Why can't you take me back to London the way Larkin brought us here?"

Sean shrugged. "Only the oldest, most powerful faeries can transport at will. The rest of us have to go through the gates."

Hidden in the darkness below the ledge where they couldn't be seen gave Tiki a slight sense of relief. "The gates?"

"Of course. The gates between the realms. The Wychwood is used often because there are so many exits, but we could go through the Goblin Market, too." Sean started walking down the path.

"The Goblin Market?" Tiki repeated faintly as she followed, taking small, tentative steps as she focused on the narrow, rocky path. She didn't dare look over the edge.

"I think you call it Covent Garden Market in London."

Tiki jerked to a stop. *"What?"*

"But the goblins are a nasty lot," he said softly over his shoulder. Seeing she had stopped he motioned for her to follow him. "They bring their fruit to market but they don't want to be paid with coin—they only want to trade—and always at a steep price."

Tiki took a few more steps down the steep slope. "But I've been to Covent Garden many times," she said. "I've never seen anyone who looks like a... like a *goblin.*"

"Ah, well. That's most likely because of the time of day you went." He reached back and offered his hand and Tiki gratefully placed her fingers in his. To plunge off the side of this trail would be all too easy and a sure death. "The Goblin Market opens at the stroke of midnight and disappears at the first light of dawn. That's the only time you can get through the gate as well." He turned on a sharp switchback in the trail and continued downward with sure steps. "Best to go through the Wychwood," his voice lowered, "though to be certain, there's risks to be found there, as well."

With a tight grip on his hand, Tiki glanced out at the panorama that lay before them. Though the forest still looked a great distance below, they were making progress down the mountain. She shuddered at the thought of traveling through the haunted wood. Her heart squeezed. Even if they survived, how would Rieker possibly find them?

BY THE TIME they reached the bottom of the trail and descended onto flat ground, the moon had sunk low in the night sky, the cloud cover making the night even darker. The trees of the forest grew right up to the base of the pinnacle of rock where the palace sat, so they were able to slip among the shadows under the trees without worry of being seen from above.

"Very few know of that trail," Sean told Tiki as he veered between giant trees, "and even fewer know of this one." For the first time that night, he smiled and in the dim light his features were transformed, as though the scars that marked his face had been erased. For a second, he reminded her of Dain again.

"How long will it take us to get through the forest?" she asked. Already the weight of her gown pulled at her waist, the hem ripped from the thorns and sodden from the night dew.

"Tonight we'll hide in a small stonecutter's cottage that has been abandoned to the thicket. We can light a fire without fear of being seen and rest for a bit before we start out again. We'll need to think about food, as well."

At his words, Tiki's stomach growled. With all that had happened, food had been the last thing she'd thought about, but she realized now she hadn't eaten since breakfast.

"Can I eat faerie food?" Stories she'd read over the years that told of mortals who had consumed faerie food and forever longed for the Otherworld flitted through her mind.

Sean raised his head in surprise. "Why wouldn't you be able to? You've got fey blood, haven't you?"

Tiki hesitated. So many things had happened in such a short period of time that she'd avoided thinking too hard on any one of them. She'd tried only to escape, to survive. She worried whether Rieker had escaped, too. She'd looked over her shoulder a thousand times to see if he might be following them—if only so she could pummel him to an inch of his life at keeping such secrets from her.

"I...I don't know for sure," Tiki finally said. The Stone of Tara had very definitely *not* roared when she'd touched it. Had Larkin made the story up just to use Tiki as a decoy for whatever game she played with Donegal? She didn't know what to believe—about anything.

"You've got the sight," Sean said matter-of-factly. "Plus, there's a reason for everything Larkin does and there's no reason for a mortal to be here, especially now."

Unless Larkin meant to do her harm. Perhaps this was the faerie's way of eliminating Tiki as her competition so she could continue her romantic pursuit of Rieker? Tiki shook her head, wishing she could shake her thoughts away too. She tugged at her skirt as it became tangled once again in the undergrowth.

"Why did Larkin want her wing back?"

Sean shrugged. "She didn't want Donegal to have it. He collects them, you see."

Tiki scrunched her nose in distaste. "He collects wings?"

"More precisely, the wings from opponents he has conquered. Usually they're dead when he takes them, though. Then he mounts them on his walls as trophies of his kills."

Tiki choked. "That is *ghastly*."

"It's a tradition that Braeden, the very first high king of the Winter court, started a millennia ago." He glanced over at Tiki. "That's why faeries don't wear wings anymore. Only the bravest—" he gave a soft snort— "or the most arrogant wear them." There was a grudging note of respect in his voice. "Larkin is both."

Chapter Twenty-Six

They followed a faint trail, winding through trees that towered above their heads. The wind blew through the branches creating a soft music and as Tiki followed Sean deeper into the forest there was no doubt she'd entered a different world.

Stunted trees stood along the path, the bark of their trunks twisted into woody faces that seemed to watch their passage. Large, vicious-looking black birds with jagged wings and beaks hooked like scimitars flew through the branches overhead with raucous cries. Tiki shivered every time their shadows brushed her back.

More than once she could hear the tap-tap-tap of what sounded like tiny hammers, pounding away within hedgerows that stretched in crooked lines through the forest. She wondered if the sounds were that of leprechauns, but if so, the workers were well-hidden.

They stopped once to drink from a brook that gurgled through the trees. The water as cold and pure as anything Tiki had ever tasted. She cupped her hands and drank more and more, not caring about the consequences, until her thirst was quenched. The wind picked up and ruffled the leaves, making them flap and flutter, like voices muttering to one another under their breath.

"Do the songbirds come out at daylight?" Tiki asked after they'd been walking through the gloom for what felt like hours.

Sean laughed. "Not on this side of the wood. It's never daylight here when the UnSeelie's are in control. It's always twilight or later." He flung his hand to the left. "When the Wychwood meets Oxfordshire you'll find birds again. And sunlight," he added, almost wistfully.

TIME CEASED TO exist as they continued through the shadows. Tiki stumbled several times but caught herself before falling. Her stomach growled with hunger, but she was used to going unfed. She'd gone to sleep too many nights in the past with a hungry belly to worry about one more. But her thoughts of Rieker and what might have happened to him couldn't be pushed away as easily.

Tiki searched for some way to learn more about this alien world to which Larkin swore she belonged. "Have you known Larkin long?"

"Yes," Sean said over his shoulder. "All of my life." His head swiveled to scan the forest as they walked. Tiki trudged along behind.

"Do you have brothers and sisters?" she asked.

"Faeries have great difficulty giving birth. I grew up without siblings and the man who cared for me died several years ago."

"Oh," Tiki said. "I'm sorry." She wasn't sure if faeries cared about things like family or not. "I lost my parents too. They died of the fever over three years ago. It was terribly difficult, but I've found a new family now."

"What kind of family?" Sean kept his eyes on the trail ahead.

"There are five of us…. and…" she hesitated, "and William. I don't know if you know, but he's quite alone, as well. Donegal… or…or Larkin…I'm not sure who anymore, drowned his family." She bit her lip, wondering why she was sharing so much with him.

One side of Sean's mouth twisted in a bitter smile. "That sounds more like something Donegal would do."

Tiki pulled her skirt free from a thorn bush that had snagged the material. "How can you be sure?"

"Larkin tends to be more efficient than most. If she wanted everyone dead—they would have been dead."

Tiki didn't have an answer for that. Had Larkin indeed saved Rieker? Had Rieker been coming to the Otherworld? Had anyone told her the truth about *anything*?

Sean jerked to a stop. "Shh!" With a shock of surprise, Tiki realized he was holding his sword gripped in one hand and a whip in the other. He was half crouched and slowly turning in a circle, his eyes searching the woods that surrounded them. "Stay behind me," he whispered. Tiki jumped to do as he asked.

"What is it?" she whispered.

"I'm not sure, but it's watching us."

Tiki exhaled slowly, trying to still the rapid pounding of her heart. "Give me a knife," she said. She slid a long deadly looking dagger with a curved blade free from his belt. "I'll take this one."

His head jerked to the side as he tried to see her over his shoulder. "Do you know how to use that?"

She clutched the knife in both hands and turned so they were back to back, circling as he did. "I guess we'll find out."

They came boiling out of the shadows. Huge, grotesque figures with double-ridged shark teeth filed to razor-sharp points and claw-like fingers with six-inch talons. Snapping and biting, they swung their deadly hands at Sean and Tiki.

Tiki bit back a cry of horror and clutched the handle of her knife tighter, waving the blade at them in a threatening manner.

Sean flicked his wrist and wrapped the end of his whip around the ankle of the first beast and gave a ferocious yank. There was a loud *pop* and the ogre exploded into a much smaller creature that only reached to his knees.

"Spriggans," Sean said, as the little creature made straight for him, snapping its jaws and trying to bite his ankles. The faerie gave him a swift kick and with a scream, the spriggan went flying into the underbrush and disappeared.

"So?" Tiki shrieked, frantically waving her knife to keep the three on her side back.

"Make contact with your knife and they'll pop." As he spoke, he sliced with his sword and another *pop* filled the air. "Their size is an illusion but their teeth are poison no matter how big they are." His breath came out in gasps as he twirled to flick his whip at one giant who was almost on Tiki. "So don't let them bite you."

Tiki slashed her knife at a particularly ugly ogre who had a line of brown drool hanging from his lips. The tip of her blade cut across his hairy arm and just like that, he became small. As soon as his feet hit the ground he was running for her, jaws snapping. Tiki screamed and kicked the little beast as hard as she could. He went flying end over end to crash loudly in the brush.

By now, Sean had dispatched the other two and only one remained. But he seemed smarter than the others and stood watching them through small beady eyes, drool hanging from the triangle teeth that lined his jutting lower jaw.

He was facing Sean so Tiki turned and pointed her knife at him as well. He stood far enough away that he was out of reach of the whip, but with his giant legs he could cover the distance in two steps.

"Be careful," Sean said, a weapon in each hand, poised to attack. "They're slow, but they can be tricky and their wounds are deadly."

The spriggan pointed at Tiki. His voice was low but surprisingly clear. "We want the girl."

A chill crawled down Tiki's spine, a shudder shaking her shoulders. The idea of being possessed by something that looked like *that* was too frightening to even consider.

"No." Sean snarled the word. "She's mine."

Surprised by his answer, Tiki glanced sideways at him. As she did, she saw movement out of the corner of her eye behind them.

"Sean!" She screamed as she twirled. Another spriggan was so close his clawed hand cast a shadow on their heads. With a wild war cry, Tiki sprang into the air and shoved her dagger clean through the creature's palm. At the same time, the spriggan who had spoken lunged toward Sean. With a mighty swing Sean sliced its head from its body. Two loud *pop*s filled the air.

Tiki and Sean stepped and kicked at the same time, sending the last spriggans sailing into the forest.

"Come on," Sean said, grabbing Tiki's hand. They ran down the path for what felt like half an hour before he slowed to a walk. "All right?"

Tiki nodded, pressing on her side where a stitch made it hard to take a deep breath. She was shaken, but unhurt. "You?"

He grinned at her in a surprisingly charming way. "Never better."

TIKI COULD BARELY drag one foot in front of the other. They'd been walking for hours and the weight of her dress seemed to get heavier by the minute. Sean had gone a short distance ahead to scout the trail when Tiki stubbed her toe on a rock and fell on all fours. Her knee slammed painfully into another rock and she cried out as she landed. In a blink, Sean was by her side, helping her up.

"All right?"

"Yes," Tiki said, annoyed with herself as she regained her feet. She started to brush her skirts then stopped. What was the point?

She wiped her hair from her forehead with the back of her hand. "Maybe we should rest for a bit?"

"The cottage where we'll stop is just ahead. But first I think we should get rid of this dress."

Tiki gazed at him in alarm. Did he expect her to walk through the forest in her undergarments? She flinched as he raised his hand at her, but to her surprise, her dress melted away and she wore a pair of brown bark trousers and a leaf patterned jacket. On her feet were shoes made of softest brown leather.

"You look like a wood nymph now," he said with a sparkle in his eyes, "though most don't wear clothes on their upper half."

"I'll be keeping my jacket on, just so you know," Tiki said, tugging the edges tight and crossing her arms over her chest. She lifted her chin at him but he chuckled and turned away.

"Not much farther now." He pointed to an impenetrable thicket. "Just there."

There was no sign of a cottage anywhere to be seen. Tiki eyed the sharp brambles and wondered how Sean thought they could possibly navigate through the thicket without being cut to shreds. As if in answer to her unspoken question, Sean snapped his fingers. Like writhing snakes, the vines unwove and became mist-like, opening a path to a stone cottage buried beneath the growth.

"After you," Sean said with an absurdly formal bow.

Tiki's lips curved in a smile. She hadn't thought there was anything she could possibly find to smile about on this day. She trudged the last few steps and pushed open a small wooden door to enter the one-room cottage. Behind her, she heard a whispering and turned in time to see the vines whip back into position to shield the cottage before Sean closed the door.

Before she could move, the faerie blew on his hands and a ball of light flew from his fingers to light the grate. Cheerful orange flames flickered toward the chimney, casting a warm glow throughout the room.

"Thank you for helping me," Tiki said with a grateful sigh, smoothing another wild strand of hair from her face with dirty fingers. She couldn't remember a time when she'd been so tired. She wondered at the look on his face as she sank onto a small chair woven from birch branches. Had she said something wrong?

Sean pulled up another chair and sat across from her. His black hair was still smoothed back behind his head and though his scars were as gruesome as ever, he looked as fresh as though they had just met in the Great Hall. He leaned back and propped his foot on a nearby round of wood, his head cocked to one side.

"Tell me—is it Tiki or Tara?" he asked, his expression unreadable.

Tiki lifted her chin. "You tell me—is it Sean or Dain?" She kept her own expression as blank as his.

Something flickered in his eyes before one side of his mouth lifted in a grudging half-grin. "Touché."

Tiki didn't smile. "Are we dueling?"

Now the smile spread across his face, though there was an underlying hint of mockery. "Life in the world of Faerie is always a duel. We know no other way."

She stayed perfectly still, measuring him. Two could play at this game. "Am I part of the prize or one of the pawns?"

His eyes glittered and she thought she caught a flash of respect. "That remains to be seen, now, doesn't it?"

A long silence stretched between them.

"It's Tara," Tiki finally said, "though I've some reason to doubt my parentage." She kept her lips closed in a firm line. "But my *friends* call me Tiki." She challenged him with her eyes. "Which name do you prefer?"

A smile played at the corners of his mouth. "I like them both."

Just like a faerie, Tiki thought. Never a straight answer. "What about your name?" She raised her eyebrows. "Or should I say name*s*?"

There was a sharp intensity about him as he looked at her through slitted lids. "You have a special kind of sight, don't you? Quite rare, in fact." He rocked the chair he had balanced on two legs. "Until recently, I'd only heard rumors that it even existed at all."

"How's that?" Tiki didn't want to show her ignorance or that her curiosity was piqued.

There was a note of awe in his voice. "You can see through glamours."

Tiki straightened in her chair. She could?

"I'm curious—what did you see about me that reminded you of Dain?" He held his hand up to his scarred face then swept it along his body. "I look nothing like him."

"It's your eyes," Tiki said. "You have Dain's eyes."

"Ah." Sean cocked his head to the side. "That is fascinating." He was quiet for a minute before he jerked his chin at her. "What about the rest of me? Do I remind you of Dain?"

Tiki mentally compared beautiful, blond Dain with the black-haired, scarred Sean and shook her head, unsure what all of it meant.

"Fascinating," he said again.

"How did you recognize William?" Tiki asked.

"I didn't recognize William. I recognized Larkin. She has used that glamour in my presence before." Sean's voice was even, not revealing anything beyond his words. "It didn't take long to catch your reflections in the mirrors—then I recognized both of you."

His gaze drifted to the fire and he stared into the flames for a long moment before he gave a sharp nod as if he'd made up his mind about something. He thumped the chair down on all four legs and waved his hand again. Before her eyes, Sean dissolved like the outer layer of an apple being peeled away. The rich smell of clover permeated the air and Dain sat before her, a mocking smile turning up the corners of his attractive mouth.

"You were right," he said, "girl-who's-not-sure-if-she's-fey-but-can-see-through-glamours." He smiled as if he'd made a joke. "I am Dain."

Tiki covered her mouth with her hands. Dain's blond hair framed a face that was beguiling in its beauty—his aristocratic nose was centered between well-defined cheekbones and above a strong chin. He was so handsome he made her breath catch—but that wasn't what she found so shocking. She knew now, why Dain had looked familiar. He was a blurry image of Rieker.

Chapter Twenty-Seven

"Now that you know—will you keep my secret?" For a second, the look on his face made Tiki's heart twist. He seemed defenseless—almost unsure. Far from the usual mocking arrogance that seemed innate to Dain. "Very few know of my dual existence. Not even William knows me as Dain—he's only met me when I'm glamoured as Sean."

"But why?" Tiki asked.

Dain pushed himself out of the chair and moved to stand before the fire. His broad shoulders and slim hips were a striking contrast to Sean's willowy frame. "I live in the UnSeelie Court as Sean. I'm known in the Seelie Court as Dain."

"You're a spy."

Dain stood frozen for a long moment, staring into the flames. Finally he turned and ran his hand through his hair, a gesture so familiar Tiki caught her breath. "Yes, I am. We are at war. The bloodiest, deadliest war this world has seen in many a millennia. I'll reveal myself eventually to William, but for his sake and mine, it's best that he doesn't know yet."

In a swift, graceful movement, he squatted next to her chair and took her hand in his. There was a raw honesty in his face, almost as if it pained him to admit the truth. Tiki thought of their conversation about his lack of family and wondered if he had no one else in which to confide. The warmth of his fingers seeped through the skin of Tiki's cold hand and she realized she didn't want to let go. Could she trust him? Was there anyone she could trust?

"I won't tell," she whispered. "I promise."

Dain gave a slow nod. "For my work in the UnSeelie court I need to be glamoured, but I get sick of the shadows—" his voice became tinged with disgust— "of the decay, the depravity." He sighed and stared past Tiki into the distance. "Sometimes I escape while I'm in London—to get some fresh air." He smiled. "I need to become myself again, if only for a short while."

Tiki searched his face. "Why did you reveal yourself to William in London?"

Dain's expression went blank. "It's better I keep that information to myself for now."

"Are you working with Larkin?" A sense of urgency filled Tiki, as if the answers were finally within reach. "Is that why you're following us? What is she planning?"

Dain held her gaze for a long moment, before he stood up. "You should sleep," he suggested. "You need some rest before we continue." Against her will, Tiki's eyes became so heavy her lids kept closing and finally she gave in and let the darkness take her.

HER DREAMS WERE terrible—Rieker was there, his beautiful face unquestionably real. She was so relieved he was safe. He was whispering that he loved her when suddenly his mouth twitched and he was laughing—laughing at her, that she'd been so foolish to believe him. Then Larkin was there laughing too, her lovely features next to Rieker's like they were a couple. They melted into an image of Clara crying and Tiki jerked awake.

Sean stood on the other side of the small room, leaning against the stone wall, watching her. His lips were pressed into a thin line, pulling the puckered skin of his face. He looked angry.

"We need to keep moving. Once we leave the Wychwood it's still a day's ride into London."

Tiki pushed herself out of the chair, stretching her stiffened muscles. From this distance she couldn't see his eyes clearly and he seemed to be every inch Sean. Had she dreamed that he'd removed his glamour and revealed himself to be Dain? Unsettled, she turned away to warm her hands by the fire, but the grate was cold, only a few dead leaves resting on the cold bricks.

"How long have I been asleep?"

"Only a few hours, but we can't delay any longer. Donegal's men are searching for you. One has tracked us into the forest." A look of regret creased his face. "I should have removed your skirt earlier. We left a trail."

She cast a startled glance over her shoulder. "How do you know?"

"I did some reconnaissance while you slept. Are you ready?"

He had left her alone? Tiki tried not to react. She could take care of herself if she needed to. "Any sign of Riek—er..William?"

Dain pushed off the wall, stepping toward the door. "He's probably in London, wondering where we are." He pulled the door open and motioned for Tiki to exit. As she approached, the vines unraveled and she slid through the small opening unscathed. She ignored her pang of disappointment. He hadn't seen Rieker. Had he escaped? A second thought came unbidden to her mind. Had Larkin?

The same shadows as before lingered in the forest. How could the UnSeelies stand to live constantly in this darkness? As they walked, Tiki noticed Sean now had a sword and other weapons strung from his belt as well as a quiver of arrows tied to his back, with a bow slung over one shoulder. She turned her head uneasily, searching her surroundings, then hurried to catch up with Sean's long strides.

"If you won't answer my questions about William and Larkin, the least you can do is tell me about you. You said you're a spy in the UnSeelie court?"

Sean whipped around and before Tiki could blink his scarred face was next to hers, his fingers pressed tight against her mouth. His eyes were slits in his face and she could hear the anger in his voice. "Watch what you say, for these woods truly do have ears. Don't say it again," he whispered. "*Ever.*"

Tiki nodded, her eyes wide. Sean stepped back and motioned for her to walk alongside him as the trail had widened. They walked in silence until Tiki heard the slow, steady sound of hoof beats echoing behind them. She turned and saw two young horses, heads bobbing as they plodded along, keeping pace with them.

"Sean," she cried, tugging at his arm, "look, there are horses—do you think we could catch them?"

The faerie never slowed in his walking, nor did he look back. "Are they wet?"

"Wet?" Tiki repeated, peered over her shoulder again. "It looks like their manes are dripping. Why?"

"Kelpies. They'll let you ride—right into the bog where they'll drown you."

Tiki swallowed a gasp and hurried to stay close to Sean, glancing once more over her shoulder at the horses, who looked perfectly normal to her.

"They'll give up after awhile," he said. "They won't stray too far from the water." Ten minutes later when Tiki looked again the horses were gone.

"Larkin said there were all sorts of fey in the Wychwood, is that true?"

"More than you can imagine and then some." Sean's expression was grim. "Did you notice those pictures on the ceiling of the Great Hall?" Images of those horrific scenes flashed before Tiki's eyes. "All replicas of actual events." His voice turned grim. "Donegal takes pride in his subjects."

As if to prove his point, a sudden rustling came from the bushes and trees ahead. Sean jerked to a stop. He already held his bow in his hands, though pointed at the ground, an arrow cocked and ready to be released.

"Name yourself," he called out.

The wind sighed through the trees, sounding like faraway whispers. Tiki stopped close to him and cocked her head to hear better, but the words were just beyond her ability to understand.

A gust blew through the branches and three women fluttered onto the trail. They stood abreast of each other, blocking the way. Their skin was weathered and brown, their leaf-like dresses revealing seductive bits of legs and arms and most of their bare chests. Long, soft hair trailed from their heads, like bits of moss, twisting in the breeze.

"We offer you shelter from the storm," the first one said, opening her long arms to Sean.

"We offer you rest from your weary travels," the second one said, cocking her leg in a seductive pose.

"We'll take your companion in exchange for passage," said the third, her long branch-like fingers pointing at Tiki.

In a languid movement, Sean drew two more arrows from his back and threaded them into his bow along with the first, though he didn't raise the weapon. His voice was calm as he responded.

"Though a tempting offer, ladies, we must decline. We need to continue on our way."

"The restless wind brings us messages from distant forests," the first one said, taking a step closer.

The second ran her fingers over her dark breasts, an inviting look on her face. She held her hand out for Sean to take. "We hear whispers of one who was meant to die at the hand of our sister but was raised instead by dark magic. Come to me and I will tell you more." The wind gusted and she floated closer.

The third one continued to glare in a threatening way, her eyes like dark knotholes in her rough and woody face. "For that—" her malevolent gaze was locked on Tiki with a hungry look— "we are owed a replacement."

"I already know of the *liche*," Sean said in a conversational tone. "That your sister, Ash, missed his heart and could not kill the creature is no concern of mine." He raised the bow ever so slightly. "Nor is the act of raising the undead. Unless you offer me a way to stop him, then I must once again decline your fine offers and continue on our way."

The women's expressions grew dark and their arms began to wave, like branches being blown in a storm. "How dare you speak to us with such insolence," the third one rasped. "We are the heart of the forest—you shall do our bidding."

Tiki took a step behind Sean. Could they outrun these wood-land creatures? In what looked like slow motion, Sean raised his bow but to Tiki's surprise, he pointed the arrows away from the women, towards the forest.

He raised his voice to be heard over the blustery wind and thrashing of nearby branches. "I spy a thorny plum, an oak and an elder tree—should I bury my arrows in their trunks to buy the answer and our passage?"

Shrieks of horror split the air that had suddenly become a whirlwind of dead leaves and twigs.

"How dare you?" screamed the second woman.

"There is only one way to kill the *liche* now—you must burn his body on a branch of Ash," the first whispered.

"Wicked UnSeelie fey." The third woman growled in a guttural voice. "Be gone from our sight." In a fierce gust of wind the three women were swept up and blown back into the forest, disappearing into the trees.

Sean lowered his bow, though he did not un-notch his arrows and motioned for Tiki to walk forward. She dashed down the trail, eager to be away from this haunted place.

"Who were they?"

"Tree Dryads," Sean said, catching up with her. "I spotted their trunks before they tried to stop us. On their own, they're shy, but the thorny plum, oak and elder together can be a deadly combination. We were lucky today."

"They knew of the *liche* that Donegal has raised."

"Yes. The entire forest is aware of the *liche*." Sean adjusted his quiver on his back and walked with his bow gripped in his hand. He scanned the area around them as they walked. "He is as feared here as he is there."

"He's the creature who attacked Prince Leopold? The creature that Donegal has sent to London to kill the Queen?" Sean turned at a fork in the trail. Tiki glanced down the other path, but the trees and underbrush looked identical to the path they'd chosen.

"The *liche* hunts in either world," Sean said in a grim voice. "Kings and queens, mortal or fey. He's not selective with his prey, though legend has it he prefers young humans. Opportunity is his master."

Tiki gulped. An assassin who killed in both worlds? "Does he have a name?"

"His name was Sionnach when he murdered the Seelie King. Translated to English, I believe he would be known as Mr. Fox." Sean moved in front of her on the trail, his head swiveling to survey the trees up ahead. "That was a helpful bit of knowledge the one shared today: burn the *liche's* body on a branch of Ash. We'd best keep out eyes peeled for an Ash tree."

Tiki longed for the safety and normalcy of the townhome in Grosvenor Square, but part of her knew even that part of her life was changing. "How much farther?"

"Not far." He pointed in the distance. "Can you see how much lighter it is over there? That's O'Donoghue's farm—the entrance and exit to this part of the Wychwood. Luckily, the Redcaps don't patrol this part of the border."

"Redcaps?"

"The worst kind of goblin. They dye their hats red in their victim's blood. Vicious little creatures who will eat you alive." Tiki shuddered at the image. "But lucky for us they live on the other side of the forest along the north border."

THEY CONTINUED ON through the forest.

"Are there villages in the Wychwood?" Tiki asked.

"Why do you ask?" Sean sounded surprised.

"There was a beggar on the path to the Palace of Mirrors and Larkin told him he'd have better luck at one of the villages in the wood. I just wondered—"

"Yes. Two on the borders and one deep in the forest. Not a place you'd want to visit." There was something dark in his voice.

"What do you mean?"

"The town has a prison called The White Tower there. It's hidden in the very heart of the Wychwood—where the damned and demented are held." He shot her a glance from the corner of his eyes. "It is said to be a place of no return."

Chapter Twenty-Eight

Tiki didn't know what to say to that so she didn't say anything at all. The trees were further apart now, with small stretches of woodland grass growing at their feet. They turned at a wide bend in the trail and she spotted three deer grazing among the undergrowth.

"Sean, look." She pulled on the faerie's arm, pointing to the graceful creatures. At her words, all three deer jerked their heads up. For a split second, their great limpid eyes fixed on them, then they turned and looked down the trail from which Tiki and Sean had just emerged. They stood frozen long enough for Tiki to wonder what they were looking at, when they turned and with great leaps bounded off into the woods.

"That's not good," Sean muttered. He looked over his shoulder in the same direction the deer had been gazing. Suddenly the low vibration of hooves became apparent and Tiki realized the deer had heard something, rather than seen something, Sean grabbed her hand. *"Run."*

Like a storm approaching, deep barks rumbled in the distance. She followed Sean as fast as her feet would take her. They zigged and zagged between the trees heading into the deepest shadows of the forest. Even clothed in her bark-like trousers the underbrush tore at her legs, but that only fueled her panic and spurred her to run faster.

It wasn't long before the thunder of hoof beats shook the earth beneath Tiki's feet forcing her heart to pound with the same rhythm.

"This way." Sean grabbed her hand and pulled her into the water of a nearby river, leading her upstream. The water was icy cold, as if melted from mountain snow, but Tiki barely noticed. The barking was getting louder and it was clear that more than one hound was headed in their direction. "Go toward those rocks." Sean huffed as he pushed against the current, pointing to a group of rocks jutting into the river. The water was getting deeper the further they went. "We need to get around the corner."

They'd just reached the turn in the river when a mournful baying split the air. Startled at the proximity of the sound, Tiki stopped and looked over her shoulder. Through the dappled shadows beneath the trees she could just make out two great black dogs, anxiously sniffing the ground on the other bank where they'd entered the river. Far behind, a horse and rider wove through the trees. Even at this distance she could see the fiery red hair of the rider.

Fingers wrapped around her wrist and yanked her around the corner.

"*Don't. Stop.*" Sean growled in a low voice as Tiki stumbled to keep her balance on the rocky riverbed. If Sean hadn't been holding her arm so tightly she would have fallen face first into the water. But his grip and her forward momentum kept her upright as he pulled her toward a group of great rounded boulders that towered over their heads.

Behind them, a man's deep voice shouted above the wild barking and baying of the four-footed beasts hot on their trail.

Sean pulled Tiki straight toward the rocks. It wasn't until she was next to the stones that she saw the thin crevice that ran between two of the giant boulders. The only part wide enough to allow them to pass through was under the water that swirled around Tiki's thighs.

"Follow me," he whispered harshly. Without releasing the grip he had on her wrist, Sean dove beneath the water, straight toward the rocks. Tiki had no choice but to follow him. She sucked her breath in with a hiss as she went face-first into the icy water. The faerie pulled her down close to the bottom of the river and swam against the current into the dark gap between the boulders.

Tiki broke through the surface and let out a gasp of air. Before she could speak Sean covered her mouth with his hand and pressed a finger to his lips. Tiki nodded her understanding. They were in a tiny pool tucked within the great boulders. Sand had built up against several of the rocks, creating small sandbars. Sean motioned for Tiki to wait on one, out of the cold water, while he stood near the edge of the crevice, trying to see what was happening outside.

In the distance she heard the splashing of the dogs as they ran in and out of the water, woofing and sniffing, trying to pick up the scent they'd lost. Occasionally, their master would shout a command.

Tiki sat on the sand with her knees tucked to her chest, her back to the stone, trying not to shiver. After awhile, the beat of her heart slowed and she was able to draw an even breath. She glanced around their hiding spot. A series of cracks and spaces arced between the rocks like otherworldly doorways, stretching away from her and disappearing into darkness.

It seemed like hours before Sean came and sat on the sand beside her. His teeth were chattering and his lips had a distinctly blue tinge to them.

"You need to warm up," she whispered. "Can we light a fire?" She hadn't forgotten the magical way he had started the fire in the stonecutter's cabin.

"N..not yet," he said. "I..I'm f..fine."

Tiki scooted close enough that her arm and leg pressed against his, trying to share her warmth. They sat huddled together in the shadows. Tiki strained to hear any noises that would indicate if whoever hunted them was still outside but she could only hear the music of the river swirling by.

"Is he gone?" she finally whispered.

"I think so. We need to wait a bit l..longer though." Sean had his jaws clamped and lips pressed together, making his scars more prominent than normal. Tiki realized she'd stopped seeing the old wounds when she looked at him.

"Who was that?"

Sean's expression was grim. "Bearach and his hellhounds. Donegal must have put a hefty price on your head if he has his *tánaiste* tracking us." He gave her a sideways glance. "What was it you were going to show Donegal?"

Tiki opened her mouth to answer, then shut it again. She didn't dare tell Sean about her birthmark. What should she say? "Larkin wanted me to distract him."

His eyes narrowed. "She brought you from London to distract the Winter King?" He scoffed. "Why do I think there's more to this story?"

Tiki gaze darkened. "I think it's better if I keep that information to myself for now."

It took a moment for him to realize she'd echoed the very comment he'd made earlier. The corner of his mouth turned up and he snorted softly. "Touché, my mysterious little friend."

SEAN WENT OUT and scouted the area before he allowed Tiki to leave the little cave. The forest was as it had been before— shadows hung like cobwebs, shifting and moving with the breeze. It didn't take long for their clothes to dry as they walked. Occasionally, Tiki saw eyes glowing from the underbrush, watching their passage. Sean stopped once and cut a branch from a tree, stripping away the symmetrical leaves and sharpening one end to a stiletto-like point. He handed her the T shaped limb. "Take it."

Tiki took the branch with a quizzical expression. "What's this?"

"A stake of Ash—for the *liche.*" His face was deadly serious. "There's no telling where he is now. He could be in London or he could be in the Otherworld." Sean's expression darkened. "You've attracted Donegal's attention. No one knows how much control the UnSeelie king has over the *liche*, or who the next target might be, but you've got to be prepared to defend yourself. I don't know how to burn someone on a branch of Ash, so aim for the heart if you have to use it."

AS THEY DREW closer to the light Tiki became more and more anxious. She needed to be home with her family, protecting them. How had Larkin ever convinced her to go to the Otherworld in the first place? And what of Rieker? Worry chewed at her stomach as questions she couldn't answer battered at her.

The trees thinned and soon they were walking through a verdant meadow. Hedgerows stretched over rolling hills and in the distance a large field of horses frolicked. Tiki shielded her eyes with her hand to watch the beautiful beasts run and kick up their heels. Even from a distance it was obvious what magnificent creatures they were. How Toots would love to see this, she thought.

Sean put his fingers to his lips and a piercing whistle split the air. A great white horse, grazing in one corner of the field raised her head and stared in their direction. The beast broke into an effortless gallop towards them. Tiki's mouth dropped open, for the horse's hooves never seemed to touch the ground. As the horse drew closer the faint sound of bells chimed in the air and she could see the red ribbons holding the bells braided into its flowing mane. The horse trotted to a stop in front of Sean, shaking its great head and blowing out its nostrils.

"Hello Aeveen," Sean said, rubbing the horse's velvety soft nose. "Have you missed me, girl?" As if in response to the question, the horse jerked its head up and down, the bells chiming with the movement.

"Wait a minute," Tiki said. "Is this the horse Toots rode?"

Instead of answering, Sean said, "D'you think your boy'd like to ride a horse such as this?"

Tiki narrowed her eyes, an accusing tone in her voice. "Are you the one who took him?"

Sean stepped away and ran his hand over the horse's withers, then across the great back. "I didn't take him," he said. "I'm the one who brought him home, remember?"

"But you know who did take him." Tiki put her hands on her hips. "Tell me now."

Sean's gaze flicked over to Tiki then returned to his examination of the horse. He bent and ran his hands down one of the back legs, gently feeling the tendons while the horse stood patiently.

"I'll tell William."

Sean straightened and cocked his head at her. "Are you threatening me?"

"Call it what you will, but I want an answer." Tiki fought the urge to stamp her foot. "Was it Larkin?"

Sean sighed. He walked back toward Tiki and stopped in front of her. "It wasn't Larkin specifically who took him, but she was behind it. She hired some fey to bring him over. She wanted to get your attention for some reason." His face darkened.

"What?" Tiki searched his eyes. "There's more, isn't there? Tell me."

Sean shook his head, a guarded expression on his face. "I don't know." He lifted his hand and smoothed a piece of windblown hair from her face. When his fingers touched her skin they lingered, then he dropped his hand suddenly. "It's one of the many things I'm trying to understand."

With a sudden burst of insight, Tiki said, "What are you? A spy in *both* courts?"

Something flickered in his eyes, then he blinked and his face revealed nothing. "What I am doesn't matter. The truth is, if we don't oust Donegal from the Seelie throne by Beltane, there will only be one court left and we will all serve one despicable king."

May First was less than two weeks away. Tiki debated about telling him what Larkin had said of the Stone of Tara but decided against it. Her life had become a chess match against players far more experienced at the game than she. Until she knew who she could trust, and what was and wasn't the truth, she'd keep as many secrets as she could.

With a snort of warm air, Aeveen pushed her head between them, nuzzling Sean, searching for a treat. In response, the faerie grabbed a chunk of mane and effortlessly swung onto the back of the great horse. He held his hand out to Tiki. "Shall we return to London?"

Chapter Twenty-Nine

Their passage through the gate from the Otherworld back to London had been almost undetectable. First, there'd been a shimmering in the air before them, reminding Tiki of a heat-induced summertime mirage. As they drew close to the wavy light, a cool breeze had caressed her face and blown her hair back, as if they'd passed through an open door. Then they'd galloped across fields as familiar as the meadow in which Sean had called Aeveen.

"How do you know your way from one side to the other?" Tiki had asked.

"It's simple," Sean said over his shoulder. "You're taught how to find the gate."

Tiki held tight to his waist as they rode. "And you taught Rieker?"

"He was keen to learn."

IT WAS NIGHT by the time they reached Grosvenor Square.

"We're back," Tiki whispered, looking around in wonder. The light of the moon was shrouded by a thick fog. Down the road a bell clanged as a carriage made its way along the cobblestone street.

The clip-clop of the horse's hooves sounded oddly distorted as they kept time in a measured pace.

Sean slid off the horse, and reached up to help Tiki down. The smell of clover filled the air and a sudden spark burned in his eyes "Your new glamour—or is it your old glamour?—becomes you."

Tiki looked down to see that her glamour had melted away upon her return to London, just as Larkin had promised. Tiki turned toward the light glowing in the window of Number Six. "I'm home," she whispered.

Sean raised a scarred eyebrow. Somehow his horrible glamour didn't look so frightening anymore. "Are you sure about that?"

"What's that supposed to mean?" Tiki asked.

He drew a long finger down the side of her face, tracing the contours as if memorizing them. "Until we meet again, Tiki," he said softly.

Tiki felt a strange tug in her chest, almost as if she wanted to wrap her arms around his neck and hold him close. "Th...Thank you for bringing me back."

His finger stopped under her chin. Tiki's lips parted to draw a breath as he leaned close. But instead of kissing her, the warmth of his lips brushed the tender skin of her ear.

"You've already thanked me once. Don't make yourself so beholden to me that I'm tempted to seek my payment." His voice was a whisper. "Because you are very tempting."

He took a step back and was magically sitting on Aeveen's back. His face was a mask.

"Be safe." Without another word he turned the horse's head and kicked the great beast into a canter. Tiki blinked and he'd disappeared into the fog.

She stared at the spot where he'd been just moments before. So many emotions churned through her it was hard to know where one started and the other stopped. Tiki turned toward the townhome and looked longingly at the lighted windows. She was home and her family waited for her.

She bounded through the unlocked front door and hurried upstairs to the drawing room where everyone would be this time of night. She rounded the corner and stopped, a rush of love filling her. Fiona sat with her head bowed over her fancywork. Shamus was asleep in a chair before the fire, his head back and mouth open. Toots and Clara were lying on the floor playing a game of checkers. The only person missing was Rieker.

Fiona lifted her head. "Tiki!" she cried and jumped from her chair, startling Shamus awake. Toots and Clara both scrambled to their feet and hurried to throw their arms around her.

"Where have you been?" Toots hollered.

"We've been worried sick!" Fiona cried. "We had to tell Mrs. B. that you'd gone to help with your dying aunt."

"Why didn't you tell us you were leaving?" Clara asked in her high voice.

Tiki wrapped her arms around the lot of them, biting her lip to stop her tears from falling.

"Welcome back, Teek." Shamus asked in his slow, steady voice. "Is Rieker with you?"

Tiki stepped forward so she could see Shamus. "Rieker's not here?"

Shamus shook his head. His face looked drawn and there were dark circles below his eyes, as if he hadn't been sleeping. "He disappeared at the same time you did."

Tiki sagged. "He never came back?"

"Where were you, Teek?" Fiona asked in a soft voice, filled with worry.

Tiki turned to her. "How long have I been gone?" Time didn't pass the same in the Otherworld. Mere hours passed in Faerie while days crept by in London.

"This is the sixth day."

Panic started building in Tiki's chest. Rieker hadn't returned. Donegal must have captured him. He might be lying injured in a prison cell now….or he might be—

She couldn't allow herself to finish the thought.

"Don' you worry about a thing, Dearie," Mrs. Bosworth said later when Tiki asked if she'd heard from Rieker. "That young man can disappear for weeks at a time—not a word." She'd patted Tiki on the shoulder with her work-worn hand. "But he always comes back." Mrs. B. had shifted the basket of vegetables she was carrying to the other hip as she walked toward the doorway to the kitchen. "Eventually."

MANY HOURS LATER, Toots and Clara had gone to bed and Tiki, Shamus and Fiona returned to the upstairs drawing room. They spoke in hushed tones, discussing Rieker's disappearance.

"Why would you ever trust Larkin in the first place?" Fiona exclaimed again, as they sat before the fire. She stabbed at the fancywork she was embroidering on a pillowcase. "Of course she betrayed Rieker, that was probably her plan all along."

Tiki picked at the seam of her skirt. She'd told them of Larkin applying glamours and taking them to the Otherworld. She'd told them of Sean returning her to London, but she hadn't told them that Sean was Dain. Even though Shamus and Fiona were family who she trusted beyond any others, she'd promised Dain she wouldn't tell, and she wouldn't break her vow. She couldn't bring herself to tell them Rieker's secret either—that he'd been traveling to the Otherworld with Sean. Not until she had a chance to talk to him for herself. If she ever got that chance again.

"It's obvious now." Tiki nodded miserably. "But when Leo was attacked, it seemed that Larkin was telling the truth about Donegal.

"Probably Larkin's doing," Fiona snarled.

"Fi—" Shamus said in a warning tone.

"Sh...she made it sound so simple." Tiki stammered. "She seemed so *sure*. I just had to touch a stone and—"

Fiona lifted her head. "And what?"

Shamus, who had been staring at the flames in the fire, raised his head to look at Tiki too, his long, straight white-blond hair shifting with his movement. He waited silently for her to continue.

Tiki hesitated.

"Does this have to do with your birthmark, Tiki?" Shamus asked.

Tiki turned to him in relief. Though quiet, Shamus had a keen eye and quick mind. He saw what many others missed. "Yes." She jerked her head up and down. "Larkin said I could help Leo and protect Rieker and all of you..." her voice died off.

"I don't understand how touching a bloody piece of rock could help anybody," Fiona said, going back to work on her embroidery. "Did you even find the stupid stone?"

"Yes," Tiki nodded, eyes downcast.

Fiona jerked her head up again. "And?" She pushed Tiki's knee with her hand. "Did you touch it?"

Tiki nodded, biting her lip to hold back the hot tears that threatened to fall.

"Well, go on—what happened?"

"Nothing," Tiki whispered.

IT WAS AFTER midnight when Fiona and Shamus went up to their bedrooms. Tiki stayed behind in the cozy drawing room.

"I'm just not ready to sleep yet," she said. "I'll come up soon." She couldn't bring herself to close her eyes in a comfortable bed, when Rieker was lost in the Otherworld.

She paced back and forth across the room, trying to think of some way to help. Could she return to the Wychwood and find him? But even as she had the thought, she knew it was a ridiculous idea. The entrance to the Wood was at least a day's ride and she wouldn't have a chance alone in that fey-infested forest, even if she could find it again. There had to be a better way.

"Larkin." She said the name out loud and waited. "Larkin!" she called louder this time. Before it seemed that anytime they'd even mentioned the faerie's name she'd appeared. Now, when Tiki wanted to see her, would she come? Tiki waited, but there was only the tick of the clock.

Tiki walked to the big paned window that looked out to the street and across to the tree-shrouded square. The wind had picked up again and blown the fog away. Tree branches swayed and moved behind the muted glow of the lamp light like dark puppets taking part in some invisible dance. Was the turbulent weather a sign of what was happening in the Otherworld? A dreadful thought crept in before she could stop it. She'd been gone six days. Was Rieker still alive? A terrible pressure filled her heart and her head, making her eyes burn, at the thought of never seeing him again.

THE CLOCK HAD just tolled three a.m. when Tiki stood at the window again, imagining the Palace of Mirrors, the crowd of faeries, the music—anything but the idea that Rieker might not be coming back. She could see the flickering torches, the towering black and gold columns with the magical mirrors lining the walls between; The sense that everything glittered with dark magic—a disturbing opulence hiding a world falling apart.

What did Larkin want from them? Had she saved Rieker that night four years ago, only to sacrifice him now for the bigger prize of winning the Seelie throne? Had they plotted together? Was

Rieker gone forever? Did she need to just walk away and worry about her own life?

Tiki clenched her fists, fighting the urge to bang them against the glass window at her helplessness. It was impossible to know the truth.

THE PINK LIGHT of dawn was sifting through the window when Tiki awoke. She was sitting in a chair before the fireplace, her head propped on her bent arm. The fire had turned to grey ashes and a chill hung in the air.

She sat up, confused, trying to sort reality from her dreams. In a rush, it all came back, like being drenched with ice water—Rieker was missing. Sadness pressed in on her again, and she shivered as she drew up the blanket that had sagged around her shoulders. She stepped to the window and peered out into the shifting colors of morning, hoping Rieker would magically appear in the square.

The dawn chorus had started, the bird song bright and sharp, even though the sun wasn't fully above the horizon yet. It wouldn't be long before Mrs. Bosworth would be up, working in the kitchen, preparing meals for another day. Geoffrey would be tending to the horses and Mr. Bosworth would be puttering around the house, fixing things, tidying others. Juliette would be making beds and the machinery of Rieker's life would be running smoothly again. Only he wasn't here to enjoy it.

The household staff were so used to Rieker disappearing they didn't give a second thought when he didn't come home now. Didn't question whether he was safe or not. Tiki was truly the only person in this world who knew Rieker's secrets. A terrible tug pulled at her heart. If she didn't take care of him, who would?

Chapter Thirty

For the first time since Rieker had asked them to stay at his townhome four months ago, Tiki planned to dress in the ragged garments she'd lived in while hiding in the abandoned clockmaker's shop in Charing Cross.

"You're not going without me," Fiona declared, when Tiki told her what she intended to do. "We've got to dress like we used to, Fi," Tiki said "We've got to be invisible to be able to go all the places Rieker goes. We have to find someone who might know Rieker; something to help us find him." Tiki bit her lip, thinking. "Do you remember him telling us about that old man he'd helped? The one who was dying?"

Fiona scrunched her nose as she followed Tiki upstairs to her room. "The faerie?"

"Yes, that's the one. Kieran was his name. Rieker told me he thought he'd found that old man but later figured out that Kieran had purposely put himself in Rieker's path."

Fiona stood next to Tiki, watching as she dug through the clothes in the drawer. "Why?"

"He told Rieker he was there to warn him. I remember Rieker's exact words: *'Kieran came to warn me about Donegal and his dark court. Of*

Larkin. Of the past. Of the future.'" Tiki sat back on her heels as she pulled out a rumbled, oversized jacket. "Sean found Rieker too. Maybe there's someone else out there, like Kieran or Sean, who knows about the Otherworld—who can point us in the right direction."

"Warn him of the past and the future? How is that possible?"

Tiki set the jacket down and began digging through the clothes in the drawer again. "I think that was the point. Kieran knew what had happened in the past, along with Rieker's link to the Otherworld and probably knew that it wasn't over yet—that Donegal and Larkin would pursue him until they got what they wanted." Tiki pulled a stained pair of ragged pants from the drawer. "Ugh. Even washing didn't get these clean." She glanced over at Fiona. "Why don't you go get your clothes from your room?"

Fiona's nose turned up in distaste. "I threw those old rags away. What will I wear?"

Tiki rummaged through the bottom drawer again. "Here." She tossed an old jacket towards Fiona. "You can wear that." She dug further. "Here's an old pair of trousers you can roll up. Put a scarf over your hair and wear a cap on top of that."

After they placed the old garments in a bag, they told Mrs. B. they were going shopping and hurried out the back door. Geoffrey was gone and they changed in one of the empty stalls in the coach house.

Tiki braided her long hair and tucked it inside her jacket. The worn boots she pulled on over her socks were more comfortable than the prim heels that hugged her feet, and she wiggled her toes in delight. She pulled a cap low on her forehead, the brim shadowing her face.

She faced Fiona. "How do I look?"

"Cor, Teek," Fiona smiled. "It's like findin' an old friend."

Tiki laughed. "I know exactly what you mean."

They scooted out the back door and ran toward Grosvenor Street. From there they walked the distance to Regent Street, busy with omnibuses and carriages, wagons pulled by tired horses. Pedestrians filled the sidewalks and no one paid any attention to two more scruffy boys scrambling through traffic.

"That one's big enough for both of us," Tiki said, pointing to a large carriage headed in their direction. "Ready, one, two, three..." They jumped on the boot as the carriage went by. Once they were settled on the small luggage platform Tiki leaned over and whispered to Fiona. "Here's to being invisible."

THE CARRIAGE TOOK them through Piccadilly Circus where it pulled to a stop. Tiki and Fiona hopped off before the driver knew they'd hitched a ride. Piccadilly was bustling with people. Wheels clacked across the cobblestones in time with the cadence of the horse's hooves. Costermongers pushed their carts down the street, crying out goods for sale. A man playing a hurdy-gurdy stood on a nearby corner, his rumpled stove-pipe hat upside down on the street, collecting coins. Children shouted, offering to sweep the street, carry packages, or fetch a cab for the upper class, some doing cartwheels in the hopes of earning a ha'penny or two.

"Where should we look?" Fiona asked, wiping her nose on her sleeve without a second thought.

"Let's walk up Shaftsbury to the Dials," Tiki said. "Rieker mentioned he'd spent time there. Maybe someone there will know something." The walk to Seven Dials, a small circular junction of seven streets, took less than fifteen minutes. As they left the hustle and bustle of Piccadilly, the buildings and atmosphere changed to worn and dark buildings where the down-on-their-luck, scrabbled to survive.

Tiki recognized the look on the faces of the children who ran in the street before them. It was a look of constant hunger. The same look had been on her and Fiona's faces just a few months ago. It didn't take long for the bits of bread and fruit she'd shoved in her pockets to give away were gone.

Though many of the children they spoke to had heard of Rieker, none had seen him lately nor knew of his whereabouts. There was no one who looked like they might know something of the Otherworld.

Tiki and Fiona wandered through the Dials, parts of St. Giles and then walked over to Covent Garden, where the fruit and vegetable traders set up their stands. Tiki tried to imagine what the place would look like at midnight, with a host of goblins hawking their magical fruit. She shuddered. It was sight she didn't care to ever see.

Fiona was chattering on about hollow columns the street children climbed to reach the top of the arcade and hide when Tiki jerked to a stop. Fi walked on a few more paces before she realized she'd left Tiki behind. She stopped and looked over her shoulder. "What is it?"

"There might be one way to find Rieker." Quickly she told Fiona about the gates to the Otherworld. Much as she didn't want to find herself in the dark of night with a bunch of goblins, it might be their only option. "Sean said Covent Garden was one of the gates. If we come back here after midnight we might be able to get through to the Otherworld."

Fiona put her hands on her hips. "And then what? Are we going to storm the castle and rescue Rieker?" She snorted. "That sounds like one of the faerie tales you read to Clara."

"But what else can we do? At least it's *something.*"

"Be reasonable, Teek." Fi slipped her arm through Tiki's and pulled her along. "Even if it is possible—I'm not going to come back at midnight and tangle with a bunch of goblins." She made a face. "It gives me shivers to even think about it."

"I know," Tiki said. "But—"

"We're not equipped to deal with faeries in their own world. Better to just see if we can find word from someone here, like Rieker did."

Tiki's shoulders sagged. Fiona was right. Even if they could get through the gate, they had no means to battle magical creatures. She didn't even know where Rieker was for sure, but she had to do something.

AFTER SEVERAL HOURS of walking the streets, they didn't know anything more than when they'd started.

"We're this close," Fiona said, a hint of color in her cheeks, "we might as well check Charing Cross."

Tiki forced a smile, though there was no part of her that felt happy. They weren't one inch closer to helping Rieker and on top of that, she couldn't seem to shake Sean from her thoughts. "What will Johnny say if he sees you dressed like this?"

Fiona gasped and looked down. "I forgot."

"Has he been about lately?"

"No. Not since we took the stew to him." Fiona wiped her nose on her sleeve again, smearing dirt across her face.

"That's probably for the best," Tiki said. They waited while a horse-drawn double-decker omnibus pulled to a stop in front of them; the crowd shifted as passengers got on and off. Fiona nudged Tiki, her mouth twisted in a small grin. Bus stops, packed with people standing tightly together, were a perfect place to pick pockets. Tiki shook her head. "Don't even think of it, Fi," she whispered.

Once the omnibus had moved on, they crossed the street, avoiding the piles of manure left behind by the myriad horses going up and down the street. "You don't have to let Johnny see you," Tiki said, "but I want to check the old clockmaker's shop, just in case. Larkin was hiding there once. I doubt she'll be there again but I have to check." Tiki veered around the small stand of a shoeshine man.

It only took a few minutes to walk the familiar path from Covent Garden to Charing Cross. As they walked Tiki had the eerie sense that nothing had really changed, that they still had to pick pockets to survive, that she and Fiona were heading home after another day of searching for a way to feed themselves and the others.

"It's almost like we never left," Fiona said as Charing Cross came into view.

"I was just thinking the same thing," Tiki admitted.

"But we're better off now, aren't we, Teek? Living with Rieker, eating every day." Fi peeked at her from the corners of her eyes. "Even though Larkin pesters you still?"

Were they better off? Or would she trade this constant fear to return to an old familiar fear of starving to death?

Tiki shrugged. "I don't know for sure, Fi. All I know is we can't go backwards. We can only look forward and try to do better." She cut to the far side of the station. "I'll go in the back way, through the maintenance tunnels. Are you coming with me?"

Fiona hesitated. "Would Johnny think less of me if he saw me like this?"

Tiki sighed. "He's a pickpocket, Fi. He's only worried about filling his belly."

Fiona made a face. "No different than what we were a few months ago."

"I'm sure he'll like you just fine, whatever way you're dressed," Tiki said over her shoulder, as she entered the alley that ran alongside the station. "He'll probably have more respect for you, knowing you can hold your own with the best of the lot in London."

They pushed their way through the narrow tunnel that led to the back of the little room where they'd lived. It was dark but Tiki knew the way blindfolded—she'd come this way so many times before. She reached the little panel of wood that marked the back entrance to the old clockmaker's shop and stopped to swing it to the side. Fiona was right behind her.

They slipped into the long, rectangular room. Tiki shivered. "It's so cold in here. The stove must not have been lit for days." Then the smell hit her. An odor she would never forget permeated the room: the smell of sickness.

Chapter Thirty-One

Tiki froze, her senses on high-alert. The watery light that spilled into the room from the three large windows on the far wall was dim and the area was full of shadows.

"What's wrong?" Fiona whispered.

A groan sounded from a pile of blankets near the cold stove.

"Johnny?" Fiona clutched Tiki's hand. They crept closer to the pile of blankets, ready to run, if necessary. "Johnny?"

Another groan. This time the blankets shifted slightly.

"Are you hurt?" Tiki asked as they took another few steps, wary of moving too close.

"Fiona?" The voice was hoarse and weak.

"Yes, it's me." Fi let go of Tiki's hand and hurried over to the huddled mass. Johnny threw back a blanket and tried to push himself into a sitting position, his face grimacing with the effort.

He froze as his gaze fell on Fiona. "Y..you don' look like Fi...." Johnny said, trying to push away, but too weak to move.

Fiona caught her breath in a gasp. "Is that *blood?*"

Convinced Johnny was alone and it wasn't a trap, Tiki hurried over and squatted down next to Fiona. She pulled the mess of dirty blankets away so she could see him. He was sweating so much his hair was stuck to his forehead, yet he shivered. Several piles of rags were heaped nearby and appeared to be soaked with blood. "What happened?"

"M..my leg." He sank back onto the floor again, his eyes fluttering closed, as though the effort to sit up was more than he could manage.

Tiki pulled the last blanket off him. The right leg of his trousers hung in shreds. Below the torn fabric, his leg was swollen and covered in blood, with deep gashes across the leg. The outer portions of the wound were black and congealing.

"Oh no," Tiki whispered, drawing a deep breath.

Fiona scooted away, covering her face in her hands.

"Stop it, Fi," Tiki said in a firm voice. "I'm going to need your help." She sat back on her heels and looked around the room. "I don't suppose there are any candles left." She leaned close to Johnny's leg again, delicately pulling away the torn fabric of his trousers to look at the wound. "I need some light."

"W..what happened?" Fiona gulped, trying to catch her breath, still huddled several feet away.

When Johnny didn't answer, Tiki leaned over and peered into his face. "He's unconscious." She put the back of her hand to his sweat-drenched cheek. "And he's got a raging fever."

Fiona crept closer. She sounded on the verge of tears. "What do we do, Tiki?"

Tiki thought fast. They couldn't leave him here or he would surely die. It was obvious he'd been alone for days.

"Does Mr. Lloyd have something that will help him?" Fiona asked, mentioning the apothecary up in Leicester Square who had provided Tiki with medicine for Clara's cough last winter.

"He doesn't need an apothecary, Fi," Tiki said, her voice tense. "He needs a surgeon. And he needs one right now." She bent forward and gently ran her hands along Johnny's leg, grimacing as her fingers became slippery and covered with blood. Johnny groaned again, but didn't open his eyes. "I don't think the leg's broken," Tiki said as she sat back. "But those are deep cuts." A terrible dread filled her. The skin on the edges of the gashes was torn and uneven, as though a claw had ripped through his leg. First Leo, now Johnny—who was next?

She wiped her hands on a nearby blanket, blood sticking between her fingers, as her mind raced to figure out how they could help the boy. "I know," she whispered. "Shamus is working today. You need to run to Binder's Bakery and pray that he's not gone on deliveries. Tell him we need him and the wagon. *Now.*"

WHILE FIONA WAS gone Tiki rummaged up every scrap of cloth she could find. Those that she could, she tore into long strips. Johnny writhed in pain and tried to stop her as she wrapped the strips tightly around his leg, but he was so weak, he couldn't put up much of a fight.

"Shhh," Tiki said, smoothing his damp hair off his forehead. Her fingers left a streak of blood across his pale skin. "I'm trying to help you feel better."

Blood soaked through the first few layers of cloth almost immediately, but Tiki kept wrapping the fabric as tight as she could. She was just finishing putting the last row of strips around his leg when Shamus and Fiona burst back through the door.

"Fi said it was an emergency. What's going on, Teek?" Shamus said breathlessly as he hurried across the room. He stopped when he saw Johnny, his gaze lingering on the boy's swollen and bandaged leg. "What happened?"

"We don't know." Tiki knotted the last strip. "He hasn't really said much since we've been here." Johnny looked much younger with his eyes closed and his face relaxed. Tiki wondered how long ago his parents had been sentenced to Debtor's Prison, how long he'd been living on his own. "Shamus, did you bring the wagon?" she asked.

He nodded. "But we can't get a drop of blood in there or Binder will have my backside."

Tiki nodded. "I know. I have an idea." She pointed to the three ragged blankets that she'd stretched out on the floor next to Johnny. "If we slide him onto the blankets, we can carry him like a stretcher out to the wagon and lay him on the floor. If he bleeds, he'll bleed on the blankets."

Shamus propped his hands on his skinny hips and stared down at Johnny. "We'll never get him through the tunnels on a stretcher." He raised his eyes to Tiki. "We can't take him through the station."

"We have to get him out of here," she replied. "He'll die if we don't."

Fiona let out a little cry of despair.

Shamus bent down and slid his hands under Johnny's armpits. He grunted as he lifted the boy's dead weight. "I'm just goin'ta carry 'im." He slung Johnny over his shoulder like a bag of flour. Johnny groaned as he dangled over Shamus' back.

Fiona scrambled to the back door and held it open so Shamus could pass through, then followed behind Tiki. Once they were out in the alley, Tiki ran ahead to the wagon and spread the three blankets out on the floor.

"Catch his head, Fi." Shamus lowered the boy to the wooden floor of the wagon. Fiona climbed into the wagon and caught the back of Johnny's head, supporting his neck and shoulders as Shamus set him down.

Once Johnny was settled, Shamus wiped his hands on his pants and looked at Tiki. "Where to now?"

"We've got to take him to hospital," Fi said. "St. Thomas' just opened last year 'cross from the Houses of Parliament down in Westminster or there are a load of surgeons up on Harley Street."

Tiki pressed her lips together. "We can't take him to a surgeon, Fi."

Fiona's mouth dropped open. "But why not? You said—"

"I've had a chance to see the wounds better now. I'm afraid a surgeon would cut off his leg." She lifted her head. "Then he wouldn't have a prayer of surviving," she finished in a whisper.

Fiona covered her mouth with her hands as tears cascaded down her cheeks. Shamus gave a slow nod of agreement.

"I think you're right, Teek."

Tiki grabbed hold of the edge of the door and pulled herself into the wagon with Fiona.

"Take us to back to Grosvenor Square."

Chapter Thirty-Two

As soon as they arrived, Tiki and Fiona dashed into the stall in the coach house and changed back to their dresses, gasping as they washed their faces with cold water from the horse's trough. Tiki left her hair in a long braid and ran into the house to look for Mrs. Bosworth.

"I remember that Johnny chap. He enjoyed my sausage and biscuits," Mrs. B. said as she rubbed her hands on a dish towel. Tiki feared ashes still clung to her face, but if they did, Mrs. Bosworth gave no sign of noticing them. "A charmer, that one. I think he had his eye on Fiona when he visited." Two dimples appeared in Mrs. B.'s cheeks, making her look younger, as she winked at Tiki. "Goin'ta be a handsome sort one day, wouldn't you agree?"

"He's had an accident, Mrs. B..." Tiki faltered, trying to think of her cover story. "I think he was hit by a carriage over on the Strand. He's got some awful cuts on his leg that need tending."

Mrs. Bosworth dropped the towel on the counter and bustled out of the kitchen. "Can he walk?"

"No." Tiki followed behind in the big woman's wake. "He's ah...asleep."

Mrs. Bosworth shot Tiki a look over her shoulder. "It sounds like it's a good thing Clara is upstairs taking a nap. I don't think she needs to see this."

"No, she doesn't," Tiki murmured. "I think Shamus can carry him to a bedroom, though."

"Put him upstairs in the guest room on the third floor. Juliette!" Mrs. B. called to the house maid who was dusting in the entry foyer. "Run upstairs and pull down the covers on the bed in the blue room." Her voice took on a determined tone. "We've got a patient." Mrs. B. whirled to face Tiki. "Where is he?"

Taken aback at her take-charge attitude Tiki pointed toward the coach house then followed her outside.

"Let me take a look," Mrs. B. said, brushing Fiona and Shamus aside. The housekeeper leaned into the back of the Binder's wagon, as if a bakery wagon in the coach house was an everyday occurrence. She placed her reddened, rough hand on Johnny's forehead and smoothed his hair back from his face. "He's burnin' up." She sized up Shamus' skinny frame. "You sure you can haul him up to the third floor? Geoffrey can help, if you need it."

"I can do it," Shamus said.

"Take his boots off here," Mrs. B. said, reaching over to untie the dirty boots that had holes worn through the soles. She sniffed. "And take everything else off without making him indecent. He needs a bath." She ran her hand over his cheek. "We need to get that fever down."

JULIETTE TOOK AN armload of clean blankets upstairs while Mrs. B. helped cut the legs of Johnny's pants away. She pointed to his wounded leg. "Who wrapped this?"

"I did," Tiki replied.

"Fine job, you did," she said with a nod. "What's it look like underneath?"

Tiki explained about the size and depth of the cuts, motioning with her hands. "The edges are very red and it seems to be bleeding a lot."

Mrs. Bosworth stopped her bustling and gave Tiki a steady look. "Does the boy need a surgeon?"

Tiki's eyes darted to Shamus's before returning to the older woman's face. "I think they'd take his leg, M'am," she said softly.

Mr. Bosworth hovered near the bakery wagon now, watching his wife work, as did Geoffrey, Rieker's driver.

There was only a split-second of hesitation before Mrs. Bosworth gave a sharp nod. "Then we'll need to stitch it," the older woman said in a determined tone.

Fiona gasped, wringing her skirt between her hands. "*Stitch* it?"

"No different than stitching a piece of fabric." Mrs. B. shot a look at Fiona out of the corner of her eyes. "You'd probably be the best one to do it."

"No!" Fiona cried. "I could never—"

"You could and you would if you had to," Mrs. B. said, waving a finger at the girl to cut her off. "Have more confidence in yourself, Fiona, you're a survivor, girl. You can do anything."

A small, satisfied grin creased Shamus' thin face and he nudged Fiona in the back.

Mrs. Bosworth started barking out orders. "We're going to need some clean cloth strips to wrap his leg after we get done stitching it up. Juliette—" she pointed toward the housemaid who had just returned. "Get to work. We'll meet you upstairs."

"Yes, mum," Juliette said with a bob and raced back inside.

"Mr. Bosworth," she turned and pointed a finger at her husband, "set a kettle to boilin' —we're goin'ta need hot water. Fiona, thread a darning needle with your stoutest thread and meet us upstairs. Miss Tara, you go find some soap and towels so we can clean this boy up." Mrs. B. looked down at Johnny, her face softening. "He stinks somethin' awful."

IT TOOK ALMOST two hours to clean Johnny up. Fiona and Shamus waited in the hallway while Tiki and Mrs. Bosworth tended to his injury.

Mrs. B. had enough foresight to put a heavy quilt, along with several thick towels, underneath the boy as they worked on him, with the plan to roll him over and gently pulled the blood-soaked blanket and towels clear when they were finished.

Tiki watched in fascination as Mrs. B. rinsed the wounds, then doused them with whiskey. Johnny woke up with a scream then, but it wasn't long before his eyes rolled back in his head and he slept again. The stitching was exactly like stitching two pieces of fabric together—looping back and forth between the two pieces of skin and pulling them tight between each stitch. The older woman never flinched once. When Mrs. B. was done, three neat seams stretched along the top of Johnny's skinny leg.

"I've been caring for people practically since I could walk," she said. "Raised four boys of my own before I lost them to the typhoid. It's what I'm best at."

With Tiki's help, she re-wrapped the wounds. She was surprised that Mrs. B. never questioned Johnny's ragged state. It was as if she took poor street children under her wing every day.

When they were finally done, Johnny was clean, his leg tightly stitched and wrapped in white bandages. For the moment, it appeared the combination of stitching and wrapping had stopped the bleeding. Mrs. Bosworth pushed off the edge of the bed with a tired sigh and brushed several strands of gray hair away from her face with the back of her hand. She reached down and smoothed the hair away from Johnny's forehead.

"We've done what we can for now. Let him sleep and we'll check on him every hour or so. By the looks of it, we're going to need to get some food in him right away, but we'll let him rest for a bit."

When Tiki tried to thank Mrs. Bosworth for her help, the older woman put her rough hand along Tiki's cheek. "I've seen what you've done for my William." Her blue eyes got misty. "I know 'twas you who brought my boy back from a living death." Her hand dropped to Tiki's shoulder and squeezed gently. "I'm glad to repay the kindness."

THE NEXT DAY Johnny awakened long enough for Fiona to get some hot broth in him and he promptly fell back to sleep. He was still fighting a fever and hadn't even asked where he was.

They took turns running upstairs to check on him, though Fiona volunteered most often. In the meantime, Tiki and Fiona played a game of chess in the parlor, though neither could really pay attention to the game. Fiona was worried about Johnny and Tiki couldn't stop thinking about Rieker. It was a relief when Mr. Bosworth interrupted to announce a visitor.

"A seamstress?" Fiona repeated. "What on earth is a seamstress doing here?"

"S'pose she's got the wrong address." Tiki shrugged, staring glumly at the black king and imagining Donegal sitting on his throne arguing with Larkin. The visitor entered the room carrying a large bag.

"Mistress Dunbar?" She was an older woman, past her child-bearing years. Curly gray strands of hair escaped from the bonnet she wore on her head. Her eyes and skin were as washed out as the dress she wore, an air of exhaustion hanging around her like a cloak. "I'm Mrs. Emerson. Here to fit your gown today." She made an awkward attempt at a curtsy, the crack of her knees loud across the room.

"A gown?" Fiona said, looking at Tiki with wide eyes. "Whatever for?"

Tiki stood up. "I have no idea."

The woman flopped the bag over the edge of a chair and was busy pulling the garment from inside. "Mr. William Richmond hired me several days ago. Rush job, it were. Had to be completed by next Friday."

Tiki sucked her breath in. She'd completely forgotten about the party to which Arthur had invited them.

"Another ball—" Fiona's wistful words died off in a gasp as Mrs. Emerson held the gown up for them to see. The fabric was a stunning shade of emerald green, exactly the color of Tiki's eyes. The sheen of the fabric seemed to glow in the lamplight. Gold ruffles swept the front of the dress and anchored on each side with elegant red roses. The wide neckline was embroidered in gold with sequins and beads that twinkled in the light, almost as if the dress itself was pleased with the surprise.

The older woman held the dress up. "You'll have to try it on, Miss, for me to measure it properly."

Tiki stood rooted to the spot. Had Rieker bought this beautiful gown for her?

"Teek." Fiona shoved her from behind. "You have to put it on."

As if awoken from a stupor Tiki hurried forward. "Of course, of course. I'll need my shoes—"

"Ohp," the woman clucked, reaching for her bag with one hand. "The young master sent matching shoes as well." She dug around and eventually produced a pair of shoes made of the same satin fabric as the dress, embossed with gold ruffles and a single red rose.

"Fer the love of Pete," Fiona whispered, turning one of the beautiful shoes over and around in her hands. "I've never seen shoes so fancy." She ran a finger along the side of the shoe, tracing the gold. "Have you, Teek?"

"Never," Tiki said in a whisper.

"If you please, Miss…."

"Yes, of course." Tiki's hands were shaking. She'd never owned a dress so fine. Not one that was actually meant to be hers. "Fiona, could you help me, please?"

THE ACTUAL MEASURING didn't take long. Mrs. Emerson had been a seamstress for many years and was quick and efficient. She exited, promising to return by Friday with the finished gown.

"Oh Tiki," Fiona cried after the woman had left. She held the skirt of her own well-worn dress out and twirled around the room. "Another ball."

"I think it's just a party, Fi."

"Will you talk to Prince Leo and Prince Arthur again?" Her eyes glowed with excitement. "And this time we won't even have to sneak you in." She giggled and fell backwards over the arm of the sofa to stretch out across the cushions. Her voice was heavy with longing. "I wonder what it would be like to go to a ball."

A twinge of guilt coursed through Tiki. Fiona had saved her when she was homeless, starving and without a shilling to her name. Fi had shown her how to pick pockets to survive, and along with Shamus, had invited her to live with them in Charing Cross. It wasn't a stretch to say she had saved Tiki's life.

"Did you see the ruffles on that dress?" Fiona sighed again. "They shone as if they were spun from real gold."

Tiki was only a year older than Fiona, yet, because of a moment of sheer lunacy when she'd stolen the Queen's ring, she had already attended a masked ball at Buckingham Palace and had actually met the Queen of England. Now she had the opportunity to attend another party with the royals—this time as an invited guest. Would she be as gracious if it were Fiona attending instead of her?

"Yes, it was quite beautiful," Tiki replied. "But the only reason I'm invited is because Arthur is afraid there's someone trying to murder the Queen or another of the royals. He wants Rieker and me to attend to see if we notice anyone *unusual*—" she raised her eyebrows— "if you know what I mean." She grabbed Fiona's ankles which still hung over the arm of the couch. "Maybe next time you can come too."

Fiona crossed her hands behind her head and rolled her eyes. "Nobody's going to believe I belong at a ball with the royals anymore than they'd believe Johnny is a lord."

"Rubbish," Tiki said. "We'll dress you up in a beautiful gown and no one will be able tell the difference between you and those society girls, I promise." But in her heart Tiki wondered if there would ever be a 'next' time. Their lives were shifting and changing as though at the mercy of the wind. And an ill wind, it seemed to be.

Chapter Thirty-Three

After not sleeping the night before, and the anxiety of finding Johnny so ill and having to bring him back to Grosvenor Square, Tiki decided it was silly to once more pace the floor of the parlor all night. But sleep had eluded her as the same questions swirled around her head: worrying about Rieker, questioning if Larkin had lied, yet again. The dulcet chimes of the clock had tolled three a.m. once again before she had drifted off.

TIKI AWOKE TO the sense of being watched.

She blinked her eyes open and slowly looked around the dark room. A shadow leaned against a nearby wall. With a startled cry, she jerked upright and scooted backwards in the bed, reaching for her dagger.

"Teek, it's me," a soft voice whispered and the shadowy figured moved closer, holding out a hand to soothe her.

"Rieker?" she whispered in disbelief.

"Yes. I'm sorry to wake you. I had to make sure you were safe."

Tiki jerked the covers to the side and leapt out of the bed. She threw her arms around his neck, ignoring for the moment all the questions she had for him. "I was so scared you'd been hurt. That they'd captured you—or—worse." She leaned back to look into his face. "I couldn't get back to help you. I was desperate—" she clung to his lapels— "I didn't know what to do."

Rieker wrapped his arms around her. "Tiki, shhh," he said softly in her ear, holding her close. "I'm fine." He smoothed her silky hair, letting the strands slip between his fingers. "It was a brave thing you did, confronting Donegal. I'd never have guessed Larkin would protect you like that."

Tiki pulled back. "Protect me? But the stone didn't roar—and she betrayed you."

He pulled Tiki down to sit on the edge of the bed with him. "Larkin made it seem like she would betray me, but in truth she didn't reveal anything that Donegal didn't already know. It was a ploy to give you time to get away from him."

"It was?" Tiki imagined the scene in her head again. Larkin, resplendent in her gold outfit, balanced on the shoulders of those beasts of men, taunting Donegal. "But who were those men?"

"The Macanna. The men and women who followed Finn centuries ago when he ceded his right to the throne."

"Why are they with Larkin?"

He shrugged. "That I don't know. Maybe they've joined with the Seelies to unseat Donegal."

"But if that's true, then she took a terrible risk for me."

"As you did for her. Even so, never forget she wants something from you, Tiki."

Tiki shuddered. Never in her wildest dreams did she ever imagine herself risking her life on behalf of Larkin. "But how could she possibly escape when Donegal had guards surrounding the entire room?"

Rieker shook his head. "I'm sure Larkin had a plan." His voice turned bitter. "She always does."

His leg pressed against hers from hip to knee and warmed her through her thin nightgown. Tiki was acutely aware of how close he sat next to her, unchaperoned in her bedroom at night. Though terribly inappropriate, there was not one part of her that wished it any different.

"But what about the stone?" She leaned against him, enjoying the warmth their two bodies created. "It didn't roar, it didn't *do* anything. Was Larkin lying about that?"

"I've been thinking about that. It all seems a bit too easy, don't you think?" His voice was cautious. "If there's one thing I know about faeries, it's that they *never* make anything easy. It's *always* a riddle—the truth hidden beneath layers of lies and plots and secrets."

Tiki knew it all too well. "What was that jester whispering about in your ear?"

"Oh, some nonsense about fate... what was it? Oh right. *'Fate never crushed those who truth never deceived.'*" Rieker laughed. "Whatever that means."

He wrapped his warm fingers around hers. "Maybe Larkin believed all you had to do was touch the Stone of Tara, or maybe that was a just a diversion to forward a bigger plot that she's brewing—I don't know. But given what they've done to protect the Seelie throne—" Rieker's words became more urgent— "to protect the world of Faerie—it seems like they would do *more* than just place a sacred stone under a throne. It was too easy for Donegal to simply kill O'Riagáin and take over. Just as it's too easy for Larkin and the Macanna to battle Donegal and reclaim the throne. There's a piece missing. But what? That's what I can't figure out."

Tiki searched his face. Was he as confused as she felt? Or did he know more than he was telling? Did he have other secrets? "Sean told me something."

Rieker threaded his long fingers through hers, the gesture somehow intimate, his touch making Tiki feel weak inside. "I'm glad you got to meet him, Tiki."

She searched his eyes, wanting to believe him. "Sean said that he's taken you to the Otherworld. That you can come and go on your own now. Is that true? Is that where you go when you disappear?"

For once, she didn't see the guarded look that so often masked Rieker's thoughts and emotions. His eyes never wavered from hers. "Yes. I hated not telling you about him, but you were so upset by Larkin stealing Clara, I knew it wasn't the right time. I didn't think you'd understand." His words rang with honesty and the cold lump she'd had in her chest since Sean had told her, eased a little.

She looked into his smoky eyes. "Understand what?"

"Why I need to know." His voice was thick with emotion. "They took everything from me, Teek. *Everything.* I have to understand why." The muscles in his jaw flexed and she sensed the determination that brewed just below the surface. "I have to understand who and what I am."

Tiki did understand. The same desire for answers burned inside of her now, making her question everything she knew.

"I had a lot of time to think while I was there, trying to get back, " Rieker said, "wondering if you'd gotten back to London safely. Time to think about everything—us—who we are—what kind of life we might have." He paused and his voice got softer. "What kind of life I might have if I lost you."

Rieker threaded her hair behind her ear with his other hand, his fingers lingering against her cheek. "We're different, Tiki," he said softly. "We're caught between two worlds and honestly, I don't know which one we belong in. But I do know this—I don't want to be either place without you."

He looked deep into her eyes. "I believe we found each other because we're meant to be together." He leaned forward and his lips covered hers. He was tender at first and Tiki's lips moved beneath his. His kiss deepened, his long fingers threading through her hair as he pulled her closer. Their tongues met, a new burst of sensations warming Tiki from the inside out. The fire that suddenly burned inside her melted away any questions of how she felt about Rieker. She couldn't hide from this truth any longer.

Long moments stretched by as they kissed until Tiki pulled back. She ran her fingertips gently over Rieker's cheekbone, memorizing his face. She soaked up the moment, when he was so close, so open. "Do you believe Larkin saved you?" Tiki finally asked.

Rieker tilted his head. "She did save me," he finally said. "There's no question about that."

"You believe her?"

Rieker ran his fingers through his hair, leaving the dark locks in tangled disarray. "Sean also told me that Donegal was responsible for the deaths of my family." He tightened his fingers into a fist, then released them. "It's taken me a long time to be objective, but it would make more sense. Larkin could have drowned me that night, but instead she held my head above the water."

Tiki wasn't sure what to think. To understand Larkin was like trying to capture smoke in your hands.

"There have been plenty of other opportunities when she could have done me harm," Rieker continued, "but she hasn't." His eyes were almost black. "The truth of the matter is that she risked her own life to save mine. When Donegal found out what she'd done he ordered her wings clamped and had her thrown in prison. In the Otherworld that's the equivalent of a death sentence."

A tangle of emotions warred in Tiki's chest. "Do you think it's because of what Kieran said? That she saved you because she loves you?"

"I don't believe Larkin is *in* love with me, if that's what you're asking, though she likes to act that way at times. I think it's a game to her. I believe I'm part of a greater plan she has that now involves you. Or maybe you've always been a part of it—I don't know anymore." He smoothed her sleeve back to reveal her birthmark. He ran a finger gently over the dark lines. "If Larkin has told us the truth, then you bear the birthmark of Finn MacLochlan. You are his heir."

Tiki watched Rieker's finger trace the pattern on her skin, his touch creating a warm tingling sensation. She raised her head. "And what do you think her plan is?"

Rieker looked into Tiki's eyes, holding her gaze. "If you are truly the heir to the Summer Court—what better way for Larkin to gain control of a kingdom than to put a puppet on the throne?"

Chapter Thirty-Four

"I told you he'd be back," Mrs. Bosworth said in a sing-song voice as she bustled around the kitchen the next morning. "He always shows up eventually, don't you, young sir?" She beamed at Rieker.

"My business took a little longer than I expected." Rieker spoke between bites of sausage. "How's the patient this morning?" Though surprised when Tiki had informed him of Johnny's arrival, Rieker had supported Tiki's decision to bring him to the town-home to recover.

"He's hungry, which is always a good sign," Mrs. B. replied. "We're going to change the wrap on his leg and check his stitches this afternoon. Fiona's been a brilliant help." She beamed at the girl who sat at the table with Rieker. "Made all the difference in that boy's recovery, I'd say."

LATER THAT DAY another storm was gathering, dimming the daylight until it was as dark as night, the air gritty with the ever-present coal dust. Thunder rumbled in the distance above Bucking-ham Palace and the dark clouds overhead threatened rain as Tiki and Rieker drove to the Birdkeeper's Cottage at the end of the lake in St. James Park. Rieker had insisted they pay a visit to Mamie, Queen Victoria's old lady-in-waiting to see what information they might glean from her.

Their shoes crunched on the gravel walkway as they approached the small front door.

"Arthur made reference to getting information from Mamie when we saw them last," Rieker said, as he rapped his knuckles against the arched wooden door. The sound echoed in the quiet afternoon. "Leo said it was Mamie who had informed him of *an fáinne sí*—the meaning of your birthmark. As children we called her the witch woman," Rieker replied in a low voice. "Even then, we knew she had knowledge that others didn't."

It was a few long moments before the door swung inward and a small, elderly woman peered out at them. Acting as a lady-in-waiting to Queen Victoria since she took the throne at age eighteen, Mamie was now in her eighties. Her hair had faded to a silvery white, like the aged bark of a birch tree, but her eyes were as bright and lively as ever in a face that was soft with wrinkles. Her lips creased with a pleased smile. "William Richmond, is that you?"

"Hello Mamie." Rieker tucked his hat under his arm. "You look well."

"Getting older all the time, but well." She cocked her head, as her bright eyes turned to Tiki. The movement reminded Tiki of a little bird.

"Allow me to introduce…" Rieker hesitated.

"Tara Kathleen, M'am." Tiki dipped her head as she curtsied.

"Tara Kathleen Dunbar." Rieker said the name as though it were an endearment.

"Lovely. So pleased to meet you." Mamie's small wrinkled hands reached for Tiki's. "A bit of Irish ancestry, then?"

"My mother's side." Tiki smiled.

"Welcome, my dear. Come in, come in. I've just made pasties. I'll put a kettle on and we'll catch up." She ushered them in with spry steps and led them to her petite living room before bustling away to the kitchen.

Tiki and Rieker situated themselves on a small loveseat that faced toward the paned windows with a view of the lake. In the far distance, a fork of lightning split the sky above Buckingham Palace.

"You must come back in the summer, when I make my famous apple pie," Mamie called from the kitchen. "The sweetest apples in all of England grow right near here on the palace grounds."

"I remember those trees from when I was a lad growing up," Rieker replied. "Leo and I used to climb them with our slingshots to keep an eye out for enemy spies." He chuckled at the memory. "Usually our only target was Arthur. Leo's sisters learned quick enough not to come near us." He jumped to his feet to assist Mamie as she carried in a tray loaded with tea and meat pies.

"Just put it on the table there, dear." The older woman settled into the floral cushions of a worn rocker. "You look well, William. So grown up now and such a handsome young man. You remind me of your father. I haven't seen you in what? Four years?"

There was a moment of silence and Tiki glanced at Rieker. His family had been murdered four years ago. Was he remembering that as well?

But if Mamie's comment dredged up painful memories, Rieker gave no sign of it. "That sounds about right," he said.

Mamie poured tea into the china cups and set the kettle down. "You've sorted some things about your family, I take it?"

"Sorted some things, confused about others." He reached for Tiki's hand as he sat down on the loveseat again. "Thankfully, I've had help."

Mamie smiled at Tiki, her eyes sharp in contrast to the soft wrinkles that wreathed her face. "I suspect you've helped each other. What brings you here this day?"

"Mamie." Rieker leaned forward, his face serious, his dark hair shadowing his eyes. "We'd like to ask you something."

She clasped her hands together. "Best to just get to it straight-away, then."

"You're aware that one of Queen Victoria's rings went missing last Christmas?"

"Of course."

"You're aware I protect the ring now?"

Tiki held her breath. Was this old woman really in Queen Victoria's confidence?

Something glittered in Mamie's blue eyes. "As you were meant to do, William. I'm sure the truce is safe in your care."

"Thank you." Rieker nodded, not questioning Mamie's knowledge of the truce held within the stone. He motioned to Tiki. "Tiki has a mark on her arm that I think you're familiar with."

Self-consciously, Tiki slid her dark green sleeve up and revealed the thin black lines that twisted and curled around her narrow wrist.

Mamie stared for a long moment at Tiki's birthmark. "*An fáinne sí*," the old woman whispered in awe. "So very beautiful." She leaned forward and rubbed her fingers gently over Tiki's skin. "And so rare."

"We've learned a bit of information about Tiki's mark," Rieker said. "We're hoping maybe you can explain what it means."

Mamie released Tiki's arm and sat back, threading her fingers together on her lap. "What have you learned, my boy?"

"Have you ever heard of someone named Finn MacLochlan?"

"Finn." Mamie said the name reverently.

Tiki shifted in her seat. "You know of him?"

Mamie's lips curved in a smile. "If you know anything about the world of Faerie, you've surely heard the stories of Finn MacLochlan."

Rieker leaned forward. "Who was he?"

"Ah, Finn. He was one of a kind, that young man." The old woman pushed her chair back and began to rock slowly. "Finn was a warrior, very fierce, very strong, but he was also a poet and said to be a seer. He had a great appreciation for the beauty of nature—" she winked at Rieker— "as well as for a beautiful face."

She laughed, her lips twisting in a mischievous grin. "Finn is practically a legend in the world of the fey. Of course he was too handsome for his own good. Made him a bit of a rogue, I daresay."

"You sound like you knew him," Tiki said.

"It's said that he was the only person to ever beat his father, Finvarra, at a game of chess. That tells you something about how clever he was." Mamie sighed. "Maybe too clever."

"Finvarra," Rieker repeated. "He was a faerie king, right?"

Mamie smiled at him. "Well done, William. Finvarra was the high king of the *Daoine Sidhe*."

Tiki rubbed her brow, trying to take in everything Mamie was telling them. "The *Daoine Sidhe*?" She pronounced the words *deena shee* as Mamie had.

"The faeries of Ireland, of course, dear," Mamie said. "Faeries are ancient creatures. It was in Ireland that the Seelie court originated, though the Scots sometimes try to claim ownership." The glides of Mamie's rocker created a quiet *shushing* in the cottage as she slowly rocked back and forth. Tiki had the eerie sense of somehow moving back through time.

"Long ago, in the very beginning, there was only one court in the world of the fey: the Seelie court—the blessed court—but there was one who did unspeakable things. His name was Braeden, which meant from the dark valley."

"What did he do?" Rieker asked.

"He murdered his own mother in his quest for power and then lied about it. There was an outrage and he was expelled from court." Mamie's mouth twisted down in distaste. "But he was so ambitious that he forcibly enslaved the fey outside the court and created an army that became the UnSeelie court. One that thrived on chaos and warfare. The dark court."

"The court that Donegal now rules?" Rieker asked.

"Yes. The UnSeelies have had other high kings over the years after Braeden, but Donegal has ruled for many centuries now. He is especially vicious." She braced her elbows on the wooden arms of the rocker and leaned forward, her voice full of warning. "Donegal is convinced that technology is replacing what magic could do before. He believes it's killing the world of the fey. He wants to destroy London and take back the space he believes should belong to the Otherworld."

"What of the Seelie court?" Rieker asked.

"For the last millennium, Eridanus ruled the court of sun and light, though make no mistake—" she pointed a crooked finger at him— "the Seelie's can be mischievous and deadly, as well. He acknowledged that their world was changing with the encroachment of humans, but the difference was he believed we had to meld the worlds—to learn to live side by side so we could all survive."

"But what of Tiki's birthmark, Mamie?" Rieker's gaze was intent on the older woman. "What of this supposed connection to Finn MacLochlan?"

"*An fáinne sí* is said to follow the lineage of the true high kings of Tara. Finn bore the same mark on his wrist. A very rare pattern indeed."

She lifted her thin shoulders. "Finn should have inherited his father's throne, and ruled the Seelie court, but he chose not to. He was young and tempestuous." She waved a wrinkled hand through the air as if to dismiss the faerie's capricious mood swings. "Finvarra had a nasty habit of womanizing and he especially liked to abduct mortal women. Finn was so disgusted by his father's disregard for these women that he left court and struck out on his own." Mamie paused to sip from her cup.

"Where did he go?" Tiki asked.

"It was said that he left Ireland and came to England. The stories were that he'd come to London to return a mortal woman his father had stolen. He was the last person to bear *an fáinne sí*." She slowed the swing of her chair. "Until now, that is."

Tiki's heart pounded in her ears, her breath tight in her throat. Mamie's words were like a weight pressing down, squeezing the air from her lungs. Maybe Larkin had told the truth. Rieker stood up and paced to the small fireplace, his height accentuated by the low ceilings in the cottage.

"There was more we learned." His voice was tense. "Tiki was told that she'd been *hidden* in London by someone named Adasara."

Mamie rocked slowly back and forth in her chair. "Adasara was one of the oldest faeries of the Seelie court. She would often shapeshift into a deer, which reflected the true essence of her spirit: a gentle, harmless creature. But make no mistake, she held great power." Mamie paused long enough in her rocking to let a small, marmalade cat jump into her lap. The cat circled once, then settled into a ball, purring with contentment. "Who is it that mentioned her name?"

Rieker told the old woman of Larkin.

"*Nimh Álainn*," Mamie said softly.

"What?" Rieker dropped down onto the loveseat close to Tiki.

"*Nimh Álainn*," Mamie repeated. "It was a nickname the other faeries gave her. It means beautiful poison. She has always had a terrible temper. Many thought she was jealous of Adasara's position and Eridanus' favor of her."

"You know Larkin?" Tiki said.

"Larkin, *Nimh Álainn*, whatever name she goes by, she has existed for a long time. She left the Seelie Court suddenly. It was whispered she left because Eridanus wouldn't make her high queen. I never heard what became of her after she joined the UnSeelie's." The old woman stroked the cat who purred contently. "It sounds as if she has taken a turn for the worse."

Tiki tugged her sleeve back over her wrist, shivering with a sudden chill. "She said she was a spy for Eridanus."

"A spy?" Surprise echoed in Mamie's voice. "*Nimh Álainn?*"

"But where does Tiki come into all of this?" Rieker asked. "If what you say is correct, this birthmark would suggest she has a fey heritage, but she doesn't remember anything."

Mamie's eyes rested on Tiki. "If Adasara hid you in London, she must have feared for your life and would have put a powerful glamour on you. If you are indeed the child of Finn, as your mark would suggest, your presence would have explosive consequences within the courts. Especially now. You must be very careful."

"But how can we find out the truth?"

Mamie was silent for a moment as she rocked. Her fingers, crooked with age, gently smoothed the fur of the cat. "If anyone would know the magic that has been cast upon you, it would be Larkin, as you call her." Mamie looked from Rieker to Tiki. "I would start there."

Chapter Thirty-Five

"It's like following a serpent eating its own tail." Rieker's frustration was evident as their carriage passed the shops on Bond Street on the ride back to Grosvenor Square. His fists were clenched on his knees, and he sat forward as if ready to spring from the coach. The rain that had threatened earlier now poured down, pounding on the roof like a million little drums beating. "Everything always seems to lead back to Larkin."

Tiki was silent as they rode, her head jostling against the cushion as the carriage clacked over the uneven cobblestones. She stared blankly out the small window at the shops as they passed, the glow of lighted windows making them appear to be a safe haven. But was anywhere safe anymore?

"Do you know if Larkin escaped that night? she asked.

"All I know for sure was that Donegal's soldiers were still looking for her when I managed to get out of the palace."

JOHNNY CONTINUED TO make amazing improvement and was able to move about the house now. Tiki and Fiona were sitting with him in the drawing room.

"Can you remember what happened?" Tiki asked him. She'd been waiting for the opportunity to find out what had caused his horrific injuries, hoping there might be a logical explanation. They reminded her of the wounds Rieker had suffered last December at the hands of an evil faerie named Marcus in that very same alleyway.

Johnny tilted his head to the side and flicked his hair out of his eyes. "It happened the day you brought me the stew."

Tiki tried to hide her surprise. That was also the day she'd met Dain in Charing Cross.

"I was going through the back alley when somebody jumped me from behind." Johnny grimaced. "They grabbed my leg—felt like they set the bloody thing on fire—and flipped me around. The next thing I knew, they'd knocked me to the ground. I couldn't see their face. I figured I was done for and then—they were gone."

Johnny shifted his gaze back to Tiki and Fiona. "I didn't see 'em run away—didn't hear any footsteps. One minute they were attacking me—the next, I was alone." For once, his expression was serious. "I don't even remember how I got home—I could barely walk."

"You were lucky you survived," Fiona whispered.

Johnny leaned back against the chair where he sat near the fire. "What was lucky was that you thought to come check on me." He gave her a warm smile. "Saved my life, you did."

Fiona's cheeks turned pink. "I'm glad for it."

Tiki sat back. There was a message of some sort in Johnny's attack, she was sure of it. "Thank goodness you're safe. For now, Johnny, I think it's best if you just plan on staying here."

THE NEXT DAY was gloomy again, the afternoon stormy and cold. Tiki and Rieker sat alone in his study before a blazing fire.

Since their return from the Otherworld, he'd taken to inviting her into the room more often.

"I've been thinking about the Stone of Tara," Tiki said, "and what you said about a puppet on the throne."

Rieker raised his head from where he sat reading the *Count of Monte Cristo* and gazed at Tiki intently. "Go on."

"Mamie said Larkin was jealous of Adasara—that Larkin wanted to be High Queen." Tiki hesitated. "Maybe Eridanus and Finn deliberately misled Larkin because they didn't trust her. Maybe they feared her ambitions would blind her to everything else—so they didn't tell her everything."

"Certainly possible."

Tiki's voice caught. "Eridanus hid the ring of the truce—one of the most important artifacts in the history of Faerie—in the mortal world. Why?" She continued before Rieker could answer. "Because it wasn't safe in the Otherworld." Tiki's cheeks warmed. "Larkin said that Adasara hid me in London."

Rieker let his breath out in a slow whistle. His hair had fallen across his forehead, reminding Tiki of when she'd known him as a pickpocket.

"They hid you—they hid the ring—" he closed his book with a snap and sat forward— "that's got to be it." His eyes glowed with excitement. "*Fate never crushed those who Truth never deceived.*" Rieker laughed for the first time in ages. "Isn't that just like a faerie? In a place where the mirrors are said to reveal the truth, they place a fake."

"Exactly," Tiki breathed, "the stone wasn't real."

Rieker pushed himself out of the chair to pace. "I'll bet a bloody thousand quid you're right—the stone in the Palace of Mirrors isn't the true Tara Stone. *That's* why it didn't roar when you stepped on it. *That's* what the Fool was saying: the 'Truth' of the

Tara Stone has never deceived anyone because we haven't found the bloody thing yet."

"And just like the ring," Tiki said in an excited voice, "it must be hidden in London."

ON SATURDAY, FIONA was putting the finishing touches on Tiki's elaborate hairdo as Tiki sat in her thin shift trying not to squirm. Clara danced around the room with her homemade wings, pretending to be wearing a gown.

"Who should I dance with next, Tiki?" the little girl asked, giggling. "Prince Arthur? Or maybe Dain?" Then she was off again, twirling and humming.

At the mention of Dain, Tiki's stomach twinged. She'd thought often of gruff, scarred Sean and the beautiful features of Dain, though she'd not mentioned him to anyone, not even Rieker. Part of her ached for how alone he was, though she knew there was nothing she could do to help him.

Tiki let out a sigh and threaded her fingers together, trying to be patient as Fiona continued braiding and pinning strands of hair.

"I'm almost done," Fiona said as she twisted another section and secured it into place. As she reached for the comb, she ran her fingers over the skin of Tiki's back. "Teek—what are these scars from?"

"What scars?" Tiki craned her head to see over her shoulder.

Fiona ran her fingers gently over Tiki's skin again, up and down in two spots. "You've got two scars back here—thin lines—between your shoulder blades. What are they from?"

"Oh, those." Tiki had forgotten about the scars. "I don't know—I've always had them. Something happened when I was a baby. Can't remember now what it was." Suddenly, Larkin's words echoed in Tiki's head: '*Adasara must have torn yours off when she brought you to London...*' Tiki chewed her lower lip. Had the faerie been right?

"They look old—they're all faded and white—but they're definitely scars." Fiona's forehead knotted in thought as she stared at Tiki's back. "Strange."

"Fi, are you almost done?" Tiki's nerves were getting the best of her. It was no small thing to be going to Buckingham Palace and especially when Lord William Richmond was one's escort.

"All right, all right," Fi said, reaching for a beautiful silk red rose that matched her dress. She stuck a few pins in her mouth as she worked to weave the red rose behind Tiki's ear where her hair gathered and then hung down her back in luscious waves.

Clara came to a spinning stop next to Fiona and rocked unsteadily on her feet as she blinked in Tiki's direction. "Maybe she should wear a crown."

Tiki held her neck and head straight for Fiona and only her eyes moved over to where Clara stood examining her. "I don't think Queen Vic would take too kindly to me showing up in a crown. I think I'll leave that bit to the royals."

"Why do they get all the fun?" Clara asked as she skipped away to twirl some more.

Fiona worked for a few more seconds then gave Tiki's hair a pat. "There. It shouldn't fall out no matter how fast Rieker twirls you." Dimples appeared on both sides of her cheeks as she grinned at Tiki.

Tiki jumped to her feet, anxious to move. All this sitting and having Fiona 'work' on her was getting on her nerves. The emerald green gown made a *shushing* noise as the silky fabric slid to the floor and puddled around Tiki's feet.

"Where are those shoes?" Tiki asked, pulling her skirts this way and that, looking frantically around the room.

"Calm down, Teek. They're right here." Fiona grabbed the shoes off a nearby table and knelt down to put them on Tiki's feet. "What is wrong with you? You weren't this nervous the first time."

"Oh, yes I was," Tiki replied. "But at least last time I didn't know anyone and I had a mask to hide behind."

Fiona backed up to survey her handiwork. Tiki held her thin arms out from her sides and twirled for her. The dress shimmered as she turned, flaring around her legs. Fiona clutched her hands to her chest. "Oh, Tiki, you take my breath away, you're so beautiful."

"The most beautiful," Clara declared.

"Let's hope Rieker thinks so," Tiki whispered.

She kept one hand on the railing and lifted her skirts with the other as she descended toward the foyer. Below, Shamus, Toots, Johnny, Juliette, Mr. and Mrs. B. and Rieker stood with upturned faces watching her.

Tiki's heart skipped a beat at the sight of her escort. Darkly handsome in his black tails and vest, Rieker's shirt was white silk tied neatly with a matching cravat. He wore a sash diagonally across his chest the same emerald color of her dress. Tall and straight, his dark hair was combed back away from his face, revealing the perfection of his features.

As their eyes met the emotions he usually worked to conceal were obvious as he stared at her with longing. Tiki's heart fluttered in response. When she reached the bottom of the stairs he took the fingers of her left hand and raised them to his lips.

"You are breathtaking." His lips on her skin warmed her and it was as if he had embraced her.

Tiki smiled and raised her eyebrows. "I could say the same of you, William."

With one gloved hand clutching his black top hat, Rieker held out the other arm for Tiki to take as he escorted her out the door to an immaculate black carriage pulled by two matched black horses. Red plumed feathers danced from their heads and their silver bridles shimmered in the moonlight. This ride to Buckingham Palace was the complete opposite of the way she had managed to sneak into the first ball she'd attended at the Palace.

As they sat next to each other on the crimson, diamond-tucked seat, Rieker reached over and slid his gloved hand over Tiki's, entwining his fingers through hers. "Are you nervous?"

Tiki leaned against his shoulder, tightening her grip. "A little. I just hope that if a—" she hesitated— "a *stranger* is at the ball tonight we'll be able to recognize them. I'm concerned if they're wearing a glamour they won't look any different than the next person."

"I know. That same thought has occurred to me. Especially if it's someone who has been entrenched within the palace for a period of time, then no doubt they'll be skilled at blending in."

IT WAS A different experience to be delivered to the grand entry of Buckingham Palace. Sentries stood lock-kneed and impassive in their red coats and tall black hats, spears clutched in one hand, as their carriage pulled through the bricked archway into the Quadrangle.

Geoffrey pulled the horses to a stop and one of the queen's men held the door for them. Rieker stepped down through the small opening first and reached back to take Tiki's hand. For a second, she felt like royalty as she gathered her gown and stepped down from the carriage.

Rieker smiled at her and tucked her hand under his arm. "Shall we go mingle?" His lips curved in a half-grin.

"Lord William Becker Richmond and Miss Tara Dunbar." The crier announced them into the ball.

Before them, a kaleidoscope of flowing skirts and black suits swayed around a huge room. Tiki caught her breath at the sheer magnificence before her. Music filled the air. Chandeliers sparkled from the high ceilings. Tall pedestals ablaze with candlelight were positioned in long rows. Soaring walls, covered with deep red wallpaper, were lined with large, gilt-framed pictures, giving the spacious room surprising warmth and intimacy. The gold ceiling above was divided into rectangles of gold and etched with deep blues and reds.

For a moment the dark images of the Palace of Mirrors filled her mind, a stark contrast to the color and brightness before her. What would the Palace of Mirrors be like when the Seelies were in power? Would it be bright and light like the vision before her now?

As they stood poised on the top of the steps Tiki became uncomfortably aware of the number of heads who turned to gaze at them with abject curiosity.

"What are they looking at?" Tiki whispered out of the corner of her mouth.

"They are looking at you, of course." Arthur's dry voice at her elbow startled Tiki.

"Hello, Prince Arthur." Tiki dipped into a curtsy.

"Because," Arthur continued, as he strolled alongside Tiki into the room, "William has never brought a female companion to a ball before." His eyes had a mischievous glint in them. "You are the first and they all want to see the creature who has captured the elusive Lord Richmond's heart."

"Arthur." Rieker' voice held a warning. "Don't be telling tales out of school. You'll fill Tiki's head with a load of rubbish and she'll be afraid to be seen in public with me."

Tiki's cheeks burned at the innuendo in Arthur's comment yet at the same time a strange pride glowed inside her chest.

A young lord, dressed in coattails of grey silk, greeted Rieker and pulled him away.

"I'll be right back," Rieker said to Tiki over his shoulder as he disappeared into the crowd. "Arthur, mind your manners."

Left alone with the prince, Tiki laughed to hide her embarrassment. "Well, if that's the reason people are staring I'm sure it won't take long for their curiosity to be sated. Then they'll wonder whatever possessed him to invite someone as plain as I in the first place."

Arthur reached for Tiki's hand. "Trust me when I say that no one would ever consider you plain. I've no doubt that jealousy will sharpen some tongues tonight, but the fact remains you are the one who is here with him." He smiled at Tiki and bowed over her fingers. "You should never forget," he added in a low voice, "that William's love for you is a powerful truth."

Tiki tried to hide her surprise at Arthur's comment. It was almost as if he'd been privy to the terrible tug-of-war her emotions had been playing inside her heart. She watched the prince's back as he departed, a new confidence filling her. If Arthur accepted her as a match for William, then anything was possible. As if in response, Rieker came up behind her and slid his arm around her shoulders, pulling her into his conversation with a different well-dressed lord and his young daughter.

"Charles, have I introduced you to Miss Tara Dunbar?" Rieker made the introductions as if there were no class distinction between Tiki and the middle-aged man. His white hair was wispy upon the top of his shiny pate and the buttons across his stomach strained against the white silk fabric as he gave a slight bow. "So pleased to make your acquaintance. Allow me to introduce my only child, Marie Claire."

The girl was about Tiki's age, with a rosy bloom in her porcelain cheeks that matched the beautiful, demure gown of pink velvet she wore. Her red hair however, would have favored a cooler color. There was a glow of excitement in her eyes as she stood next to her father. The girl's cheeks turned even pinker as she curtsied to Rieker, clearly smitten. "She is sixteen now, after all," her father said, "and allowed to attend parties." Charles smiled fondly at her, clearly doting.

"So nice to meet you," Tiki said with a smile. The girl reminded her of a well-fed, prized hen. She could imagine the sheltered life in which Marie Claire had grown up. Tiki couldn't help but picture how beautiful Fiona would look, dressed in a similar gown.

After Charles and Marie Claire left, Rieker turned to Tiki. His lips twisted in a teasing smile as he moved close and lifted her chin. The intimate pose brought a sharp memory of Sean tilting her chin in a similar fashion when they'd returned to London. For a minute, Tiki thought Rieker was going to kiss her in public. "Now, Miss Dunbar, where is that dance card?"

"William, surely you're not going to let her monopolize you the whole evening, are you?"

Rieker and Tiki turned together to find Isabelle Cavendish standing there, familiar blue-green eyes staring back at them. Larkin. Tiki's stomach surged with an unfamiliar emotion as her gaze swept the girl from the ground up. Was she glad the faerie had escaped Donegal? She didn't know for sure.

Isabelle was wearing a striking gown of blue silk, the color of a sapphire. Her brown hair was pinned up in an elegant hairdo that cascaded in perfect sausage ringlets around her neck. Her long fingers toyed with an ivory cameo pendant that hung against the perfect skin of her chest.

"Larkin." Tiki said. "I shouldn't be surprised."

Chapter Thirty-Six

Larkin twirled once, sending her skirts flying about her ankles. "I always do love a party. Especially when you're here, William." She laid a gloved hand on Rieker's chest and smoothed the silk lapel of his black jacket.

For a second, Tiki's stomach surged with a jealous twist. How could Rieker resist someone so breathtaking? But she knew that was exactly what Larkin wanted her to feel.

"You haven't answered the question," Rieker said in a tight voice. "Why are you here? Your gambit with the stone and Donegal didn't pay off. Frankly, I'm surprised you escaped."

Larkin gave Rieker a shrewd look. "You don't enter the pit of the snake unless you have an exit strategy."

"Of course not. But surely, you're done with us now."

"I'm debating our next steps. We must push forward as time is of the essence." A fan dangled from one of Larkin's wrists and she tapped Rieker on the chest. Her eyes were as turbulent as the sea crashing to the beach. "It's only days until Beltane and there's already been an attempt on Leo's life. Your queen is in danger as are both of you." She snapped the fan open and shielded her face from all but Tiki and Rieker. "I need you alive." Her gaze flicked over to Tiki. "Sadly, I need both of you." Then she walked away.

"Arthur must have been right about 'other forces' being involved," Rieker said under his breath. "I don't think she's here because of us."

"No, she doesn't seem to be." Tiki watched the back of Larkin's dark blue dress until she disappeared in the crowd of people.

"Let's try to keep an eye on who she's talking with tonight."

The orchestra struck up a waltz and Rieker led Tiki into a throng of dancers. She slipped her right hand into Rieker's much larger, gloved hand, as he rested his other hand on her tiny waist. With a slight nod, he began the dance. At first, Tiki had to concentrate and count the steps of the waltz in her head. But after a moment, she began to relax and the steps came naturally. The music soared around them, Rieker guiding her across the room.

The dance ended and Rieker twirled her to a stop. For just a second he slid his arm around her waist and pulled her close so their bodies pressed together, his cheek warm against hers. Then he stepped back and bowed, a perfect model of decorum.

"Thank you for the privilege of dancing with you, Miss Dunbar." He grinned at her. "As light on your feet as I imagine a faerie might be."

Tiki smiled. "Who would know better than you?"

Rieker chuckled as he lifted two drinks off the silver tray of a passing footman and proffered one to Tiki. "Let's go mingle with the crowd and see if we can spot anyone else who seems out of the ordinary. And remember to sip that. As I recall, you have a nasty habit of choking on fine wine."

Tiki smiled and slid one hand under Rieker's arm as he led her through the room. It was easy to talk with people she didn't know with Rieker by her side. He seemed to know everyone in the room. They chatted with lords, barons, dukes and duchesses, all with more titles than Tiki could track, as if they were old friends.

She could see the curiosity burning in their eyes as Rieker introduced her, but aside from a few questions about her family, which she and Rieker had practiced answering before attending tonight, their conversations were pleasant and superficial.

"WHAT DO YOU think?" Rieker asked several hours later as he pulled Tiki into a secluded corner. He cast a glance around the room, frowning. "I haven't seen anyone beyond Larkin who looks questionable to me."

Tiki brushed a piece of lint from the lapel of Rieker's coat, letting her hand linger. "Only Larkin."

"Wait here. I'm going to go ask Arthur if we can see Leo now." Rieker strode off into the crowd and Tiki moved toward the wall to sit on an upholstered bench. It felt good to rest her feet. Though the shoes that matched her gown were beautiful and exquisitely made, they had very tiny heels on which she had to balance and the pointed ends pinched her toes. The old pair of boots she'd worn as a pickpocket had been shabby and the stitches were starting to give but at least her feet could breathe and she could run for her life, if necessary. A smile curved her lips at the thought of trying to flee in these shoes. She would be forced to run on her tiptoes. Or, better yet, she'd kick them off and run barefoot.

"You look like you're enjoying yourself." Larkin—in Isabelle's glamour—slid onto the bench next to Tiki.

"Where did you come from?" Tiki asked.

"Oh, I've been here and there, watching the crowd."

It irritated Tiki at how vague Larkin always chose to be. For once, Tiki wanted to get some answers. She raised her hand to shield her mouth. "What do you know of the assassin Donegal sent after the Queen?"

To her surprise, Larkin didn't hesitate. "I know he's here in London." The faerie's voice was low and serious. "I'm expecting something to happen tonight. Donegal isn't sure who is guarding the ring now but it doesn't really matter anymore. His plan is simple enough: decimate the royal family, leaving London in chaos simply from lack of leadership. Sooner or later he will find who guards the ring of the truce and dispose of them as well." She gave Tiki a sideways glance. "Then the UnSeelie king will claim another throne."

Tiki squirmed in her seat. "There must be something that can be done."

"Perhaps," Larkin said. "Donegal plays a dangerous game. To raise a *liche* from the night, you have to give over part of your own body. This one was said to have already been staked when he was found. Donegal must have made a significant offering to revive him."

Tiki cringed. "Is it true he's eating the hearts of his victims?"

"Yes, that's the one." Larkin fanned herself and gazed around the room. "He could be here tonight."

Tiki's heart thumped against her ribs. "How is he stopped?"

"You can drive a stake through his heart, but there is only one way to guarantee he won't return—you have to destroy the body of the *liche* so he can never be raised again."

The whispered warning of the Dryad came back to Tiki. It was what she had said as well. She thought of the Ash stake that Sean had given her which she'd hidden in her bed chamber—just in case. That flimsy piece of tree hardly seemed enough to kill such a vicious creature.

Larkin tapped her fan against her knees. "We need a way to lure him to us. Creatures of his type often seem to have a predilection for young people." She gave Tiki a calculating look. "We need someone to be our bait."

Tiki scowled at the faerie. "I hope you aren't suggesting me."

"Actually, I wasn't." Larkin snapped her fan closed. "You're too important to draw Donegal's attention to you again." Larkin toyed with the pendant that hung around her neck. "I was thinking of that girl who lives with you. The dark-haired one. What's her name?"

The hair on the back of Tiki's neck stood up. "*What?*"

"Oh, look." Larkin pointed into the crowd. "Rieker has found a friend."

Tiki followed the line of Larkin's finger to the dance floor. It only took a second to recognize Rieker's tall shoulders and dark head among the swirling skirts and coattails. He was dancing with a young woman with long dark hair. She wore a gown of red velvet with an off-the-shoulder neckline that emphasized her well-endowed chest.

Tiki gasped. "Is that—"

"Yes," Larkin said in a voice that did little to hide the pleasure she was taking in the moment. "I believe it is Pashan. You met her before, didn't you? Though her glamour does a good job of making her look mortal, don't you agree?" Larkin's teeth glittered as she smiled, reminding Tiki of fangs. "I guess everybody loves a party."

Against her will Tiki's gaze returned to the dance floor in search of Rieker and Pashan. Though they moved in and out of the swirl of other dancers, it was easy to track Pashan's red dress. Even from this distance it was obvious what a striking pair they made, with Rieker's tall, dark looks and Pashan's exotic beauty.

Rieker's hand rested on the faerie's hip in a familiar way and it looked to Tiki like he was smiling into her eyes, just as he did with her. Tiki fought to keep her voice even.

"How did she recognize Rieker? He was in a glamour when she met him in the Otherworld."

"Oh that." Larkin fluttered her fan in front of her face, as if suddenly warm, though Tiki knew the faerie rarely felt a moment of discomfiture. "I invited her here tonight. Every set of eyes is helpful right now."

Tiki bit the corner of her lip, willing herself not to ask the question but she couldn't stop. "But how did she recognize Rieker?"

Larkin shrugged. "I doubt she does. I pointed William out and told her to keep an eye on him. I guess she takes her job seriously." Tiki watched as the couple twirled, both laughing at something that had been said. "Though William does seem to be enjoying himself. That's the happiest I've seen him look all night."

Chapter Thirty-Seven

Without another word, Tiki pushed herself off the bench and hurried through the crowd. She didn't know where she was going but she wasn't going to sit there one minute longer and let Larkin fill her head with poison. It didn't matter that Rieker was dancing with Pashan. Larkin just wanted her to think the worst.

Tiki clutched the fine silk of her skirt as she navigated the crowd, trying to cool her anger. And to suggest that Fiona be used as bait. The faerie was as heartless as she was beautiful. Tiki came to a stop in a corner of the large room, maneuvering so she was hidden behind a group of women chattering. She released the death hold she had on her skirts and took a deep breath to calm down as she tried to smooth the wrinkles away.

"Tiki?"

She turned and recognized him instantly. Slouched against a nearby wall, he was dressed in a black suit with long tails, his sun-kissed blond hair falling carelessly across his forehead above familiar blue eyes. He held a half-full glass of wine, and slowly swirled the burgundy contents as he watched her.

"Dain?"

"Or perhaps I should say Miss Dunbar?" He pushed off the wall and reached for her hand— "so nice to see you again." He bowed and kissed her fingers, his mocking eyes locked on hers.

Tiki's breath caught in her throat. What was he doing here? She wondered if he'd thought of her half as many times as she'd thought of him since she'd returned to London. Tonight he looked every inch the charming and handsome aristocrat—so different from the gruff and wounded Sean. "How are you?"

"Still alive, which is saying something anymore." He straightened, releasing her hand. "And yourself? No worse the wear for your adventure?"

Tiki threaded her fingers together, trying to maintain her composure. "Fine, th—" she swallowed her words. "Yes, just fine." There was a magnetism to him that was as compelling as the first time she'd met him, but there was also a sharp edge tonight, as if he were angry.

Dain smiled, his expression softening. "Had I not met you in London before and seen this different glamour I would never have recognized you tonight—though you are breathtaking in either form. Your gown reminds me of the hills of Ireland, though even the lady *Ériu* herself doesn't hold a candle to the beautiful green of your eyes."

Tiki felt like a fly caught in the snare of a spider's web—a beautiful spider who she tried to convince herself not to trust.

"I see William found his way safely back to London, as well," he said.

Tiki forced herself to take a step back. She needed to remember he was dangerous.

"Yes." She fingered the dance card that hung from her wrist as she wondered if Dain recognized the similarities in his and Rieker's features, as well. "What are you doing here?"

The faerie measured her over the rim of his glass before he took a long draught of wine. "In case you haven't heard there's a war going on."

"And you felt the need for fresh air?"

His lips twisted in a half-smile. "Usually that is the case but my presence was requested tonight." He reached out and fingered the edge of her dance card. "Actually, I wanted to see you."

Tiki's heart skipped a beat. "Me?"

"I'm afraid I've been caught in your web," he said. There was something breakable in his face. "You haunt my thoughts like no other." Dain's gaze traced the contours of her face then dropped to the pale skin of Tiki's chest where the swell of her breasts rose and fell above the low-cut gown with the erratic beat of her heart. His gaze burned a path as tangible as a fingertip caressing her skin. She shivered—whether in pleasure or fear, she was unsure.

His words were soft. "Maybe it's because I've placed my life in your hands." He took her hand, turning her palm up and ran his fingertips gently over her skin. "Have you kept my secret?"

Tiki stared into his eyes, powerless to look away. "Yes," she whispered.

"Tara—there you are." Arthur's voice caught her by surprise and Tiki jerked around with a guilty start. The prince nodded at Dain. "Pardon me for interrupting but I need to steal Miss Dunbar away."

"Oh, yes h...hello, Arthur," Tiki stuttered. "William was looking for you." She nodded at Dain. "A pleasure to see you again." She turned and followed Arthur. She didn't need to look over her shoulder to feel the weight of Dain's gaze upon her back.

"Where is Wills?" Arthur craned his neck.

Tiki pointed in the direction of the dance floor. "He met an old friend and they've been catching up."

"Yes, well, he does know most of the group here tonight. He's been missed." Arthur lowered his voice. "Leo is anxious to talk to the both of you. Why don't I take you to him and then I'll come back and find Wills?"

Arthur escorted Tiki from the room. As they walked through the ornate hallways the image of Dain replayed in Tiki's mind. Why was Dain here? Behind the sarcasm had that been longing in his eyes? Tiki's thoughts were a confusing blur as the prince led her down grand hallways lined with paintings, oversized pots of the finest porcelain and marble figurines frozen in various poses.

"Here we are." An armed guard stood at stiff attention outside a door. At Arthur's arrival the guard pulled open one side of a giant pair of doors. Arthur motioned for Tiki to enter the room. "After you."

The space was very large, with grand ceilings and paired columns around the perimeter. One small sitting area had been carved out of the enormous room, with chairs circled around a hearty fire to create the illusion of an intimate setting. The back of Leo's brown head was visible in one of the seats.

Tiki hurried across the room, wishing Rieker was with her. Arthur called to his brother.

"I've brought Miss Tara up to talk to you. I'm going to go round up Wills and bring him up as well." Arthur disappeared back out the door, shutting it quietly.

"Leo?" Tiki called.

"Lovely Tara." Leo's voice sounded weak, but he raised a hand to signal he was aware of her approach.

Tiki rounded the corner of the chair to face Leo. He wore a purple silk dressing robe with the royal insignia of a lion and a unicorn emblazoned on one breast. A rich satin blanket of purple and gold covered his knees.

She was shocked at how thin he'd become since she'd seen him last. His brown hair lay limp on his head. Though he sat upright in the chair, his shoulders sagged and Tiki wondered if he had the strength to stand on his own. His neck was encased in a white shirt with a high neck of ruffles, but underneath Tiki could see layers of white padding wrapped around his throat.

"Forgive me for not getting up. These blasted wounds have sucked the life out of me," Leo said. His eyes still held a hint of mischief in them, as he held his hand out to her. "It's so good to see you again, Tara. You grow more beautiful, if that is even possible. You are indeed a sight for sore eyes."

Tiki dropped into a curtsy that Leo waved away. "Pull up a chair so I can feast my eyes upon you before Wills arrives and gets all territorial. I'm sorry I'm not at my best at the moment."

Tiki pulled a chair up and sat down, spreading the folds of her skirt so they wouldn't wrinkle. "You've been through a terrible ordeal."

The large door leading into the drawing room swung open and Rieker hurried into the room. His long legs crossed the room in quick strides. Tiki didn't miss the questioning look he sent her way before he hurried to Leo's side, clasping his hand.

"Well, Leo, you still look like something the cat drug in."

Leo gave a weak laugh as Rieker pulled a chair close and sat down, flipping his tails out behind him. "As it turns out, I feel more like something the cat coughed up." The smile faded from Leo's lips as he propped his elbow on the arm of the chair and rested his head against his fingers. "I'm lucky to have survived. I know that much. He wanted to kill me—I could feel it."

The young prince reached a shaking hand to grasp a glass of water that sat on a nearby side table. He closed his eyes for a moment, as though in pain.

"I forgot to ask before, did he speak?" Rieker asked.

"There was a hoarse sort of breathing—disturbing, really, but I don't recall him saying any words." Leo picked at the fabric of the blanket that covered his knees before he cast a sideways glance at Rieker. "Was he—" he hesitated— "human—do you think?"

Rieker hesitated, running his hand through his hair, creating tousled waves. "It's hard to say."

Leo nodded. "I thought not."

"Everyone in the royal family needs to be guarded at all times until we catch him," Rieker said. "But I doubt he'll be back soon. He knows you'll be watching for him now."

Leo let out a heavy sigh. "They were right, weren't they? It's more than the bloody ring this time."

Rieker nodded. "Much more. It's a fight for the power to control all of the Otherworld, as well as the British throne. That's what Donegal wants."

Leo's face was gray and Tiki could tell their visit was exhausting him. Rieker stood up, holding a hand out for Tiki.

"Not to worry, Leo. We'll get this sorted. This battle has waged for centuries. We're not about to give up what is ours." Rieker leaned forward and patted Leo on the knee. "In the meantime, you just focus on getting well."

Leo reached for a small bottle on the table. A cork stopper was shoved into the top of the clear glass. "I saved this for you, Wills. Been meaning to give it to you each time you've visited." He held the bottle up for them to see. "I wager you're the only one around here who might be able to make use of it."

Rieker's brow furrowed as he squinted to make out the contents. "What is it?"

"A handful of hair I apparently ripped from the head of my assailant. They found it clutched in my hand after the attack." Leo held the bottle out to Rieker. "Here, you take it. Perhaps it will help you in recognizing him." His lips wavered in a thin smile. "Look for the chap with a bald spot on one side."

Chapter Thirty-Eight

"What are you going to do with that?" Tiki motioned to the bottle in Rieker's hand. Upon closer examination they discovered the bottle held strands of jet black hair.

"I have no idea," he said as he slipped the container into his pocket.

"It's a bit gruesome, don't you think?"

He shrugged. "We might find it helpful later." Rieker slid an arm around her shoulders and pulled her close as they walked down the secluded hallway. "Where did you go?"

"For some reason Larkin delights in antagonizing me. Tonight I didn't feel like listening to her, so I left." Tiki told him of running to hide in the corner, but made no mention of Dain. "Then Arthur found me and insisted that I come right then to see Leo."

"Well, I apologize for my delay." Rieker lowered his voice. "It turns out there are others besides Larkin here tonight. Do you remember that dark-haired faerie who was so chummy with Sean when we were in the Palace of Mirrors?"

Tiki's reaction was guarded. "Yes."

"She's here tonight, as well. I noticed her in the crowd when I went looking for Arthur. She approached me and told me she was a friend of Isabelle's and suggested we should dance. I didn't really know how I could say no, especially as there were others watching us. I figured it was a good opportunity to see what information I could get out her."

"Did you?"

"I asked her point-blank why there were two faeries here tonight—" he chuckled under his breath— "I wish you could have seen the look on her face when she realized that I knew what she was—and she said 'two? I thought there were five of us.'"

Tiki put a hand on Rieker' arm and pulled him to a stop. "*Five?*"

"Of course, when she realized that I hadn't known, she clammed up. She told me to ask Larkin. But obviously, they must be expecting something to happen."

"That is exactly what Larkin said too. That they expected something to happen tonight." Tiki glanced around the deserted hallway, eyeing the shadows gathered in the corners. "The entire palace is under guard," she said in a low voice. "I can't imagine anyone trying to attack a royal here but it concerns me you might be a possible target."

"I hardly think I'm going to be attacked in the middle of a party." Rieker said. "But it does make me wonder what they know—or what they think they know."

As they returned to the dance floor Tiki couldn't shake the thread of worry tightening around her. The ballroom was more crowded when they returned. The wine had loosened the inhibitions of many in the group and gales of laughter rang out over the roar of conversation and music. Tiki followed Rieker through the teeming couples, scanning the crowd for any sign of Dain.

They were halfway across the dance floor when the orchestra struck up a lively polka. The area was suddenly swarmed with couples chasing and hopping in time with the music. As they kept being stopped by people dancing in front of them, Rieker finally swooped Tiki into his arms, dancing her in a polka across the room and to the opposite edge of the floor. Tiki giggled as they spun to a stop. Her skirts swirled about her ankles and she clutched Rieker's arm until the room stopped spinning.

She looked up to find herself standing next to Dain.

"Oh, Dain," she said, without thinking, "there you are." For once, the vivid color of his eyes seemed shrouded.

"Who is your friend, Tiki?" Rieker asked, a strange note in his voice. "I saw you talking to him earlier."

Tiki's heart dropped into her silk shoes. Rieker had seen her talking to Dain? She imagined what that must have looked like from a distance, with Dain holding her hand as she stared into his mesmerizing eyes. With a start she realized Rieker had danced them next to Dain on purpose.

Dain held his hand out. "Lord Brendain Browne."

Tiki looked at Dain in surprise. He was a lord, too?

Rieker clutched the offered hand in a firm grip. "Lord William Becker Richmond."

Silence as heavy as a stone filled the space between the two young men as they measured each other.

Seeing the two of them standing together face to face caused an uncomfortable twisting in the pit of Tiki's stomach. They were the same height with shoulders that filled the outline of their jackets, hinting at the strength that lay beneath. Their faces were chiseled with good looks, though Rieker's nose leaned ever so slightly to the right and Dain had a slight hook to the bridge of his nose. The differences were subtle, however. Their hair color varied, though the texture was the same. But the similarities stopped with their eyes: Rieker's were smoky and filled with shadows while Dain's blue eyes were as clear as a cloudless summer sky.

"William, this is Dain," Tiki said.

"Tiki has mentioned you." Rieker said, releasing his hand. Tiki noticed he didn't smile and the muscle along his jaw line flexed.

"Strange," Dain replied with a half-smile, "she hasn't mentioned you."

Tiki's mouth dropped open at his lie. A grin teased the corner of his lips as he gave her a sly wink.

"I see you two have finally met." Larkin appeared out of nowhere. Unsmiling and tense, she stepped between the two of them and slid a hand under each of their elbows. "William, you're looking a bit hostile. I thought you might be pleased to meet Dain."

Larkin lifted her chin at Tiki. "You see it, don't you?" The faerie, disguised as Isabelle, didn't wait for Tiki's answer. "Unfortunately, we don't have time for reunions right now." Her expression darkened. "We have more important matters to attend." She reached for Tiki's arm. "We're about ready to make our move against Donegal, but the Macanna want to meet you. They need proof you exist."

Tiki jerked her arm away and stepped back. "Am I to be your bait, then?"

Rieker's voice simmered with anger. "She's not going with you."

Larkin's expression turned black. She ignored Rieker and faced Tiki. "You are *needed*. Without the Macanna, what remains of the Seelie court has no hope of overcoming Donegal. He's become too strong." Her lips pressed together in a thin line as she tried to control her anger. Through gritted teeth she said, "They need a reason to believe."

"She has a family here that needs her, as well." Rieker took Tiki's hand and held it firmly. "She went to the Otherworld once for nothing and was almost captured by Donegal. It took her days to get back—no thanks to you. You can fight your own battles now."

Larkin's anger felt like a wave washing over them. "Why can't I make you understand, William, that what happens in my world affects your world? If Donegal continues to rule both courts we are *all* doomed to a never-ending war. You think what you saw last winter was something to be concerned about?"

Her eyes flashed fire. "You can't even imagine what devastation Donegal can wreak on London if there is no one to stop him." She moved a step closer to Rieker. "You've seen the storms. Donegal won't stop until every Seelie is dead or enslaved. Then he'll finish London." Tiki's hand felt cold in Rieker's as Larkin's voice got sharper. "Natural disasters: fires, earthquakes or perhaps a tainted water supply? He can kill thousands. He can wipe out half of this city in a blink."

She pointed a razor-sharp finger at Rieker. "Don't think for a second that he won't send the *liche* after you, William." She flung her arm in Tiki's direction— "or after her when he learns the truth. It's only a matter of time."

"What exactly does Tara have to do with our world?" Dain's voice was a sea of calm and Tiki let out her breath. "There seems to be some question as to whether she is mortal or fey."

Larkin jerked her head towards him as if she'd forgotten he was there. Her eyes were poisonous chips of blue-green ice. "There's no question. She is fey. There's not a drop of mortal blood in her veins."

Tiki wavered on her feet. Not a drop of mortal blood. Larkin's words shook her to the core. Both Rieker and Dain reached out an arm to steady her. Tiki didn't miss the warning glare that Rieker shot him.

Dain held his hands up as if in surrender. "Apparently that's news to some of us. Why is she so important to this war?"

"Because she is marked with *an fáinne sí.*" Larkin spat out the words. "Just like Finn."

For the first time Tiki saw a truly spontaneous emotion on Dain's face. He swept Tiki with a bewildered look. "*Her?*"

"Show him." Larkin commanded.

Tiki stood paralyzed.

"If you don't, I will." Larkin moved so fast her hands were a blur. One second she was standing several feet away, the next she had yanked Tiki's sleeve up to reveal the thin black lines that twisted and swirled around her left wrist.

Dain's expression shifted from shock to wonder. He whispered words that sounded like Gaelic before he bowed his head. "I am your servant."

"*Stop.*" Rieker voice was ragged with fury. "This has gone far enough. We're done here. Leave. Us. Alone." He pulled Tiki from Larkin's grasp and slipped an arm around her shoulders, leading her away from the two faeries.

"Guttersnipe."

There was something in Larkin's voice that made Tiki look over her shoulder.

"I know about Clara."

A wisp of fear flamed in Tiki's stomach as the blond faerie's lips turned up in a gloating grin.

Chapter Thirty-Nine

O utside Buckingham Palace, the killer waited patiently, hidden among the shadows as if wrought from darkness. The Queen and her family were too closely guarded to reach tonight, but there were others who would feed him until the right opportunity presented itself.

One young girl in particular had caught his eye. Mr. Fox licked his lips in anticipation.

Chapter Forty

The ride home in the carriage was cold and quiet. Tiki huddled alone on the seat, clutching her cloak around her shoulders, trying to stop Larkin's parting words from echoing in an endless loop in her head.

Rieker sat across from her, jaw clenched, staring out the window. The last time he'd been this angry was months ago when, not knowing his family was dead, she'd had accused him of being spoiled.

But now, there was another worry. Larkin had said she knew about Clara. It had been a threat—but what exactly did Larkin know? Tiki closed her eyes and shuddered as goosebumps crawled across her skin like tiny spiders. Clara was hers. How did Larkin know something about the little girl that Tiki didn't?

They arrived at Grosvenor Square and Rieker stalked in ahead of her. Tiki followed more slowly. How could she make things better? They were both upset about Larkin—by her manipulations and her secrets. But right now, Rieker was acting like he was jealous. Not without reason, a small voice whispered in the back of her head. Tiki sighed. What was it about Dain that drew her to him?

She kicked off her shoes and walked barefoot down the hallway, her dress dragging behind with a quiet shushing. Maybe tomorrow things would make more sense.

Upstairs, Tiki checked that Toots, Johnny and Shamus were asleep, before tiptoeing up another level to check on Fiona and Clara. When she stood next to Clara's bed and stared down at the mass of blond curls on the pillow and the contented smile on the little girl's face, a surge of love brought tears to her eyes. Larkin didn't know anything. Clara was exactly where she belonged.

THE NEXT MORNING Clara screamed with laughter as Toots chased her through the house, trying to steal her homemade wings. Shamus was gone building school furniture for Rieker's free school.

"Johnny's taking a nap," Fiona announced, coming into the parlor where Tiki sat by the fire. "He's feeling better."

"He seems much better lately," Tiki said.

"Mrs. B. said she thinks the worst is over," Fiona said with a broad smile.

Tiki nodded. She'd been thinking about Rieker and Dain, the two of them standing there glaring at each other, like matched bookends. Larkin was never far from her thoughts either—like a nightmare from which she couldn't awake.

"Do you think Rieker will send Johnny back to Charing Cross when he's well?" Fiona asked.

Tiki turned toward the other girl. "I couldn't say, Fi." She hadn't seen Rieker today. Apparently he'd left before dawn. "But I hope not."

"Teek." Clara shrieked as she ran into the room and flung herself onto Tiki's lap. "Save me," she giggled. "Toots is trying to get my wings. He wants to hide them from me." Tiki glanced towards the empty doorway as she pulled Clara onto her lap.

"I think you've flown too fast for him. I don't see any sign of Toots."

The little girl gasped for breath. "That's because he went with Dain but he'll be right back."

Tiki froze. "What?" Had Dain been here? A mix of emotions rose in her chest. Had Larkin put him up to this?

"Dain again?" Fiona gave the girl a sideways glance. "Did he ride his white horse?"

"No, I didn't see the horse. Her name's Aeveen." Tiki blinked in surprise at Clara's knowledge as the little girl smoothed Tiki's long hair with her fingers. "He said maybe I could come next time but I told him I couldn't go without askin' you first." She leaned close and whispered, "I told Toots he better not go without askin' either, but he just laughed at me."

Tiki took a deep breath and forced herself to remain calm. She twisted one of Clara's soft curls around her finger. "That was very good of you to stay home. I'll talk to Toots when he comes back about telling us before he leaves next time."

"He won't be gone long. Dain just wanted to show him something." Clara's face glowed with excitement. "Maybe it's another horse?"

"Could be." Tiki pretended to be unperturbed by news of Toots's departure. Why would Dain take Toots? Was this another ploy to manipulate her into doing what Larkin wanted?

"I wonder what color the horse is?" Clara mused. "The white one had bells tied to its mane with red ribbons and…" Clara chattered happily.

Tiki's mind raced. Where could she send Fiona, Clara and Toots to hide until she and Rieker got this situation resolved one way or the other? Was there any place that was safe? Would Mr. and

Mrs. Bosworth consent to be their chaperones? Or should she send them with Shamus?

Less than thirty minutes had passed when the sound of Toot's boots echoed down the hallway in their direction. He catapulted through the door and rushed toward Tiki.

"What're you on about?" Fiona asked, raising her head from the embroidery she was working on to give him the once over. "Clara's been talking about that Dain chap again."

Toots flopped on the floor in front of the fire and held out shaking fingers to the flames as if chilled. Instead of the euphoria that the boy had experienced on his last trip to the Otherworld, this time Tiki could see that he was horribly upset.

"Toots?" Tiki asked. "What is it?"

There was a long moment of silence then Toots jerked around to look at her. His freckles were bright against his pale skin as his face furrowed into a knotted expression. Tiki could see he was trying desperately not to cry.

"Dain came again. Asked me to go with him for a bit." He looked guilty. "So I did."

Tiki nodded. "That's what Clara said."

"I thought maybe I could get that golden bridle for you, Teek. You know—" he motioned to the room around them— "so we could live in a flat of our own if Rieker kicks us out. But—"

"Yes?" Tiki kept her voice gentle, but her heart was thudding. Something was very wrong.

Toots burst into tears. "They killed all the horses. Those beautiful horses that could run like the wind—" a gut-wrenching sob ripped from his throat— "they're dead."

Tiki almost spilled Clara onto the floor. *"What?"* Visions of those beautiful creatures in the fields of O'Donoghue's farm at the entrance to Wychwood Forest filled her eyes. "What are you talking about? Who killed them?"

Tiki carried Clara on one hip as she went and crouched by Toots on the floor, putting her free arm around him. Clara clung to Tiki and wrapped her other little arm around Toots as far as she could reach, resting her head on Tiki's shoulder.

"Dain said Donegal did it." Toots sobbed against Tiki's chest. "He wanted me to tell you it's only the beginning." The young boy took a shuddering breath. "He said to tell you that Donegal will destroy everything of beauty in his quest for the Seelie throne."

"Shhhh." Tiki rested her cheek on the top of Toot's head and rubbed his back as she rocked, trying to calm him. "Don't think about it. I don't know why Dain would show you something so awful."

"Because—" Toots leaned back, his tear-streaked face a mute testament to his sorrow— "he said you're the only one who can stop Donegal."

Chapter Forty-One

"Tiki!" Rieker hurried into the parlor later that afternoon, an excited look on his face. He'd just returned home, his cheeks ruddy from the cold air. He gave no indication he'd been out of sorts the night before. "Can you join me in the study for a minute?"

Tiki pushed out of the chair and followed his tall form down the hallway, pulling her black shawl tighter around her shoulders. Another storm was brewing over London and this one threatened snow. The temperature had dipped below freezing, almost unheard-of weather for late April in England. Even with the fires burning heartily it was hard to keep the cool air at bay.

"I've got something to tell you, too." She was still horribly upset by the fact that Dain had taken Toots without her knowledge and at the news Toots had shared upon his return. She'd been waiting for Rieker's return to tell him.

Rieker held the door to the study then closed it softly behind Tiki. "I've been doing some research," he said, as he sat down next to her, more animated than she'd seen him in a long time. "I've found a stone in London that might be what we're looking for."

Tiki slumped back against her chair. "Oh, you're not on about that, still, are you?" She fingered the carved chess pieces on the table between them, frozen in an unfinished game. "That story about the Stone of Tara must have been something Larkin fabricated just to challenge Donegal. There are more important things to worry about."

Rieker's brows pulled down in a perplexed frown. "If that were the case, what would it gain her? And what more important things?"

Tiki shrugged. "Who knows with Larkin? I fear I was simply the diversion she needed to get those men from the Macanna into the hall and ask for her wing back. She doesn't want Donegal to hang it on his wall like a trophy." She waved her hand. "It doesn't matter. I don't believe the stone is real. I don't believe anything Larkin says." She raised her eyebrows. "A stone roar? Ridiculous."

"I see," Rieker said slowly. "What are the 'more important' things you mentioned?"

Tiki recounted Toots' story of Dain taking him to see the dead horses and the message the young boy had returned with.

Rieker's eyes narrowed as he listened. "That is exactly why we can't stop looking for the Stone. It's the one piece that might give us a bit of power, instead of always being at the mercy of the fey. " He stabbed his finger in her direction. "You are part of this, Tiki, whether you want to be or not. If you weren't—Larkin wouldn't be wasting her time on you."

He leaned across the table. "Listen to what I found out. There's a stone in the City that is considered to be the 'heart' of London. A place where deals are sworn and oaths are forged." He raised his eyebrows. "There's a myth associated with it that says if the stone is safe, so then is London." Rieker reached for one of the chess pieces and slid the white Queen across the board to an open square in front of Tiki. "That sounds like a stone that might be important to both mortals and the fey."

Tiki sat up. Rieker was right. If there was some way to turn the tables, to not always be waiting for Larkin to reveal another piece of the puzzle—then perhaps they could protect themselves—protect the ones they loved. "Does the stone have a name?"

"They call it the London Stone. Apparently there are references to the stone that date back to the Middle Ages."

"You don't really think—"

Rieker's voice turned eager. "What can it hurt to go lay a hand on the thing and see what happens?"

"Where is it?"

"Just over on Cannon Street. Set in the wall of a church there." Rieker stood up and grabbed her hands. "We can be there in less than half an hour."

SNOWFLAKES DRIFTED DOWN from a leaden sky as their carriage made its way across the City.

"Snow in April," Rieker said with disgust. "That tells you something's not right with the world."

Tiki pressed her nose against the window. "I love the snow. It's like magic falling from the heavens." She cast a cautious glance at Rieker. "Maybe it's a sign?"

One corner of his mouth turned up in a grin that somehow looked slightly wicked. "We'll soon find out, won't we?"

The carriage slowed and Rieker was on his feet and out the door before the wheels stopped rolling. He offered a hand to Tiki, helping her down the narrow steps. The church had a brick façade with an arched entry, tucked between two other buildings. A bell tower stretched skyward to the right of the entry and the bells began to toll as they neared, their clappers clanging against the copper sides.

"St. Swithin," Tiki read the nameplate on the side of the building. "I've never heard of this church before."

"Not unexpected, given there's a church on every bloody corner in London," Rieker said.

Snowflakes landed on Tiki's hair and eyelashes then melted away. She lifted her face to the sky but Rieker grasped her hand and led her up the three stone steps into the entry.

"Come along," he said, clearly trying to hide his excitement. "We can enjoy the snow after you touch the stone." He tugged on the great door, holding it open for Tiki to pass through.

A quiet hush greeted them as they entered the church. It was almost like going back in time to a place that had not been overrun with humanity and poverty.

Tiki tilted her head back to stare up at the ornate arches of the nave. "Do you know where the stone is?"

"Right there." Rieker's voice was quiet as though to match the silence of the church.

Tiki turned to where Rieker was pointing. Sure enough, sitting at waist-height in an alcove built into the wall of the church, sat a large chunk of stone. It was off-white in color, almost yellow, and somewhat square in shape with rounded edges. There was nothing remarkable about its appearance.

Rieker led Tiki up close to the rock.

"Can I help you?" A priest, with a round, friendly face, approached them.

"Yes, hello." Rieker motioned toward the alcove. "We were wondering—is this the London Stone?"

"Oh, you've heard of it, then?" the older man asked. He wore simple robes of grey with a brown mantle that reached to his knees. His brown hair was cropped short. He rested a hand on the stone's cratered surface. "It's quite famous, you know, a landmark here in Cannon Street for centuries. They say it was part of an altar that Brutus of Troy used when he founded London back in 1070 BC."

Tiki inhaled sharply. "Really?"

The priest smiled. "It's also said to be the stone from which King Arthur drew his famous sword."

"Excalibur?" Rieker sounded equally impressed.

The priest nodded as he patted the rock like a pet. "One of the many legends associated with the stone." He clasped his hands in front of himself and stepped back. "Feel free to stay as long as you'd like."

"Thank you," Tiki and Rieker said at the same time. The priest nodded and went back the way he'd come, his shoes silent on the stone floors.

"Could this be what Larkin was looking for?" Tiki stared at the stone in fascination. "It certainly sounds important, though it doesn't look like much. And—" she turned and gazed around the church— "it's not really hidden."

"Only one way to find out." Rieker tipped his head toward the rock. "Touch it and see what happens."

Tiki looked from Rieker to the stone. "You can't believe that hunk of rock is going to make a sound?"

"I didn't believe in faeries a few years ago," Rieker said.

"All right, all right." Tiki took a step closer and held her hand out. Her breath caught in her throat and her heart was suddenly racing like a steam engine. Far above their head the church bells rang out for the quarter hour and Tiki let out a squeal and yanked her hand back. "It startled me," she said defensively.

"Just do it, Teek." Rieker stepped closer. The peals of the bells faded away and they were enveloped in quiet again.

Tiki nodded. She took a deep breath and stepped forward, placing both hands squarely on top of the stone.

Silence.

The stone didn't roar.

She stepped back and wiped her hands, her cheeks suddenly warm as a mix of emotions rushed through her: relief, disappointment, embarrassment. "I knew it was ridiculous to think a stone would make a noise."

Rieker's shoulders slumped. "I thought this might be it." He slid an arm around her shoulders and pulled her close. "We'll just have to keep looking."

Chapter Forty-Two

"Leo," Arthur looked up from his desk where he sat writing some notes. "It's good to see you up and about. Are you feeling better?"

Leo nodded as he slowly walked across the room and sank into a chair opposite his brother. He wore a dressing robe over his pajamas, a white bandage still taped to his neck. "I think the bleeding has stopped."

"Excellent news. You'll need to take it easy for a few more weeks to rebuild your strength." Arthur's forehead was creased with worry.

"What is it?" Leo asked. "What's happened?"

Arthur's shoulders sagged. He shoved the pen he was holding into the inkwell. "Another attack—the night of the party."

"Here?" Leo asked in surprise.

"No. In the early hours of the morning. The police are suggesting he followed her from the palace."

Leo sat up and gripped the arms of his chair. "Who was it?"

Arthur shook his head, his features twisted with regret. "Charles Bagley's daughter, Marie Claire."

"The girl?" Leo's jaw dropped. "Is she—"

"Regrettably so."

Leo's words were a whisper as he slumped back in his chair. "Tell me he didn't take her heart."

A long sigh escaped Arthur's lips as he rubbed his forehead with both hands. Though muffled, his reply was still audible. "He did."

Chapter Forty-Three

"We need to talk." Tiki stood in the doorway of Rieker's study.

He paused in mid-step from where he was pacing in front of the cold fireplace. His sleeves were rolled above his elbows and his dark hair was mussed as though he'd run his hand through the strands over and over.

Rieker pulled his chair back, the legs scraping against the wooden floor and sank into the seat. "You've made some decisions, I take it?"

Tiki nodded. She moved into the room and sank into a high-backed leather chair across from him. "I can't stand by and do nothing. If I need to go to the Otherworld to help Larkin stop this madman—that's what I'll do."

Rieker nodded, his smoky eyes were dark with shadows. "It's a big decision."

"I've heard about that girl from Arthur's party. Mrs. Bosworth was talking about it." A twinge of guilt clutched at Tiki's chest as she remembered thinking the girl to be spoiled. "She was my age. It could've been Fiona." She took a deep breath. "The next one could be you."

Rieker's voice was sober. "We've certainly seen how dangerous some of the fey can be. Donegal seems to be the worst of the lot. Are you sure you want to take the risk?"

"I have to go. I couldn't live with myself if I stood by and did nothing while others died." A quiet hush filled the room, as if they were the only two people in the world. "If I go, do you think I can make a difference? Larkin seemed to think the Macanna needed to see me. Do you think I could just show myself to them and return?"

Rieker took her hand in his long fingers. "Nothing is ever that simple with the fey, Teek." He took a deep breath. "But I agree, we can't stand by and wait for the next murder to happen." He was silent for a long moment. "I've a small manor house west of London. The Bosworth's could take the children there."

Tiki hesitated. "Is it where Larkin found you before? Where your family lived?" The grisly tale of Larkin appearing at Rieker's estate and asking him to help her the day before his entire family was drowned crossing the English channel was forever etched into her memory.

"No. It's in a town called Richmond. I keep some horses there. A stable. I don't think Larkin knows of it."

Tiki didn't ask why a town had the same last name as Rieker. At times, the magnitude of his wealth was overwhelming and seemed a chasm between them.

"You think they'll be safe there?"

Rieker nodded. "The Bosworth's can go with them. They might enjoy getting out of the City." His eyes were bright and Tiki wondered if it was excitement she saw gleaming there.

MOVING THE OTHERS to the manor house in Richmond was surprisingly easy. Toots never spoke of the terrible sight of those dead horses. Instead, he spent more time than ever in the coach house with Geoffrey, helping to care for Rieker's horses—almost as though he could protect them.

The idea of having horses to ride and fields to play in was almost more than Toots, Fiona, Johnny and Clara could imagine. Even Shamus came along. Mr. Binder had agreed to allow him some time off and he planned to work on continuing to build furniture for Rieker's new school there.

They'd told the Bosworth's that she and Rieker were going to Paris for a few weeks to check on a family estate there. For Tiki, it was a huge relief to have Shamus and Fiona know where she and Rieker were really going. If they didn't make it back, Shamus and the Bosworth's would see to it that the children were cared for.

Tiki fought tears as they hugged everyone goodbye. She could see the worry in Fi's eyes.

"Don't stay long, Tiki. Clara and Toots need you here." The changes in the fifteen year-old girl in the last few months were astonishing. Since Johnny had started living with them she was more scrupulous about washing and dressing. Her wavy brown hair shone as did her clear skin. Her face, which had been painfully thin, was now angled in an attractive way, her high cheekbones accenting the sparkle in her eyes.

"I promise, I'll be back as soon as I can," Tiki whispered as she hugged Fiona, now like a sister to her.

"Don't you worry, Miss Tiki," Johnny stood behind Fiona, leaning on an old wooden cane. "I'll keep an eye on things." His hair was still a wild tangle of waves but three good meals a day and a warm place to sleep at night were making a difference in his appearance. His face was less gaunt and Tiki didn't get the same sense that he was planning some sort of dodgy activity.

Shamus had said his goodbyes earlier, disliking any public display of emotion. He'd held Tiki's hand for a long moment, almost as if he could hold her there. "Stay close to Rieker, Tiki," he'd said in his slow, steady way. "He needs you as much as you need him."

It was a strange statement, coming from Shamus, who rarely gave advice. But little escaped Shamus' watchful eye and his words warmed Tiki's heart.

She leaned forward and kissed his cheek. "I promise, Shamus."

Saying goodbye to Toots was easier than she'd expected. He was so excited to be in the country with real live horses that he could hardly contain himself.

"Teek, did you see the bay with the black mane? Mr. Bosworth said she was just my size an' that I could ride her tomorrow. Can you believe it?" He jumped up and down as if he was about to burst at the seams with enthusiasm.

"I'm sure you and the bay will become fast friends. When we get back you can show us everything you've learned."

Saying goodbye to Clara was a different matter. The little girl's lower lip quivered as she patted Tiki's shoulder and smoothed her hair. "But I don't understand *why* you have to go. Why can't I come with you, Teek?" Her young voice was higher than normal and thick with emotion. A large tear escaped her lower lid and rolled down her pale cheek to plop onto Tiki's hand. "I could help you. I *know* I could."

Tiki bit her lip to hold back her own tears. She would give anything not to leave Clara. She was so little still—she needed Tiki to be home with her. But Tiki knew she had to go, or they would forever live with one eye open at night, fearful of who or what might be looking for them.

"You help Fiona with her stitching and keep an eye on Toots while he rides. We'll be back before you know it." Tiki pressed her lips together to stop their trembling. "And Mrs. Bosworth always needs help in the kitchen." Her voice cracked and her eyes filled with tears. She motioned to Doggie, the stuffed animal that Clara had clutched in her arms. "You can take Doggie for a walk every day. She'll like living in the country."

Another tear broke free and streamed down Clara's face. "Okay Tiki." She rubbed her hand on Tiki's shoulder as if to console the older girl. "I'll be good while yer gone."

TIKI SOBBED ON the way back to London. Rieker sat next to her in the carriage, his arm wrapped protectively around her shaking shoulders.

"I know it's for the best," she choked as she rested her head against his chest, "but I just don't want to leave them alone, unprotected."

"That's why we're going, Teek. Because we can't protect them the way things are."

Tiki blew her nose. "You're right. I won't cry again."

THEIR BREATH CAME out in clouds of white smoke as Tiki and Rieker walked the few blocks down Upper Brook Street and across Park Lane over to Hyde Park. The grounds were practically empty in the chilly weather, with even the most stalwart vendors seeking warmer doorways and locations to hawk their wares as twilight descended upon the City.

A jittery nervousness filled Tiki as they walked. She was doing the right thing—she was sure of it—but she was afraid, as well.

"Tell me what you're thinking," Rieker said, walking close enough to Tiki that their shoulders brushed. His gloved hand reached for hers.

She clung gratefully to Rieker's fingers. "I'm wondering if we'll find Larkin. About what will happen—if we can stop Donegal—stop the *liche*. About all of it." They turned into The Ring and followed the well-worn path beneath towering trees laden with a sparkly layer of snow, reminding Tiki of frosting. "If only I knew whether to believe Larkin or not. I would know whether we've made the right decision to get involved."

"You don't have a choice." A voice interrupted. "You've been involved."

Tiki whirled around to find Larkin standing behind her. The faerie was dressed in a slim black dress, her blond hair hidden under a black head wrap. A smoky veil covered the lower half of her face. Black gloves covered her long fingers making her appear to be encased in shadows. She didn't twirl or dance. There was no mocking note to her voice or in her smile. Instead, she was grim and focused. Only her blue-green eyes were familiar.

Tiki wasn't surprised to see the faerie. It was the reason they'd come to this place.

"How do the Macanna know about me?" Tiki asked. The idea that others—people she didn't know—believed she was Finn's daughter with a claim to the Seelie throne was hard to believe, not to mention unsettling.

"They've heard rumors about you for a long time," Larkin said. "They've been hoping for your return."

"Tell us about Finn," Rieker said.

"Finn was the last gatekeeper. A powerful and dangerous young man—to both the Seelie's and the UnSeelie's."

"You knew him well, then?"

"Finn left the Seelie court centuries ago. He didn't agree with his father so he left Ireland and started his own troop of faeries called the Macanna—a court of renegades who claimed Finn as high king." Larkin's voice softened. "I remember those times well. Crafty and clever, those lads were. The Macanna are a wild bunch and brave to a fault. Some called them a band of misfits, but others swore they could travel on the wings of the wind." She sighed with something that almost sounded like longing. "It was rumored that Finn inherited his mother's ability to see the future. That and the fact he was marked as a true high king and could control the gates to the Otherworld made him very powerful."

Larkin continued. "Donegal feared he would return and try to take control of the UnSeelie court. He was afraid that Finn wanted to reunite the courts as they had been in the very beginning." Larkin ran her fingers along a low-hanging branch, the snow falling in a white cloud to the ground. "Even the Seelie king, Muiratach, was afraid of him. Afraid of the war he might start."

Rieker cleared his throat. "But if he was so powerful, how did he die?"

"It's a sordid tale, that," Larkin replied. "Finn was murdered by the five sons of Urmac. But it's whispered it was Muiratach, his own uncle, who contracted with Urmac to kill him."

Tiki gasped. "His uncle?"

Larkin gave Tiki an arrogant half-smile. "And therein lies the best part of the story. Though all believed he was mortally wounded in that battle, Finn didn't actually die. His great steed, Lioch, carried him to safety where my sister nursed him back to health in secrecy." She leaned forward and whispered, "It's one of the greatest secrets of the Faerie world."

Tiki's heart jumped into her throat. "He still lives?"

Larkin heaved a regretful sigh. "I fear not. Finn was instrumental in helping Eridanus overthrow Muiratach and reclaim the throne. They shared a similar belief that faeries and mortals needed to work together to save both our worlds. But he was too ill for many years to assume any kind of command. It was all he could do to stay alive. Unbeknownst to him, a shard of an iron arrowhead had become embedded in his lung during the battle and was slowly poisoning him. It took years before a healer realized the problem but by then, Finn was so ill he couldn't recover."

"So he helped put Eridanus on the throne instead?" Rieker voice echoed with surprise. "And no one knew?"

"A very few knew the truth, of course, but not many. They didn't dare take the chance." Larkin adjusted the veil that covered her head. "You have to remember, faeries are often immortal. He thought he had forever."

Snowflakes swirled in the air around them.

"Together they had a grander plan for the future of Faerie—until he died." The faerie tilted her head to one side, eyes bright and sharp. "Legend says that even now he's not really dead, but sleeps below London, waiting to be called back to battle in the time of Faerie's greatest need."

"So the Macanna wait for a sign that Finn lives on?" Rieker frowned, the skin creasing between his eyes.

"It has been a bloody battle these last few years and little has gone the way of the Seelie court." Larkin's gaze settled on Tiki. "Proof that Finn lives on would be a powerful motivator for those who are asked to risk their lives for the sake of the court."

They stood frozen, dark shapes in a world of white.

Finally Tiki spoke. "I can't stand by and watch as Donegal continues to kill people. What would I have to do?"

"I need you to come to where the Macanna gather now. They hide and plan for the day, very soon, to take back what Donegal has stolen. I just need you to show yourself, show your mark—give them something to fight for."

For the first time ever, Tiki saw a side of Larkin where the girl seemed to care about something other than herself. Or was it all part of her quest for the Seelie throne?

"All right, I'll go."

"I'll go too." Rieker stepped close to Tiki. "We're to stay together at all times, is that understood?"

Larkin considered Rieker through half-slitted lids. "William, be careful or you'll smother your butterfly before she's grown her wings."

"Don't riddle me, Larkin. Just vow Tiki and I will be together in the Otherworld. I need to be able to protect her."

The corners of Larkin's lips quivered as though she was fighting not to smile. "What makes you think you have the power to protect her? Perhaps it should be the other way around?"

"In case you've forgotten," Tiki said coldly, "the stone didn't roar, Larkin. What makes you think you're right about my heritage?"

The mocking grin slid off Larkin's face. "Enough talking. We need to go now."

She reached for Tiki's wrist and took a firm hold with her long fingers. Once again, Tiki was surprised by how soft Larkin's skin felt—like the velvet smooth texture of a rose petal. "Grab hold of each other."

Rieker threaded his fingers through Tiki's and gave her hand a squeeze. Where Larkin's hand was cool, Rieker's hand radiated warmth. Tiki clung gratefully to his fingers.

"Ready?"

Tiki nodded. A soft breeze caressed her skin and the trees of Hyde Park shimmered out of sight.

Tiki blinked. She was standing in a sunlit meadow before a grass-covered mound with an entry made of stones. White flowers dotted the grasses of the meadow and nearby she could hear the sounds of a river as it wound its way through the trees. The music of songbirds filled the air along with a sweet, succulent fragrance. It was as if they'd stepped into the middle of summer.

"Welcome to the Plain of Sunlight—home of the Seelie Court," Larkin said. She pointed in the distance. "Wydryn Tor rises toward that horizon. The UnSeelie's Plain of Starlight is beyond that."

In the far distance rising against the sky Tiki saw the sharp rocky pinnacle of Wydryn Tor. From the peak, the sides dropped away as sheer cliffs before hills angled into dense forest. They were too far for her to make out the palace that she knew stood on the top of the mountain.

"Look around," Larkin said as she dropped their wrists and shifted like a shadow toward the opening in the mound. "Memorize this spot—because for now this is the safest place we've got. Make sure you can visualize it—you may need to find your way back on your own at some point."

Chapter Forty-Four

O n her own? Tiki didn't even want to think of that possibility. She looked for unusual trees, or standing stones
that might be remarkable, but aside from a few hedgerows
in the distance, the sunny meadow was non-descript. The mound
before her could have been any mound, in any meadow, in the country outside of London or in the Otherworld.

"Follow me." Larkin ducked low to enter the narrow passage
and Rieker followed her. Tiki glanced doubtfully at the small hill.
Surely, they weren't going to hide in this dirt mound?

Rieker reached back for Tiki's hand. "Stay close to me."

The tunnel was dark and sloped steeply downhill. Tiki struggled to draw a deep breath as darkness closed around her like hands
pressing the air from her lungs. As they moved further into the
tunnel, small torches, embedded along the dirt walls, lit the way.
The flames wavered and flickered as they passed, dancing as though
alive. The passage smelled of freshly dug dirt, yet the walls were
hard-packed as if they'd existed for centuries.

They went down and down and down.

Ahead of her, Rieker finally stopped. Tiki peered around his
shoulders. Larkin was talking to two men who appeared to be

guards. They gripped razor sharp spears and stood before a weathered plank door. Larkin murmured something to the men, then pointed toward Tiki and Rieker.

One of the guards eyed them, his gaze lingering on Tiki, before he motioned to the other to open the door and allow them to pass through. Against her will, Tiki's gaze was drawn to his face as she neared. To her surprise, he dropped his eyes and inclined his head in a small bow.

Unsettled, Tiki hurried past, staying close to Rieker. They traveled down a hallway then stopped again. Tiki stared down a short flight of stairs that encircled the spectacular hall below her. The ceiling stretched high and candles in great wooden wheels cast a bright light over the room. Men and women ate at long wooden tables. A loud buzz of conversation echoed off the walls as the group ate and talked. Pairs of armed guards stood at attention around the perimeter of the room.

Larkin stepped to the head of the stairs, her head held high. As a few noticed her presence they nudged each other and nodded toward her. One by one, everyone in the room quieted to hear the news.

Larkin raised her hands. "My Macanna brethren. We have fought long and hard against a formidable foe. Tonight, there is light cast here among the darkness." She paused for three heartbeats. "I return with Finn MacLochlan's daughter." Whispers rippled through the crowd like the wind through the rushes. "A true high queen of the Seelie Court is among us again at last. Together we will ensure her destiny." Larkin swept her hands toward Tiki. "May I present Tara Kathleen Dunbar MacLochlan."

There was a split-second of absolute silence as every pair of eyes focused curiously on Tiki. Her cheeks grew warm and her head suddenly felt light. She tightened her fingers on Rieker's as if she could draw strength from them. It was just like Larkin not to warn her that she intended to present her like this.

"She don' look like Finn," someone yelled from the back of the room.

"She's just a girl," somebody else yelled.

A deep voice came from the left. "Where's she been all this time?"

One woman sat close enough that Tiki could see the way her eyes raked her up and down. "How do you know we can trust her?"

"SILENCE!" Larkin swung her arm through the air and snapped her fist closed. In that instant the room became silent as though she'd cast a magical enchantment. "I know you have questions. I know you want proof." She looked from one face to another, almost daring anyone to question her. "You shall have it. And then, *together*, we will dispose of Donegal once and for all."

Tiki stared at the toes of her boots, trying not to make eye contact with anyone in the room. She understood why they were questioning her. It was the same question she was asking herself. What if Larkin was wrong again?

For a second the room remained quiet, then conversation burst out across the hall, though no one yelled any more questions in Larkin's direction.

"Come along." Larkin walked down the steps to lead them through the hall. The stares pressed on Tiki as she followed Larkin across the room. After having lived the last few years of her life hiding from attention it was unsettling to be the focus of such intense scrutiny.

Larkin spoke to no one but led them to a private table, set off by itself, at the far end of the hall, already laden with plates of food. She pulled out a chair, its wooden legs scrapping against the floor, and sat down.

"Eat while you can. We'll be on the move tomorrow as there's only two days before Beltane."

As she ate, Tiki felt the eyes of the Macanna on her. She kept her gaze focused on her plate. Of course they were curious. She would be too if she were in their position. But if they came to believe she was Finn's daughter, what would these people expect from her? How could *she* lead *them*?

"How are you keeping apprised of what's happening?" Rieker asked Larkin. He dug into the food without a second thought.

"We have spies within Donegal's ranks," Larkin said. "Spies pretending to be UnSeelie's in the Palace of Mirrors as we speak. Dain, for one." Larkin barely skipped a beat. "Though, I believe you've known him as Sean."

Tiki's fork clattered against the plate.

"What?" Rieker's face darkened as the faerie's words sunk in.

Larkin raised her eyebrows at him. "Surely you don't expect him to spy in the UnSeelie world without the benefit of a glamour? No one in their right mind would ever believe Dain is UnSeelie."

Against her will, a twinge went through Tiki at the thought of beautiful, blond Dain being undercover in Donegal's court at a time like this. An image of his gruff exterior as Sean filled her head.

"Who is he, Larkin?" Rieker clenched his fork. "We're risking our lives for you and your people. The least you can do is tell me who—"

"He's your brother." There was no emotion in Larkin's response. She shoved another bite of food in her mouth and swallowed a great gulp of wine as though she had nothing more important on her mind than to fill her stomach.

Rieker froze.

Tiki cringed at the faerie's choice of words. She knew what an emotional impact the word 'brother' had for Rieker, especially after his two younger brothers had been murdered.

Rieker struggled to keep his expression neutral. "Surely you must mean a distant relation? Someone who also carries the bloodline of Eridanus?" He crossed his arms, his face now guarded and unreadable. "I'm sure there are many, but certainly not a brother."

Larkin checked the neighboring tables to see if anyone was listening to their conversation but all the other tables were on the other side of the room. Convinced that no one was paying any undue attention to what was being said she spoke softly.

"Your father spent time in the Otherworld before he married." She lifted her shoulders in a careless shrug, as if sharing the day's news. "He was descended from Eridanus and knew of his own connection to the fey—diluted though it might have been. When he was presented with the opportunity to visit our world, he took it."

Rieker sat back in his chair with a *thump*.

Anger burst in Tiki's chest like a match to a flame. How dare Larkin manipulate Rieker like this—in the most painful way possible. Tiki set her fork down, trying not to reveal her shaking fingers. She'd suspected there might be a connection between Rieker and Dain, but *brothers*? Surely Larkin was mistaken.

"Are there others?" Rieker tone was even.

"No. He's the only one." Larkin replied. She raised an eyebrow at him. "Your father was only here for a short time."

The muscles in Rieker's jaw flexed. "Who might Dain's mother be?"

Larkin hesitated before she let out a small sigh. "Her name was Breanna."

"Was?"

Larkin chewed her food without speaking. Tiki got the impression she was debating how much information to reveal. Finally, the beautiful faerie nodded. "Perhaps it's best if you know. The time feels right."

"Know what?" Rieker ground out.

"Breanna died in childbirth. Your father was grief stricken, for he was very much in love with her." Larkin ignored Rieker's sharp intake of breath. "He chose to return to London. Apparently, it was there he thought he could best carry on."

The façade of calm that Rieker had maintained up until now cracked and Tiki could see the anguish in his eyes. "He abandoned his own child? He left Dain behind? My father wouldn't do such—"

"Actually—" Larkin cut him off with an upheld finger to motion for him to wait as she took a drink of the blue wine that filled her glass. Tiki wanted to reach across the table and shake her. The faerie enjoyed her moments of power too much. Larkin set the goblet down. "As you know, it's rare for faeries to give birth. Twins are virtually unheard of in the Otherworld."

Larkin leaned back and contemplated Rieker through half-slitted eyes. "I suspect it was due to the influence of mortal blood." It was as if an explosion had suddenly rocked their table and Larkin's words rained down on their heads like stones.

"*What?*" Rieker gripped the edge of the table.

"In any event," Larkin continued with an airy wave of her hand, "Eridanus would only let your father return to London if he left one of you behind. Insurance, I suspect." There was a smug smile of satisfaction on the faerie's lips. "Your father chose to take you."

Tiki clutched at Rieker' arm. "Larkin, are you saying that Dain and Rieker are *twins?*"

Larkin took another bite of food, chewing thoughtfully. "Fraternal, of course. It does seem obvious though, doesn't it?" She smiled. "Now that you know the truth." She raised her wineglass to Rieker. "Here's to newfound family. Bit more faerie in your blood than you thought, eh?" With a grin, she took a deep swig and drained the contents of her glass.

Anguish was etched across Rieker's handsome face, as if someone had drawn lines of pain across his skin.

Tiki's mind rushed in dizzying circles. If what Larkin said was true, then Rieker had much more than a thread of faerie blood in him. This confirmed why he could disappear in London on a whim; why he was chosen to guard the ring of the truce. Perhaps even why she had such a strong attraction to him. "Why did Eridanus decide to split them up?"

Larkin waved her fork toward Rieker. "Isn't it obvious? William doesn't look as much like a faerie. Apparently took after his father's side. Dain, on the other hand—" she paused to drink from her glass again— "would have more trouble explaining his pointed ears and other features to some of those aristocratic types in London. But Eridanus was extremely clever. I suspect he believed having a child in both worlds would ensure your father's loyalty as well as a necessary commitment to secrecy." She cocked her head at them. "Perhaps he even thought you might be a liaison for the future?"

Rieker leaned toward Larkin, the intensity of his emotions like a wave rolling across the table. "But if Breanna died, what became of Dain? Who raised him?" Though his face was pale, his words were steady.

Larkin motioned to a servant to bring more wine. "Dain was raised by a faerie named Kieran. He loved that boy like he was his own child." She shuddered. "Unnatural, if you ask me."

Rieker choked. "*Kieran?*"

Tiki had to bite her lip not to gasp out loud. The faerie who Rieker had cared for during his dying days had raised his brother?

The servant refilled Larkin's glass. "Leave the bottle," she said. "I suspect we're going to need it." With a short bow, the servant set the twisted wine bottle on the table and departed. She held up the green glass. "Can I fill your cup, William? You look like you need a nip."

Rieker ignored Larkin's offer. "Where is Kieran now?"

Tiki was amazed at how calm he sounded, though she recognized that guarded tone of voice. He was not going to let Larkin see how he really felt. He had mentioned to Tiki more than once that many of the things Kieran had told him had not made sense. That it was as if the old man had expected Rieker to know of things he didn't. Now to find out that Kieran had raised Rieker's twin brother—

Larkin shrugged. "Kieran disappeared a few years ago while I was working within the UnSeelie court. I never did hear what became of him. I don't think even Dain knows, but I assume he is dead, like so many others." She nodded at Tiki. "Exactly the reason why she is needed here—to help put a stop to the killing."

Tiki remembered what Rieker had told her. Kieran had been dying when he had met him. Believing him to be homeless, he had cared for the older man. It had been Kieran who had told Rieker there was a rumor of someone marked with *an fáinne sí* hidden in London.

Rieker's voice sounded brittle and forced; more of a statement than a question. "He knew we were twins?"

"It wasn't common knowledge," Larkin said. "Eridanus told those who knew of your birth that you had died. But Kieran knew the truth of where you went. I always suspected he kept track of your father." She leaned back, one arm draped over her chair, her wine goblet held loosely in her long fingers. "The fey have a terrible time curbing their curiosity." The corner of her mouth quirked. "Perhaps he dreamed of reuniting the two of you. Wouldn't he be pleased now?"

Below the table, Rieker's hands were drawn into fists, his knuckles white. "Does Dain know?" His voice revealed none of his inner turmoil.

"I'm not sure exactly what Kieran told him, but no—" Larkin shook her head— "I don't believe Dain knew he had a brother until recently." She took a long drink of wine. "Then he couldn't help himself—he went to London as Sean in search of you."

"Does he know he's half mortal?" Tiki asked, remembering how Dain had questioned her about her own heritage.

"I have no idea what he does and doesn't know." Larkin shoved her plate to the side. "Enough of Dain. We need to talk about our plan."

"So Dain is in Donegal's court right now?" Rieker pressed. "In danger?"

Larkin jerked forward, suddenly angry. "We are *all* in danger, William," her voice was razor-sharp. "Dain is willing to risk his life for what he believes, as are all the Macanna." Her lips pulled back from shiny teeth that were suddenly pointed, making her look feral. "Are you?"

Tiki dropped her eyes and stared at the table. She didn't want to confront Larkin. But if what she had just told them was true, then Tiki knew she'd made the right decision to come. If it was in her power, she would not let anything happen to Rieker's only living relative.

Chapter Forty-Five

"Johnny!" Fiona shouted across the field as she ran, the hem of her dress clutched in one hand and held high above her knees so she wouldn't trip. Overhead, storm clouds gathered on the horizon, black and threatening.

He turned from where he was perched on the fence, watching Toots ride the big brown bay in circles around the corral. Mr. Bosworth stood in the center of the gated area, holding the lead as he shouted instructions to Toots.

Johnny climbed down and hobbled to meet Fiona. Something in her tone made the skin crawl along the back of his neck just like when a bobby was paying too much attention to him.

"Fi, what's wrong?"

"It's Clara." Fiona's chest heaved, her voice coming out in choking gasps. "Have you seen her?"

"Clara? No." He motioned toward Toots. "I've been out here with the horses. Why?"

"I can't find her." Fiona gasped for breath, seemingly unaware that she still clutched her skirts well above her knees.

"Could she be with Mrs. B.?"

Fiona shook her head. "Mrs. B. hasn't seen her since breakfast."

"What about Shamus?"

"Shamus is working in the barn on his furniture. She's not there." Fiona shoved past him and jerked herself up on the fence posts until her head was over the top rail.

"Toots!" Her cry pierced the afternoon air like the cry of a hawk. In the distance, thunder rumbled.

Toots jerked around in surprise.

"Where's Clara?"

"How should I know, Fi?" Toots swiveled his head as the horse continued to prance around the circle. "Can't you see I'm learning how to ride?" Mr. Bosworth slowed the horse to a walk and turned his weathered face in Fiona's direction.

"You sound distressed, Miss."

Johnny climbed the rails to look into Fiona's face.

"Why are you so upset?"

"Toots." Fiona's voice held a wild note of hysteria. "She's *gone*. Do you understand me? *Gone*. By herself."

Toots' eyes narrowed in a frown as the horse came to a stand-still, jerking his head to loosen the reins. "Gone where?"

"She's gone to help Tiki."

Toots gripped the saddle horn. "How do you know? How could she?"

"She *told* me she was going to go." Fiona kicked a leg over the top rail so she could balance on the fence. "She said Larkin revealed her true name and told Clara if she ever needed her to call her and she'd come. But I didn't believe her. I thought she was just missing Tiki."

"But how could she get anywhere, Fi?" Johnny asked. He climbed a rung, balanced below where Fiona sat perched. "She's just a little girl."

Fiona bit the corner of her lip. "If she called for Larkin, she would come. She *has* to come. Larkin would take her."

Next to her, propped on the fence, Johnny's brows scrunched in confusion.

Sitting on the horse, Toots' face blanched. "Are you sure?"

"*Yes*. I've looked everywhere."

A frown creased Mr. Bosworth's wrinkled forehead as he led the horse toward Fiona. "Does the missus know the little girl is gone?"

Fiona stared at Toots. "Larkin *has* to come when her name is called. All she had to do was grab Clara and leave again."

"But why would Larkin take her?" Toots asked.

In the distance, white forks of lightning speared the sky. Fiona jumped as deep-throated thunder followed a second later. "Don't you understand? She took her before. She's a way for Larkin to get Tiki to do what she wants."

"Slow down now. Who's this Larkin person yer keep referring to?" Mr. Bosworth looked from one to the other, the edges of his white hair lifting in the sudden breeze. "Is she a neighbor?"

Toots kicked a leg over the horse and slid down from the saddle. He raced around the front of the animal and headed for the fence. "Thanks a lot, Mr. B.," he called over his shoulder, "but we've got to go find Shamus right now." He scrambled through the gate as Fiona climbed down. It only took Toots a moment before he was racing across the grass with Fiona, headed for the barn where Shamus worked on his furniture.

Johnny tried to hurry with his crutch behind them.

Left alone with the horse in the middle of the corral, Mr. Bosworth frowned and rubbed the bay's nose as he watched the receding backs of the children. "Guess we better go tell the missus." He gave the lead a tug and led the horse toward the gate.

Inside the barn, Toots and Fiona raced to Shamus where he sat sanding a flat piece of wood that looked like it could be a desk top.

"Shamus!" Fiona cried as they slid to a stop on the straw covered floor. Her words came out in a rush. "Clara's gone missing."

"What should we do?" Toots asked, his chest heaving to catch his breath.

The tap-tap of Johnny's crutch could be heard as he entered the barn.

Shamus lifted his white-blond head and rested the slab of wood across his knees as he contemplated the three of them. "Have you checked with Mrs. Bosworth? Are you sure she's not off playing with her wings somewhere?"

Fiona jerked her head up and down, her brown curls waving with the movement. "She said she was going to call Larkin because she wanted to help Tiki—but I didn't think she'd actually do it."

Shamus was silent. Knowing how he liked to think things over Fiona and Toots waited impatiently, the young boy hopping from one foot to the other.

"Well, if Larkin has taken Clara to—" Shamus glanced at Johnny— "*away*, I don't think there's anything we can do about it but wait here. We've no way to follow and no way to get in touch with Larkin ourselves." His lips twisted into a line of worry. "Unless the two of you can think of some other way to track Clara down, I think we're stuck waiting."

"What about going to The Ring in Hyde Park?" Fiona said in a whisper. "The fey are always there during storms."

CONVINCING MR. BOSWORTH to let Shamus take a wagon loaded with children into London during a storm was not easy. It was, in fact, impossible. In the end, they had to sneak away. Fiona bit her fingernails down to the quick on the ride into the City, worrying about what the elderly couple would say when they returned.

Thunder continued to boom overhead and the closer they got to London the more prominent the smell of smoke became.

"What's burning?" Toots asked, looking in all directions for the smoke that would indicate the location of the fire.

"It must be a massive fire to smell all the way out here," Johnny replied.

"I wonder if Mr. and Mrs. B. know we're gone yet?" Fiona said in a fretful voice.

Shamus continued to drive, remaining silent.

IT WAS SEVERAL hours later when they arrived in Hyde Park. Dusk was just beginning to set. Shamus steered the horses around the Serpentine to the area in the northeastern section of the park called The Ring. The leather rigging on the wagon creaked as Shamus pulled to a stop.

"Which way?" Toots called.

"Over here," Fiona cried, as she jumped down from the wagon and headed toward a band of trees.

"Should we just shout her name?" Johnny asked.

"Larkin! Larkin! Larkin!" Their voices were sharp, desperate, like cry of birds. The name seemed to bounce across the park and disappear into the shadows under the trees as Fiona and Johnny went one direction and Shamus and Toots went the other. Overhead, thunder rumbled, like an answering echo.

FIONA AND JOHNNY had been calling for almost twenty minutes when a tall man with black hair, dressed in a long dark coat and black trousers, approached. He carried a thin black cane and wore a black top hat, the dark colors making him blend with the rapidly approaching night. Like a leaf caught on the wind, he moved soundlessly toward them.

Chapter Forty-Six

Servants moved among the tables in the great underground hall, removing dishes, filling wine glasses. They remained silent and didn't make eye contact—making it easy to look through them. Tiki wondered who they were. Mortals? A lower class of faeries? One girl in particular had a familiar cast to her features, though Tiki couldn't place where she might have seen her before.

"Now, this is what we have to do." Larkin rattled off orders. "Tiki needs to speak to the Macanna. She needs to show them her birthmark and convince them she is Finn's daughter—" Larkin's expression was steely with determination— "without her glamour."

A spider web of dread filled Tiki's lungs making it difficult to draw a deep breath. She gave a short nod. "Fine." There was no other choice.

TIKI'S LEGS SHOOK. She stood in a small room with Rieker and Larkin, not far from the great hall where the Macanna were gathered. She had changed into a shimmering gown the color of ripe cranberries, shot through with threads of gold and glittering with embroidered gold sequins.

"You need to shed your glamour here," Larkin said. She was still draped in shades of black and grey – somehow making her form indistinct. "We need to reveal your true features to the Macanna so they know what you look like—who they'll be protecting and fighting for."

"They still have to be convinced that I'm Finn's daughter," Tiki said.

Larkin made a small noise at the back of her throat. "They'll believe."

Rieker squeezed Tiki's hand to reassure her. She clung to his fingers, trying to deny the fear that flooded her, threatening to drown her.

"The first order of business is to shed that glamour," Larkin said again.

Tiki dug her fingernails into the flesh of her palms. Could she do it? What if she looked like a monster? She was so nervous she wasn't sure if she could push one more word out of her mouth. "How?"

"It might take a few tries since you've been subconsciously producing this glamour all your life. However—" Larkin reached into a pocket buried within the gauzy dark folds of her gown and pulled something free— "you've maintained your present image because that's what you *believe* you should look like."

The faerie lifted a small, flat object. For a moment, Tiki thought it was a piece of painted wood, but as Larkin turned the object a shaft of light reflected off its surface and shot across the room. "I've this. Maybe if you know what you really look like, you'll be able to shed the glamour more easily."

Rieker grabbed Larkin's wrist to still her hand so he could see what she held. "What is it?"

"It's a mirror." Tiki answered for Larkin. "It's from the Palace of Mirrors, isn't it?"

Larkin smiled and for a second she was her old self: Enigmatic. Mocking. Breathtakingly beautiful. "I stole it especially for you, guttersnipe. I knew one day you'd be ready to use it." She held her hand out, the mirror resting on her open palm. "Take it."

Tiki saw the glint of curiosity that glowed in the blue-green depths of Larkin's eyes. "Take it," she coaxed. "You must wonder what you really look like."

The mirror balanced on Larkin's outstretched hand.

Tiki didn't move. Was she ready? This would change everything.

She drew in a shaky breath. Her heart pounded so hard she feared Rieker would hear her ribs rattle.

She snatched the mirror from Larkin's hand and held it up to her face.

Tiki blinked once.

Twice.

Then exhaled in a sharp gasp.

The face staring back was the girl she'd seen in the Palace of Mirrors right before Dain had taken her down the back hallway and out the side door. Without knowing it, she'd been looking at herself in one of the enchanted mirrors.

Vivid green eyes stared back with a mixture of curiosity and fear. Large and almond shaped, they were emeralds glowing beneath sooty lashes. Skin as opalescent and beautiful as her mother's well-loved string of pearls gleamed in the reflection. Her features were sharply etched by razor-sharp cheek bones, a thin straight nose and a lush mouth—one meant to be kissed— making her look older, and much wiser than she was. Yet, somehow, the face looked familiar, too.

With a rush of unexpected emotion she realized she was as beautiful as Larkin. But where Larkin was blond and ethereal, she was darkly exotic and mysterious. What was the word Rieker had told her Prince Arthur had used? An enchantress.

"*Well?*" Rieker burst out. "What do you see?"

"We could look over your shoulder to see the reflection," Larkin suggested.

Tiki turned her head to the side and pulled her hair back, still staring into the mirror. "I've got pointed ears."

Rieker let out a sigh of exasperation. "What about your face? Will I recognize you?"

Tiki dropped her hair and looked straight in the mirror again, contemplating his question. Though some of her basic features were the same—the color of her eyes, the shape of her nose had always been straight, but not quite as long or dramatic. Now, however, the sum of the parts caused her to look strikingly different.

With a start, Tiki suddenly realized why the face in the mirror looked familiar. She dropped her hand to her side and stared at Larkin. "I look like you."

Larkin lids lowered and she gave what looked like a forced shrug. "I'm not surprised. You are my niece after all."

"You look like *Larkin?*" Rieker said in a dazed voice.

Larkin ignored him. "Do you think you can shed your glamour?"

"I can see a resemblance," Tiki said to Rieker. She turned to Larkin. "I don't know.

"The glamour you wear now comes from the essence of your faerie soul. It will take a great effort to shift magic as profound and organic as that which you've accomplished for sixteen years." Larkin's tone was oddly respectful. "It is a powerful magic that can innately shift for that long."

"So what should she do?" Rieker asked.

Larkin looked at Tiki. "Let the layers melt and peel away. Use the power of your mind to dissolve that which is no longer necessary."

Tiki thought of what Rieker had looked like when she'd first met him as a pickpocket. His face and clothes had been dirty, his accent rough. He'd had a dangerous air about him and Tiki had been unsure whether to trust him for the longest time. But over the days and weeks, as she had gotten to know him, the layers had peeled back and she'd found the true Rieker: A dependable, loyal, handsome young man.

She brought the mirror up again and gazed at the alluring girl staring back at her. Her heart fluttered in her chest like the wings of a bird trying to break free. She closed her eyes to concentrate. It was time to find her true self. She imagined rain falling on her, rinsing her clean. In her mind, streaming torrents of water drenched her, flooding her with watery hands, washing away the illusion she'd been cloaked within.

She imagined peeling layers back, like a flower unfurling, to free someone hidden within a skin that didn't belong to them. A skin that held them captive.

Tiki held her hands out from her sides, as if to shake the remnants away—to reveal the girl who had stared at her from the depths of that mirror. The air around her seemed to warm and the smell of clover filled the air as she focused her energy on the image she had seen—mentally releasing the past until she could feel herself *becoming* that person.

"God bless the Queen," Rieker said. "Tiki, is that *you*?"

Tiki's slowly opened her eyes. She felt different. Free, somehow. She saw Larkin's stunned expression first. She had never truly seen the faerie look shocked before. As if she couldn't believe her eyes.

Rieker looked dazed, but there was a fire, a hunger, in his eyes that spoke louder than any words.

Tiki glanced down at her hands. Her fingers were long and thin, much like Larkin's. She reached up and felt the contours of her cheekbones and nose recognizing the face in the mirror by touch.

"Teek—" Rieker seemed at a loss for words as he took a step towards her, his arms open— "You were beautiful before, but now—"

Larkin blinked rapidly and sucked her cheeks in to hide any emotions she might be feeling. "Now—" she cut Rieker off— "you look like Finn and Adasara."

Rieker cupped Tiki's face in his hands, a look of wonder in his eyes. He ran his thumbs over her eyebrows and along the side of her nose. "It's you, but you've changed. You're so... so..."

"Faerie-like?" Larkin sounded annoyed. "We need to keep moving. Every second we're here is another second that Donegal will gain more power, enslave another Seelie or murder a mortal." She swept towards the door. "Come along."

Tiki didn't move. "Is there some place where I can see myself first?"

"This way." Larkin motioned over her shoulder and jerked the door open. For the first time, Tiki didn't worry about the blond faerie's mercurial mood. Larkin never reacted in a predictable fashion.

She led them down a hallway to another room. Rieker held Tiki's hand as they walked. Out of the corner of her eye Tiki could see him casting quick glances at her.

Larkin pushed open an unmarked door and led them into a furnished chamber. "There." She pointed to an ornately framed mirror that hung on a nearby wall. Tiki approached with a confusing mixture of excitement and dread churning in her stomach. What if she didn't recognize her own face?

She hesitated then pushed herself forward. There was no time to waste on foolish fears. What was done was done. She moved in front of the looking glass. The girl from the Palace stood before her but now instead of looking startled, she had an air of confidence. She looked self-composed and sure of herself—almost regal.

Tiki tilted her head to the side and was surprised when the image in the mirror moved too. It was her. She examined the arch of her slender neck, the cut of her jaw line. She put her face close to the mirror to stare at the dramatic green of her eyes. Even her hair appeared different—what had been dark brown waves before, like her mother's hair, was now wild tangles of blackest ebony.

"Did Finn have black hair?"

"As black as midnight," Larkin replied. Tiki wondered at the emotion she heard in Larkin's voice.

The contrast of the rich cranberry fabric of her gown gave her pale skin a luminescent glow, making her features appear flawless. Her beauty was mesmerizing in the most powerful way. But she recognized it for what it was: a tool to bend mortals to do her bidding.

"Well? Are you satisfied?" Larkin spoke from behind her. "You bear a striking resemblance to Adasara, though your green eyes and black hair are all Finn."

How could she not be satisfied? She'd never dreamed in a million years that she could have a shred of the otherworldly beauty of Larkin, but now—

SHE WASN'T SURE what to expect as Larkin led her back into the great hall.

"We'll start with the Macanna accepting you as the next high queen. Once we find the Stone of Tara then all of Faerie will be forced to bow to you as the Seelie queen. That is the way we will ultimately beat Donegal."

They entered from a passageway that was cleverly tucked behind several columns, almost undetectable from the huge room.

Larkin led them to stand on the top step again, overlooking the tables. She grabbed Tiki's wrist and pulled her to stand next to her on the steps. Rieker flanked Tiki's other side, his tall form towering next to hers.

This time there wasn't a gradually quieting.

The room went silent in a single instant.

The silence was deafening as everyone in the room stared at Tiki. She tried to remain calm and unafraid, her fingers threaded together in front of her. She belonged here. She was one of them. And now she believed it.

"Look." A large man, his skin weathered and creased from years in the sun, sat near where Tiki stood. He pointed to where Tiki's sleeve was pulled back, exposing her wrists. "She's marked with *an fáinne sí.*" He turned and shouted to the room. "She bears Finn's birthmark!"

A buzz of whispers exploded throughout the room as everyone craned their necks to catch a glimpse of Tiki and her birthmark.

Then a single voice shouted in a thick accent over the din: 'TARR-UH.'

Tiki jumped. It sounded like a battle cry.

Rieker leaned close and whispered in her ear. "It's your name."

"Tara is the place where our kings and queens have been crowned for centuries," Larkin said quietly. "There's a reason that Tara was the name given to you by your parents."

A great hulk of a man slid to his knee in front of Tiki.

"My queen."

There was a shuffling across the room as everyone dropped down and bowed toward Tiki.

Tiki sucked in her breath. A chill ran up her arms. Were these powerful beings bowing to *her*?

"Rise and rejoice," Larkin called out, raising her arms above her head. "Your faith and patience have been rewarded this night." Her voice held a power and a passion that Tiki had never heard before. "Tomorrow—together—we reclaim our throne."

Another cry swept through the room, gathering momentum until the wooden rafters shook.

"TARR-UH!"

Chapter Forty-Seven

"Are you seeking Larkin?" The killer's voice was low, almost seductive. Johnny and Fiona whirled together to face him. Overhead the storm had moved closer and lightning split the sky in a jagged fork of white light. Thunder boomed loud enough to make the ground shake.

Johnny limped towards the man. "D'you know Larkin? We've got a bit of business with her tonight. Be much obliged if you could point us in her direction." Fiona tugged on Johnny's jacket, pulling him in the opposite direction. He swatted a hand behind his back at her, trying to get her to release him.

"I'd be glad to help you, young man." His voice was smooth and melodic. The stranger moved closer, his long jacket oddly still in the sudden gust of wind that blew Johnny's hair back from his face.

"Is she here, then?" Johnny swiveled his head to look from side to side, but there were only the deepening shadows suddenly pressing closer to him.

"Johnny," Fiona's voice was threaded with fear. She pulled on his jacket again. Harder this time. "Johnny—we should go."

"No need to be afraid, dear." The stranger tilted his head to see around Johnny to where Fiona was half-hidden. "I'll be glad to help you." There was something in the possessive way he said 'you' that raised the hackles on the back of Johnny's neck.

"Now wait a minute." Johnny held a hand up to stop the approach of the man who was beginning to circle around him, his eyes locked on Fiona. The man was obviously upper class, well-dressed and moneyed, but still—there was something unsettling about him. "You look like a right upstandin' gentleman and all, but—"

The stranger held out a hand to Fiona. "Come with me. I will take you to Larkin." His lips spread in a grin revealing teeth that glittered in the waning light. Johnny glanced back at Fiona. Instead of being afraid, she was staring at the man as if hypnotized. Her eyes were glassy and the look on her face reminded Johnny of those charmed snakes that danced in baskets before a flute player.

Fiona slowly lifted her hand.

The killer chuckled deep in his chest as he reached for her fingers. "That's a good girl."

"Stop that!" Johnny cried, swatting Fiona's hand out of the way. "You don't need to touch her! What are you on about?"

Fiona fell back with a small shriek. She grabbed Johnny's jacket as she stumbled backwards, tugging at him as she tried to put distance between them and the stranger.

The stranger lunged for Fiona.

Johnny hurled himself at the man. "Fi, run!" he cried. "Run and find Shamus!"

The stranger jerked around with a hiss and for a second it looked as though his teeth were fanged. "You've made a mistake, my young friend," he said in a low voice. A sudden gust of wind caught the man's black cape and it swelled around them until everything went black.

Chapter Forty-Eight

It wasn't long before Tiki was swept into the crowd—everyone wanted to see and talk to her. Larkin disappeared into the swirl of people shortly after introducing Tiki, but Rieker made a point of staying close. Though he appeared relaxed, Tiki could feel the tension coiled in his muscles, ready to defend her, if need be.

"Tara."

The word was a whisper, floating on the air behind her. Tiki recognized the voice and whirled around.

Dain stood before her, his blond hair slouched over his forehead but the usual sardonic twist to his mouth was missing. His eyes widened as he took in her new appearance and to her surprise, he dropped his head in a small bow. "My queen."

"You're safe," Tiki blurted out.

Dain voice was gruff as he stood. "I know my way around." His usual teasing manner was absent.

"But Larkin said—"

Dain cut her off. "That's why I'm here. I've news."

Rieker stepped closer. "What is it?"

Dain flicked a cold glance at him then focused on Tiki. "The *liche* was spotted in Hyde Park. Apparently someone was calling for Larkin and he answered the call."

Tiki clutched at Dain's arm. "Was he captured?"

Dain shook his head. "He has escaped back into the Wych-wood—"

"No!"

Dain held his hand up. "There are others on his trail. Larkin also responded to the call of her name. She is one of those chasing the *liche* now. We think he will eventually return to Donegal. I only came here because I thought you should know he took someone with him when he ran."

Tiki tightened her grip, unaware of her fingernails digging into the fabric of his jacket. "Who?"

"It's the young chap who lives in Charing Cross. The one Larkin roughed up to get your attention."

"Johnny?" Tiki said.

Dain nodded. "That's the bloke. He's been taken."

"*Larkin* was the one who attacked him?" Rieker said.

"What can we do?" Tiki cried. "We've got to help him."

"The best thing you could do is find the bloody *Cloch na Teamhrach*," Dain muttered, "but until then you'd be smart to go back to London and watch over the rest of your family."

"You don't think—" Tiki turned from Dain to Rieker, panic blanching her face. "But they're hidden—"

"Could they have gone to Hyde Park with this Johnny fellow?"

Tiki put her hands to her mouth. "I don't know." She couldn't draw a deep breath. She could barely think straight. She'd left her family unprotected. "We've got to go back to London—*now.*"

Rieker spoke calmly to Dain. They were the same height and looked at each other eye-to-eye. "Larkin brought us over. Where is the nearest gate from here?"

Dain only hesitated for a second. "There is a gate from the Plain of Sunlight to Hyde Park in London. It's an easy walk if you know the way."

THEY FOLLOWED DAIN from the underground hall back to the sunlit meadow where they had arrived with Larkin.

"It's that way—" he pointed in the distance— "follow the river through those trees and you'll end up at The Ring in Hyde Park. You know your way from there, yes?"

"Yes." Tiki said. She paused, her hand on his arm. "Thank you for coming and telling us."

Dain shrugged, sliding his hands into his pockets. "Seemed important for you to know."

"Be careful," Tiki whispered. "You do have family who cares about you, you know."

Dain's eyes flicked to Rieker, who stood silently, then back to Tiki, but his expression remained inscrutable. "Once Donegal is off the throne we'll talk more." He glanced over his shoulder. "But for now—"

"You need to go," Tiki finished for him. On impulse, she slid her arms around his broad shoulders and hugged him close. "Stay safe," she whispered.

Dain stood stiff in her arms, but when Tiki stepped back, she caught something raw and painful in his eyes. He nodded at Rieker then turned and disappeared back into the stone opening.

IT WAS A surprisingly short walk through the trees to reach Hyde Park. Tiki knew they'd slipped from one world to another when the weather suddenly changed from sunshine and singing birds to black storm clouds overhead. The wind blew fierce and harsh as they hurried through the trees and it wasn't long before she began to recognize familiar landmarks.

She looked at Rieker in surprise. "Do you really think it's that easy to go back and forth?"

"I think when you're one of them, the path becomes clearer."

One of them. The words echoed in Tiki's head. She thought of the Macanna who had embraced her as Finn's daughter and the vision of herself without the glamour she'd always known. It couldn't possibly have all been an illusion—could it?

They hadn't spoken of Johnny, or the others. Tiki couldn't think of anything to say, though her heart raced with fear. She had to get to Richmond and make sure everyone was all right. Then they'd figure out what to do next.

Rieker glanced down at her. "You'd better change your appearance before we go any further."

Tiki put her hands to her face. She'd forgotten. She quietly muttered the words that Larkin had taught them and the smell of clover filled the air. She glanced up at Rieker.

"All right?"

He nodded, a glow in his eyes. "So much more than all right.'"

THE RIDE FROM Grosvenor Square to Richmond seemed to take forever, though in reality it was less than an hour. Every roll of the wheel across the cobblestones made Tiki want to pound on the window and yell *faster!* It wasn't yet noon when they pulled up to the manor house, but rain was pelting from the skies.

Tiki pushed the door open before Rieker could get to it and jumped to the ground, unmindful of the puddles that had formed on the gravel lane. She yanked up her skirts and dashed for the entry. She burst through the door without knocking.

"Fiona! Shamus! Toots! Clara! Are you here?"

The scramble of footsteps could be heard in response to her calls.

Toots was the first one in the hallway, his eyes red and his face blotchy.

"Teek, you're home!" he cried as he dashed toward her. He wrapped his arms around her waist and buried his face in her skirt.

Clara was next, her bare feet pattering on the wood floor like the sound of mice.

"Tiki, Tiki, Tiki," she said in her high, little-girl voice. "Yer safe!"

"Of course, I'm safe." She bent down to wrap her other arm around the little girl, choking back a sob.

Shamus rounded the corner of the drawing room, his face lined with worry. He reached out to shake Rieker's hand as he walked in the door behind Tiki. "Glad to see you made it back."

"Where's Fi?" Tiki asked sharply, looking around. Her heart pounded as she waited for their answer.

"She's upstairs crying," Clara said. "She's been crying since Johnny disappeared."

Tiki straightened and looked at their faces. "But you lot are all right, yes?"

"We're fine," Shamus answered. "We thought we'd lost Clara but she was playing in the woods and fell asleep."

"Larkin made me stay here," Clara whispered.

Shamus' face twisted with uncharacteristic emotion. "Johnny's missin' though."

"Let me go upstairs and talk to Fi and then you can tell me everything that's happened."

Rieker reached down and scooped Clara in to his arms. He put his big hand on Toots's thin shoulder. "Has Mr. Bosworth taught you how to ride yet? Because I've been looking for someone to ride with..."

Toots' eyes got round with hope. "I've been on the bay a few times."

"Let's go in the drawing room and you can tell me about it."

IT WAS TWO days later and Tiki sat with Rieker in the warmth of the kitchen eating a bowl of potato soup with some fresh rolls. There'd been no word from Larkin or Dain, no news of Johnny.

"May I see the ring?" Tiki asked.

Rieker fumbled at the chain around his neck, pulling it over his head to drop it, along with the Queen's ring, into her hands. "By all means. Maybe you can see something that will tell us what to do."

A familiar tingling warmth infused Tiki's fingers as she picked up the golden ring and peered into its depths. The flames of the fire danced brightly in the heart of the stone, almost as if the ring lived and breathed.

Tiki twisted the band in her hand so she could read the inscription inside: *Na síochána, aontaímid: For the sake of peace, we agree.*

"I've been thinking about it. There's got to be a clue here." She tilted the ring to the light. "Did you hear Larkin in the Palace of Mirrors? She said the ring held other secrets." Tiki slid the band onto her finger and stared into the blood red depths looking for a something—*anything*. "Finn and Eridanus gave this ring to the rulers of England. Someone's got to know something."

Rieker sucked his breath in with a quiet hiss. "That's it."

Tiki glanced up. "What?"

"The royals have the stone." Rieker's voice rose with excitement.

"They do?"

"*Of course.* It's so obvious now. Finn and Eridanus believed our worlds had to meld—that we had to learn to live together. It only makes sense that the stone which marks the high kings and queens of the Otherworld is also associated with the high kings and queens in the mortal world."

He grinned at Tiki. "Somehow, *Cloch na Teamhrach,* is connected to the royals. That's where we need to look."

It did make sense. "Do you think Leo or Arthur would know?" Tiki asked.

"There's only one way to find out." Rieker pushed back his chair with a screech and jumped to his feet. "I want to check and see how Leo is faring, anyway."

THEY LEFT WITHIN the hour and headed for Buckingham Palace. Tiki sat next to Rieker in the carriage, reassured by the pressure of his shoulder next to hers. The guards at the Palace saluted Rieker as they allowed the carriage to pass. The doorman bowed his head in acknowledgement as he swept the door open for them to enter. It was only minutes before they were being escorted into Leo's chambers.

Arthur met them at the door. Though there were tired circles under his eyes, he was his usual neat and tidy self and there was a smile on his face.

"How is he?" Rieker asked in a hushed voice.

"Slow to recover but definitely better." Arthur nodded at Tiki and reached for her hand. "Miss Tara. Always a pleasure to see you."

Tiki dipped in a small curtsy. "And you, Sir."

"What's been wrong with him?" Rieker peered over Arthur's shoulder into the spacious bedchamber. "Is it still the cut on his neck?"

"The physicians have had a devil of a time getting the bleeding to stop." Arthur kept his voice low so his brother wouldn't hear. "Nothing was helping and I finally became convinced they didn't know what to do—" he lowered his voice— "so I sought Mamie's help."

"Ah, the witch woman." Rieker nodded as though not surprised. "And what was her suggestion?"

"The first thing she did was take him off the man-made aspirin the physicians had prescribed and she made some kind of poultice using a concoction of natural ingredients: bilberry, grape seed extract, stinging nettle, witch hazel, yarrow and who knows what else." He shrugged, then grinned. "He began to improve almost immediately."

THEY DIDN'T STAY long in Leo's room. Tiki was shocked at his appearance. His brown hair looked thin and wispy. Huge dark circles filled the hollows under his eyes reminding Tiki of a skeleton. His skin was like translucent wax and appeared to be stretched across the bones underneath. Though he pushed himself into a sitting position at their arrival, it was obvious that he was still very weak.

"Leo." Rieker bent close and grasped the young prince's hand. "You're looking spry."

A smile stretched Leo's lips and a weak laugh escaped. "Bollocks, Wills, but it's bloody good to see you." He reached for Tiki's hands. "And the lovely Tara, more beautiful than ever."

Leo's hands were cold when he clasped hers and Tiki held tight to his fingers for a moment, trying to send her own good health to him. "I hope you're feeling better soon, Leo, because I've saved a dance for you.

Leo raised his eyebrows. "That is all the motivation I need to leap from this cursed sick bed." He raised his eyebrows at Rieker. "I may yet steal her heart from you, Wills."

Rieker smiled but his eyes slid to Tiki. "I hope not."

"Yes, well, after your disaster at the Masked Ball last Christmas Leo, we'll make sure you're not holding any wine near her," Arthur said in a dry voice, but his face was lit with a fond smile.

SOON AFTER, ARTHUR escorted them out of the room. "Believe it or not, he's made amazing improvements since Mamie started tending him," the prince said as he walked down the spacious hallway with them. "She was the one who got the bleeding to stop."

"Arthur," Rieker began, "not to sound unconcerned about Leo's condition, because I am, dreadfully so, but I need to ask you about something else, if you have a minute."

The prince glanced over at him. "Of course. What is it?"

Tiki walked along on the far side of Rieker, staring in wonder at the opulence that surrounded them while she listened to their conversation. Worry for Leo burrowed a hole in her heart. She remembered his gay, infectious attitude when they'd first met at the Masked Ball last winter. The memory of that young man was a far cry from the ailing prince to whom she'd just spoken.

"I'm looking for a stone that is somehow important to the royal family."

Arthur frowned. "A *stone*, you say?"

"Yes. I think it's something that could be used to name a new king or queen, or perhaps be—"

"Oh." Arthur interrupted him. "You mean the Stone of Scone."

Rieker stopped abruptly and pulled Arthur to face him. "The stone of what?" Tiki moved closer, wanting to hear every word. Her heart was suddenly racing as if she were running.

"The Stone of Destiny, of course." Arthur gave him a surprised look. "Haven't you ever heard of it? It's housed in King Edward's chair."

"Do the stone and chair still exist?" Rieker choked out.

Arthur let out a chuckle. "I should think so. King Edward's chair is also called the Coronation Chair. It's the throne on which every English and British sovereign has been seated at the moment of coronation since 1308."

Tiki put her hand to her mouth to cover her gasp. Could it be true?

"The Coronation Chair holds the Stone of Destiny?" Rieker echoed.

"Yes. It has for centuries. Legend says it came from Ireland originally by the Gaels who settled Scotland." Arthur started walking again, clearly enjoying the subject. "It's really quite a fascinating history. They say there's a connection between our Stone and the *Lia Fáil* – which is the coronation stone of the Kings of Tara over in Ireland. I can't say it looks like much more than a chunk of rock, though, if you ask me."

Rieker almost sounded giddy. "You've seen it?"

Arthur gave him a puzzled look. "Of course I've seen it."

Rieker's words came out in a rush. "Where is it?"

Arthur clapped him on the shoulder, a smile tweaking the corners of his mouth. "Wills, I don't know why you find this topic so exciting but it's in Westminster Abbey, where it's always been."

Chapter Forty-Nine

Tiki could hardly sit still on the carriage seat she was so excited.

"Do you think it's the Tara Stone?" she asked for the tenth time.

Rieker's eyes were positively glowing. "I do. Hidden in plain sight." He grabbed her hands and squeezed. "I think we've found it, Tiki. I really think we have."

"Where in the Abbey did Arthur say the chair was located again?" Tiki shivered. Could they possibly be this close to the Stone of Tara? Had they found the secret that Finn and Eridanus had hidden in London?

"He said the Coronation Chair was in the Chapel of Edward the Confessor." Rieker peered out the window. Outside thunder roared overhead and the sky was weighted with black clouds that threatened rain at any moment. "It's right in the heart of the abbey. We shouldn't have any trouble finding it."

The clip-clop of the horses' hooves kept a steady rhythm as the wheels clacked along the cobblestone streets. Tiki's heart jumped with every jingle of the reins. Her mind raced in circles. The stone was housed in a chair that had crowned English royalty for almost six hundred years. She could still hear Arthur's words as if he whispered in her ear: *'Legend says it came from Ireland originally...'* Tiki almost didn't dare to allow herself to think about it—but would happen when she touched the stone?

THE STREETS WERE unusually quiet as they exited the carriage and approached the grand north entrance to the Abbey. A gust of wind caught Tiki's skirt, blowing it and her long hair behind her.

Tiki stared at the imposing structure that arched before them. She'd been past the Abbey many times before in her travels but she'd never really paid much attention to the building. Grand cathedrals such as Westminster Abbey were not for the likes of pickpockets like her. These buildings were meant for kings and queens.

Spires stretched toward the sky on each side of the intricately carved entry like massive sentinels standing guard.

"Rieker." Tiki pointed. "Look at that huge circular window. The giant circle is made up of smaller circles, made up of more circles. Even the stonework above has circles within circles." Her voice was hushed. "It's as if the ring belongs here."

Rieker reached for her hand and laced his fingers through hers. "Time will tell," he said in a quiet voice. They left the chaos of the wintery weather behind as they slipped through the oversized black doors into the hushed splendor of the grand entry.

"It's like entering another world," Tiki whispered. Rieker nodded. This was a world of quiet and peace; of secrets and promises, of things greater than themselves.

Their footsteps were muted against the stone tiles on the floor. Tiki stopped and stared up in awe at the arched ceiling that towered above them. Brown stone columns held up fluted cream-colored stone arches that stretched above them to a breathtaking height, creating a dizzying framework of architectural glory.

The bright color of the ornate, gilded chairs of the choir drew Tiki's eyes to the right as they passed through the north transept. The high-backed chairs stretched away from her in staunch rows, like a line of soldiers standing at attention. The chairs reflected the light from the arches above, creating the impression of room full of gold.

"Teek, look." Rieker whispered as he pointed to a section up ahead. "That's Poet's Corner. It holds the tomb of Geoffrey Chaucer and other great writers. They just interred Charles Dickens a little over a year ago."

Chills ran up Tiki's arms. They were surrounded with greatness—kings and conquerors, lords and ladies, artists and authors. Did she even belong in a place like this?

"This way." Rieker pulled Tiki to the left. "Arthur said The Chapel for Edward the Confessor is to the left of the Choir." They spoke in hushed tones, as if instinctively trying not to disturb those who had been laid to rest in these halls. Tiki couldn't shake the feeling they were the only two people in vast building. She glanced about looking for moving shadows, for obscure faces staring at her from a distance, but there was only the ancient grandeur that surrounded them.

Rieker led her into an ornate enclosed chamber. Centered in the middle was a large stone shrine. On the walls, carvings of saints surrounded them. Vibrant stained glass figures broke up the repetition of the lead paned windows and Tiki got the impression more than one set of eyes watched her every move.

Rieker stopped in front of a dark, gilt-encrusted chair. "This has got to be it." The chair was large and looked quite ancient. The lavish gilded paintings that had once graced the wood were faded and hard to decipher. The back of the grand chair stretched up in a commanding triangle to frame the head of anyone who sat there. Each of the four feet stood on a gilded base protected by golden lions. The chair looked like a throne.

But that's not what caught Tiki's eyes.

A sturdy gold shelf had been built directly beneath the seat. On the shelf sat a thick slab of stone.

Rieker squeezed her fingers.

"Do you think—" Tiki whispered.

"There's only one way to find out." Rieker pulled her close and pressed his lips against her forehead. "I think you should remove your glamour," he whispered. One side of his mouth lifted in a teasing smile. "Just in case anybody's watching."

Tiki was so scared her fingers were shaking. What if the stone didn't roar? What if the stone *did* roar? She wasn't even sure what to hope for. She whispered the words to remove her glamour and inhaled the fresh scent of clover. She glanced down to see the same shimmering crimson gown she'd worn when meeting the Macanna.

Something flickered in Rieker's eyes as he gazed at her in her true form. "You look like a faerie queen," he whispered. He raised her hand to his lips, his eyes locked on hers. The sleeve of her dress fell back, revealing her birthmark of *an fáinne sí.* His kiss was warm against her skin, sending an arrow of heat through her veins.

Tiki clung to him, suddenly frightened. If she sat on the chair would she gain the power to stop the war in the Otherworld? If she let go of Rieker's hand would she lose everything they'd built together over the last year?

"What's going to happen?" she whispered.

"Everything will change," Rieker said softly, his smoky eyes intent upon hers, "but our love will remain the same." He smiled as he helped her step up toward the seat. "Allow me to assist you, m'lady."

Tiki's heart was pounding so hard she expected it to burst from her chest at any second.

"Should I touch the stone or just sit?"

"Why don't you sit down and then just put your hand on the stone and see what happens?" Rieker's eyes gleamed with excitement.

Tiki nodded and took a deep breath. She put her foot onto the platform between the tails of the two golden lions that guarded the front legs of the Coronation Chair and stepped up.

Rieker released her hand and bowed as he stepped away. "My queen."

"William." Somehow only his true name sounded right in this place. Tiki tried to laugh and sound disapproving at the same time but her voice came out in a whisper, sounding more like a plea. She clutched the skirt of her dress and lifted the fabric. Keeping her eyes on Rieker she held her breath and sat down.

She didn't get a chance to lean down and touch the stone.

A roar erupted into the air and vibrated around them, so loud the stone arches above their heads shook.

"TARR-UH!"

Chapter Fifty

Rieker looked as shocked as she felt. The roar of "Tara" echoed in the air around them. Shadows began shifting through the room. Mist crept, twisted and swirled around them. Then, as if someone scratched a match and ignited a flame, faces and bodies began to appear. Within seconds, the entire room was filled with faeries.

Tiki saw numerous members of the Macanna along with dozens of unfamiliar faces. For a split-second Tiki thought she saw Mamie in the back of the room, but the crowd shifted and the diminutive woman's wrinkled face was gone. There was no sign of Dain.

Larkin appeared, in all her golden glory. She gripped what looked to be a golden scepter, a large ruby capping one end. She came to stand in front of Tiki where she sat on the throne. Larkin's lips curled in a mocking half-smile but her eyes glowed with victory.

She spoke low enough that only Tiki could hear her. "It looks like you've claimed your place, guttersnipe."

"It appears you told me the truth about my relationship to Finn," Tiki said, pretending to be calm.

"There are other relationships we've yet to discuss, but for now, we have a war to win." Larkin's eyes glittered like fire opals in the half light of the cathedral. She leaned close and whispered, "And by the way, your little thief friend is still alive."

"You saved Johnny?" Tiki could hardly contain her relief.

"He's alive," Larkin said drily. "Whether he survives still remains to be seen." She snorted in disgust as she stepped on a stone platform next to Tiki. She spoke from the corner of her mouth as she turned to face the crowd. "Mortals. So unfortunately fragile."

"Thank you," Tiki whispered. "But what of the *liche*?"

Larkin's lips twisted in distaste. "Still alive too—if you can call an undead creature alive. They took the boy as bait to draw me to them, but it's difficult to outsmart a dove with the heart of a fox." A smirk twisted her lips. "You'd be wise to remember that."

The beautiful faerie raised her scepter. "All Hail the High Queen. Hail to Queen Tara!"

As one, every person in the room, including Larkin, got down on one knee and bowed to Tiki. Then they shouted, "TARR-UH!"

Before the echoes had died away the Macanna encircled the chair where Tiki sat, like a protective wall. Their muscled shoulders and arms, their warrior-like stance and battle-scarred faces set them apart from the others in the room who were beginning to push and shove to get a look at the new queen. In the back of the room a flute began to play a lively jig.

Whispers flitted through the air like buzzing insects:

"Is that *the* Stone of Tara under her seat?"

"But what of the stone beneath the Dragon Throne in the Palace of Mirrors?"

"Did *she* make the stone cry out?"

"Who is she?"

"Why is it in London?"

"Who is she?"

"Who is she?"

"Who is she?"

As if given an unseen signal, the rumblings and excited whispers suddenly fell silent. Even the music died away until there was only the hush of stillness. All eyes turned toward Tiki.

Cries of *'speech', 'speech'* filled the air.

Tiki swallowed the nervous lump that suddenly filled her throat, threatening to choke her. They wanted her to speak? What was she supposed to say? She reached for Rieker's hand, wanting to feel the reassuring warmth of his skin. He laced his fingers through hers and squeezed. Though most of the faces before her were unfamiliar, a common expression was mirrored in their eyes. An emotion that Tiki knew all too well: hope.

Suddenly, Tiki realized what they were hoping for: someone to lead them to peace.

She cleared her throat. "We have been at war too long." Her voice was loud and crisp as though amplified. "It is time to stop the killing and reunite once again. To find peace."

Heads leaned close. Whispers rustled and flew about the room.

A short rotund man near the front stepped up. His green pants were held up by suspenders and a pair of well-made leather shoes covered his long feet. He bobbed his head in a low bow to Tiki before he spoke. His voice was surprisingly gruff.

"Beggin' your pardon, your majesty, but Donegal's killed our loved ones, our families. He's taken our homes and possessions." The man waved long fingers toward the group behind him. "Enslaved some of us."

"Donegal don't want peace." Someone shouted from the back. "He wants to *own* us."

The short man cleared his throat and bobbed his head again. "Forgive me, Majesty, but we don't want peace." His next words were steady and strong. "We want revenge. This is *war*."

In a rush, Tiki realized she'd been wrong. These people weren't hoping for peace. They were hoping for someone to lead them in battle against Donegal. Before Tiki could speak, another, louder voice interrupted.

"So the rumor is true." A giant of a man stood at the back of the room, a head above the others. His mass of copper locks appeared burnished in the last bits of daylight that leaked in through the arch-top windows. "A second stone exists."

As one, heads turned to see who spoke and just as quickly people shuffled to the side to make way for him to pass.

"Bearach." Larkin's said, her mouth turned down in a sneer. "Donegal's self-proclaimed protector."

Tiki recognized the fiery red hair that capped the man's head. It was this man who had hunted her and Dain in the Wychwood with his hellhounds.

Larkin straightened and faced the newcomer. "At last we've found the true Stone of Tara." Her voice held a dare. "We've got a message for you to deliver to Donegal." A taunting smile stretched her lips. "Tell him he is no longer king of the Seelie Court."

The crowd parted to allow the giant of a man to approach.

"Stop where you are," Rieker said as the man moved to within fifteen meters of where Tiki sat. Rieker pulled two daggers from inside his sleeves. At his movement, the Macanna shifted as one to form a tight wall in front of Tiki, swords, spears and spiked mauls suddenly appearing.

"Your men can relax." Bearach said in a deep, booming voice. "I'm not here to fight. I've brought a message for you, as well." His beady eyes narrowed in a glare beneath bushy red eyebrows. "Donegal has a friend of yours."

"And who might that be?" Larkin asked in an icy tone.

"A spy." Bearach spit the word out like it was poison. "Hiding in the UnSeelie Court. I don't know the name you might call him, but we know him as Sean ó'Broin—the Raven."

Tiki sucked in her breath and dug her fingernails into her palms to stop herself from crying out. They had Dain.

"I know not of who you speak," Larkin said in a scathing tone. "Perhaps he's not really a spy but someone who'd like to defect to the bright light of the Summer Court?"

A buzz went through the crowd of faeries at Larkin's insolence, waiting for Bearach's reaction.

Tiki straightened and mimicked Larkin's ice cold façade as she spoke to Bearach. "What does Donegal want in exchange for this prisoner?"

Bearach turned his gaze toward her and to Tiki's surprise, the giant faerie bowed, his big body much more graceful than seemed possible. When he spoke, his words were tinged with respect. "The cry of *Cloch na Teamhrach* was heard throughout Faerie. A new queen is among us. Welcome."

"TARR-UH," the crowd cried in answer to his statement.

Tiki inclined her head. She felt like an actor in a life-or-death play. "The answer to my question?"

Bearach's face was resolute. "There are no exchanges for spies. Only death. Donegal has marked him to be the Seven Year King."

The crowd gasped and Tiki jerked toward Larkin for an explanation.

The faerie's face was rigid with anger. She spoke in a low voice. "The UnSeelie Court must pay a tithe every seven years to the Seelies to remain a separate entity and avoid servitude to the Summer King or Queen." Her eyes narrowed. "Usually, the sacrifice is a mortal. They are named the Seven Year King."

"What is going on in here?" A night watchman stood in the doorway, surveying the room with a shocked expression.

In a blink, the entire room emptied, save for Tiki and Rieker.

"Wait a minute—where did everyone go?" The watchman said in a confused tone. He pointed to the far corner of the room. "There were people there. I saw them. Now—" he swung his arm wide— "everyone's gone."

"We've got to get out of here." Rieker took Tiki's arm and hurried toward the door. As they approached the guard Rieker spoke in a smooth, convincing tone. "I'm afraid we have no idea what you're talking about."

The guard's gaze locked on Tiki.

"Cor, you're as beautiful as a queen, miss." He stared, mesmerized.

"Glamour," Rieker said in a low voice as they ran for the door leading outside to the carriage.

With a flick of her wrist, Tiki assumed her familiar glamour, her thoughts not on the magic she could perform so effortlessly, but on the shocking bit of news she'd learned: Dain, as Sean, had been found out in the UnSeelie Court and was facing death.

The little man had been right tonight.

This was war.

Author's Note:

Though THE TORN WING is a work of fiction, many parts of the story are based in reality. In addition to the note shared at the beginning of the book, you might find it interesting to know that the Coronation Chair, (also known as King Edward's Chair) and the Stone of Scone or the Stone of Destiny (referred to as the Stone of Tara in the book) are real. Both chair and stone have been used to crown almost every English monarch since the coronation of Edward II in 1308. They were last used for the coronation of Queen Elizabeth II in 1953.

The chair is still on display in Westminster Abbey, though in 1996 the Stone was taken to Scotland and is now housed in Edinburgh Castle. Provision has been made to transport the Stone to Westminster Abbey when it is required there for future coronation ceremonies.

Legend holds that this stone was the coronation stone of the early <u>Dál Riata</u> <u>Gaels</u>, who brought the stone with them from Ireland when settling Scotland. The more historically supported story is that Fergus, the first King of the Scots in Scotland, brought the stone from Ireland to Argyll to be used in his coronation.

There are additional legends associated with the stone but most present a transport from Ireland and include a connection to the stone <u>Lia Fáil</u>, the coronation stone of the kings of Tara.

Thank you for reading THE TORN WING. Tiki's story continues in book three, THE SEVEN YEAR KING.

Kiki Hamilton
April 9, 2012

Acknowledgements

I am thrilled to have the opportunity to continue to share Tiki's story with interested readers. Special thanks goes to Peggy King Anderson, for her spot-on editing, thoughtful comments and wonderful encouragement.

Thanks also to Mark and Carly, and Doby and Gramps for always supporting my writing efforts and believing in me.

Thanks to the many, many fantastic bloggers, librarians, booksellers and readers who have offered their support in promoting this book and THE FAERIE RING. I couldn't do this thing I love so much without you guys!

Finally, to the many wonderful readers who have written such sweet and heartfelt notes — your kindness means more to me than words can describe. Thank you!

About the Author

Kiki Hamilton believes in faeries. And magic. Though she has a B.A. in business administration from Washington State University and has worked in a variety of management positions over the years, her first love is writing young adult stories. Kiki lives near Seattle, Washington, where it only rains part of the time. (A *large* part of the time...)

Visit Kiki's website and blog at www.kikihamilton.com. For more information about Tiki and the faerie ring, visit www.thefaeriering. com.